THE JEWISH HOSPITAL

THE JEWISH HOSPITAL

JONATHAN HAMMEL

Skyhorse Publishing

Skyhorse Publishing books may be purchased in bulk at special discounts for sales promotion, corporate gifts, fund-raising, or educational purposes. Special editions can also be created to specifications. For details, contact the Special Sales Department, Skyhorse Publishing, 307 Fifth Avenue, 4th Floor, New York, NY 10016 or info@skyhorsepublishing.com.

Visit our website at www.skyhorsepublishing.com.

10 9 8 7 6 5 4 3 2 1

Library of Congress Cataloging-in-Publication Data is available on file.

Cover design by David Ter-Avanesyan
Cover photo by Nathalie Raffet

Print ISBN: 978-1-5107-8644-8
Ebook ISBN: 978-1-5107-8645-5

Printed in the United States of America

Praise for *The Jewish Hospital*

"A gripping, intriguing World War II novel capturing the loss of innocence of a young Jewish girl. I cried. I raged. I despaired. Ultimately, Jonathan forces us to believe humanity can exist in the most evil of times."

—**Heather Morris**, *New York Times* bestselling author of *The Tattooist of Auschwitz*

"Hammel's vivid imagery and deft storytelling remind us that there are infinite grey areas between the extremes of good and evil. Suspenseful to the very end, *The Jewish Hospital* will quicken your pulse as each life-altering decision unfolds."

—**Georgia Hunter**, *New York Times* bestselling author of *We Were the Lucky Ones*

"A fine and deeply moving novel—riveting from beginning to end. Hammel brings 1940s Berlin vividly to life and gives us a portrait of an ordinary person caught in extraordinary events. I was reminded of *All the Light We Cannot See*, which I hope is taken as the high praise it's meant to be."

—**Graeme Simsion**, *New York Times* bestselling author of *The Rosie Project*

"Inspired by the extraordinary true history of Berlin's Jewish hospital, Jonathan Hammel blends meticulous research with vivid imagination to create a gripping and deeply affecting novel. His portrayal of Jewish life in Nazi Berlin—and of the fragile sanctuary the hospital provided—is unforgettable."

—**Daniel B. Silver**, author of *Refuge in Hell*

"Evocative . . . a must-read."

—**Carly Schabowski**, *USA Today* bestselling author of *The Rainbow*

"A moving and dramatically intense novel."

—**Serge Klarsfeld**, Nazi hunter, lawyer, and historian

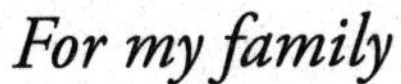

For my family

To those who lived
And to those gone too soon
May your stories be told
And the world be forewarned

Berlin, 1942

• • •

As the world rages in war, Germany's Jews find themselves ensnared in a vise. Stripped of their nationality, expelled from their homes, robbed of their businesses, imprisoned, beaten, and humiliated—those fortunate enough to escape did so before the borders were closed. For the rest, survival is now a daily struggle.

A year earlier, the first deportation trains departed Germany, bound for the east. In Berlin, the very heart of Nazi power, only two Jewish institutions are still allowed to function: the Weissensee Cemetery and the Jewish hospital. Within the walls of the two-hundred-year-old hospital, doctors and nurses try their best to perform their work, even as the world outside descends into madness.

Lena is one of those nurses. This is her story.

PART 1

1

• • •

Monday, September 28, 1942, 6 a.m.

Motionless, she watched the night. Her large yellow eyes, split with a vertical pupil, finally spotted movement. There, down below, near the great oak. The dry grass had moved. She tensed her claws, causing the stone to screech, and leaped into the void. Her feathers caressed by the wind and wrapped in a silence only the night knows, she veered toward the lawn and shot forward, a stealthy and deadly arrow, parallel to the cold-cracked ground. A new rustling of grass confirmed what she already knew. Driven by the smell of flesh, by the sound of the small heart beating amidst the bushes, she gave one last flap of her wings, and she was upon her prey.

Ten minutes later, the eagle-owl was back on her perch. Night was her kingdom, harboring a silence necessary for the hunt. She had chosen this large park bordered by brick buildings as her playground long ago, but for a few years now, her sleep had been disturbed by new and terrifying sounds. Cries of pain, the staccato of leather boots. So when darkness fell, she stretched her wings, clicked her beak, and around her, nature finally exhaled. She blinked and tilted her head.

The sky was still thick and dotted with stars, but she knew, by a subtle change in the air's humidity, that soon, the dark would be tinged with blue. She jumped off. Carried by the currents, she circled the weathered trees one last time, and, spotting a window ledge, she landed. Then, perhaps excited by her own reflection, she tapped the glass with little pecks.

Tap tap, tap tap.

Lena Schild opened her eyes and spotted the shadow at the window. She leaned on her elbow and tilted her head, mimicking the raptor's movements. *Good morning, little owl,* she whispered, barely moving her lips. *Are you awake, too? Shh, don't make too much noise, you'll wake Sophie . . .*

She cast a protective glance at the bed next to hers. The wool blanket gently undulated in the unmistakable rhythm of sleep.

Sophie looked so peaceful, lost in dreams. Though they had only known each other for a few months, Lena could barely imagine life without her. Their paths had been different ones, of course, but both had been uprooted from their families and thrown headlong into the chaos of working life. And what a life it was . . . Lena felt so lucky. From the very first day, Sophie had taken her under her wing, offering the lay of the land.

"That one? She's trouble, steer clear. And that doctor—he looks austere, but he's a regular straightshooter. Do as he asks, and you'll be fine. But whatever you do, never bring up his family. He lost his daughter in a bombing."

Sophie Gollschmidt, the sharp-witted Berliner who seemed to know every secret nook of the city and had promised to show them all to Lena someday.

An only child, Lena had never had the opportunity to share her room. Even a few months earlier, when she and her father had had to live with an aunt in Munich—already so far from her village—she had set up a mattress in a corner of the living room, between the piano and a cast-iron radiator, creating her private, personal space there. But sharing a room? No, never . . .

What strange months those had been. Her father spent his days in the city, running between the consulate, the bank, and other meetings he preferred not to mention. Her old aunt, if she had welcomed them out of familial duty, still demanded rent from them, and Lena spent her days performing various household tasks for this woman who seemed to feel no love for her. And to think that not that long ago, she had still been a high school student with a bright future ahead of her! But the school didn't want her anymore . . . well, she still had her Papi, her dear father, in whom her trust was absolute.

One evening, he had burst through the door, hung his worn coat on the rack, and, in the excitement of the moment, had forgotten to take off his hat. With gleaming eyes, he had grabbed his daughter's face. "Lena, I've finally found a solution! There's an open nursing position at the Jewish hospital in Berlin!"

She could still feel his warm, rough palms firmly placed on her cheeks. Her heart had played a thousand tricks on her—fear, excitement, joy, disbelief . . . so, did her father no longer want her near him? Still, being a nurse would surely beat washing her auntie's underwear all day. But, Berlin, really? She wasn't too knowledgeable about politics, but despite the exciting prospect of finally seeing the capital, she couldn't help but wonder, was the city safe for people like her?

None of these feelings had found their way into words, and to the surprise of her father, who had—he would never tell her—used all his contacts and incurred many debts to get her that position, she had only said, "Will I have to share my room? That will be very new for me, Papi . . ."

The man had then smiled and stroked his daughter's hair.

All around her, dozens of young girls were dozing on camp beds, their breathing creating a regular symphony of snores. If someone had told her she would manage to sleep in such cacophony, she would never have believed it. But her days were so exhausting that come evening, all she had to do was close her eyes and the world faded instantly. Furthermore, Sophie was beside her. Even on her first night, she'd had no trouble falling asleep.

Well yes, little owl, I have a best friend now!

She couldn't help but think back to her village, her home—the house she had loved so much. She hadn't seen it since that terrible day in November, when that scary Sturmabteilung (SA) man had forced them out, only to settle himself in their apartment, while Lena and her family were thrown into the streets.

They had thought themselves safe in Ansbach, a quiet haven tucked deep in the heart of Bavaria. It had been a peaceful place, where for centuries Jews, Protestants, and Catholics had lived side by side in harmony.

They had owned a lofty apartment in the center of town, and her mother, despite her illness, had kept a neat household, while her father had poured his heart into his work as a kosher butcher. He had set up his workshop in the courtyard of their apartment building, surrounded by the wildflowers that seemed to spring up out of nowhere between the moss-covered stones. Yellow and purple—"as if the sun had dyed its hair," Lena used to say—and she loved to gently run her fingers along their stems, letting the sunlight warm her skin.

But things had changed so quickly.

Lena lay on her back and stretched her toes, wondering about her father. What was he doing at this very moment? Was he awake, was he thinking of her?

Silently, a hand reached through the dormitory door, fumbling a bit before flipping a switch. The tall, wide room was suddenly flooded with a cold light, and the owl, blinded in its own realm, disappeared without a sound.

"Up, ladies, up!" said Ingrid, the head nurse, in a voice that opera would not disown. Her plump body had trouble weaving between the camp beds. Her fingers manipulated a tiny bell with a metallic ring. "Up, ladies, up!"

Sophie groaned, rolled over in her bed, and buried her head under her pillow. "I don't believe it . . . I feel like I've barely closed my eyes! The boss has read her clock wrong! I'm not budging from here."

But Ingrid had found her rhythm and was now moving between the beds with the implacability of a Panzer running down a wheat field. Her voice grew more intense with each repetition. "Up, ladies, up! Up!"

2

• • •

Monday, September 28, 1942, 6:30 a.m.

LENA THREW OFF HER BLANKET, GATHERED HER MOMENTUM, and swung her body with agility, placing her feet on the cold parquet floor. She rubbed the tip of her nose with the palm of her hand, a childhood gesture she had never quite outgrown.

"Oh, Sophie, I slept so well. I had the most amazing dream. I was on vacation with my parents, and we were jumping in the waves, under a radiant and pleasant sun . . . for someone who has never seen the ocean, it's quite funny, don't you think?"

Sophie unfolded her elastic body, propped herself up on an elbow, and blew on a rebellious strand of hair. She tilted one corner of her mouth, revealing white, powerful teeth.

"Yes, I see, my little dreamer. How lucky you are. When I finally do fall asleep, all I see is darkness. And that's a best-case scenario."

"Really? You don't dream?" Lena asked.

"Not as beautifully as you do. But don't you mind that. If we want a spot at the sink, we'd better head for the bathroom as quickly as possible."

Around them, bodies still warm from sleep yawned and stretched. In small groups, the women disappeared for a few minutes before reappearing, their faces fresh and moist, their hair freed from its nocturnal disarray. They put on their uniforms, adjusted their caps, and trotted toward the dormitory door.

Fifteen minutes later, Lena and Sophie were moving along the wide corridor, eager to reach the breakfast hall. The wooden floor creaked under their feet. Despite the war, the hospital—now over two hundred years old—had managed to maintain a certain guise of dignity. No barbed wire surrounded the high brick walls of the seven-building complex, and the sign at the main gate, ignoring the madness of its surroundings, still proudly read "Jüdisches Krankenhaus." Tall windows punctuated the corridors at regular intervals, offering beautiful views of the awakening park.

But this was hardly the time for contemplation. Lena tried to keep pace with Sophie as, surrounded by their peers, they made their way down the central staircase. Each floor was lined with long hallways leading to various wards. Surgery, dermatology, internal medicine . . . the hospital had miraculously maintained a wide range of treatments, even in the midst of war. The third floor was reserved for nurses, well-separated from the doctors' quarters, located in an adjacent building. Of course, this didn't stop a few adventurous souls from sneaking through the underground passages at night to meet with their sweethearts . . .

They reached the ground-floor cafeteria in record time, joining the breakfast queue as they crossed the vast room under the light of bare yellow bulbs and the first daylight filtering through the windows. Most of the tables were already full. On one side sat the doctors' table, on the other, the nurses' table, dispersed among them were a few administrative staff, medical assistants, and janitorial workers.

The queue inched forward. Moshe, the young kitchen helper, extended a thin arm toward Lena.

"Good morning! Oh—you look very well today, Nurse Lena!"

His face turned beet-red, and he instantly regretted the remark. He reminded Lena of the baby roosters she sometimes saw in her parents' farmyard—skin both pale and flushed, eyes anxious—creatures she had always found both endearing and slightly off-putting.

"Good morning, Moshe."

"Good morning, Moshe," Sophie echoed, putting on the expression of a lovestruck schoolgirl as she jabbed an elbow into Lena's ribs. "Oooh la la, is this loooove?"

"Hush! Don't say things like that!" Lena muttered, grabbing a piece of bread and sinking her head into her shoulders.

Sophie let out a bubble of laughter, and together they headed toward the nurses' table. "Well, enjoy, my dear," Sophie said as they sat down. They always started the first meal of the day—sometimes habits form quite quickly—by warming their hands on their hot mugs, breathing in the bittersweet scent of the ersatz coffee.

They ate in silence. Mornings were not usually conducive to confidences or muffled laughter. Instead, along the big wooden table, there was a common excitement, a desire to do well, and the small jaws ground the food meticulously, all the while being careful not to soil their beautiful white uniforms.

Lena thought of all the breakfasts she had shared around the wooden table back in their Ansbach apartment. Oh, how she'd loved that table. One afternoon, when she was home alone, she had carved her name into the soft, worn wood with an old kitchen knife. When her father had discovered it, she had feared he would get angry—and for a moment, his face had flashed with irritation—but then he'd taken a deep breath, and his face had softened into a grin. "Well, now I guess we can never leave this apartment!" Her mother had laughed, a sound so pure and filled with joy that it had forever imprinted itself in Lena's memory. But of course, they'd had to leave.

A hand landed on Lena's shoulder, like a bear caressing a poppy. She jumped out of the past and was resolutely faced with her present once more.

"Stefan! You scared me!" she said with a smile.

Stefan was a tall man with broad shoulders, his striking curly hair framing his angular face as dark petals might a weathered marble sculpture. Lena and Sophie had first met him during one of his frequent walks in the park—a privilege reserved for the psychiatric patients—and a bond had quickly formed between the three of them.

"Hi, there!" he said, pinching her cheek. "Good morning, Sophie!"

"Good morning, Stefan. You look very elegant today," Sophie replied.

"Thank you, you're too kind . . . just a simple white shirt I was able to salvage during my last trip to Prague. But it has one advantage. It's very roomy."

He leaned forward, lifted his shirt, and pulled out two slices of dry bread stuck together.

"Look, Lena," he whispered, showing her the bread. "I fixed the clock in the pediatrics department. They gave me a jam sandwich as a thank you, and I want you to have it."

His eyes, two black nuggets struck with golden reflections, surrounded by heavy lashes, shimmered with happiness. His breath smelled of warm cinnamon. "Promise me you'll enjoy it thinking of me! And share it with Sophie!" he said, standing back up.

"Oh no, keep it, Stefan! You've earned it!" Lena said.

"Sweetheart, look at you! You're so delicate. You need all the calories you can get," Stefan replied with a grin. "And don't you worry about me! Uncle Stefan is built like an ancient oak tree!"

He burst into a carefree, booming laugh that turned a few heads at the doctors' table.

"Well, I must leave you, my darlings, otherwise my good doctor will wonder where his favorite patient has disappeared to."

He planted a kiss on Lena's forehead—which quickly turned her crimson—gave a short curtsy, and left.

"He's so strange, your Stefan," said one of their neighbors, shaking her head. "Does he wear makeup or something?"

A twinge—the innocent's reaction to injustice—clenched Lena's chest. She wanted to reply, but Sophie placed a hand on her arm. "Maybe he does! What's it to you? Mind your own business. It's 7:27, and if you don't hurry, you'll be late to your department. And believe me, with Dr. Hirsch, that's not something I'd recommend."

The girl, taken aback, looked up at the wall clock and scurried off without a word.

"Oh, you didn't need to scare her . . . I'm sure she meant no harm," Lena told Sophie.

"Believe me, she'll get over it. Here, just like anywhere else, you must avoid getting pushed around. Never forget that, okay? Come on, we need to go as well. See you at lunch break?"

"As if you had a doubt!" said Lena, getting up.

She hadn't let go of her precious sandwich. "Do I have time to drop this off by my bed?"

"No time! Off to the department! Here, put it in your front pocket . . . there. Haven't you figured out yet that no delay is tolerated? And here I thought you were a quick learner!"

Within minutes, as if moved by some kind of primal instinct, dozens of young women left the comfort of the cafeteria to pour into the central staircase. With each floor, the crowd thinned, and soon, leaving Sophie to continue on her way, Lena entered the general surgery department.

Working in a hospital had not yet taken on the feel of reality for her; it felt like just yesterday she was still in her room, leaning on the windowsill, her gaze lost in the twinkling of constellations, her soul still warmed by childhood. Sometimes it felt as though life had suddenly sped up, and her body was now wrapped in a nurse's uniform before her mind had fully caught up.

"*Schwester* Lena, are you daydreaming?" said a voice behind her. "I told you the rounds are starting!"

Lena turned around, muttering something unintelligible. Dr. Weiss, the head of general surgery, was a stern and demanding physician, and his mere presence was enough to make her tense up.

"Let's go, *schwester*! What can you tell me about the patient in bed number 1? Is his wound finally starting to heal?"

"I . . . yes, Dr. Weiss. I haven't yet received the handover from my night shift colleague; I was just about to change his dressing."

Lena felt her stomach tighten. What could she possibly tell the doctor? After all, she had only been a nurse for a few months. What if he took a dislike to her? Oh, how she missed her dear Papi in moments like these.

They approached a bed occupied by an ageless man with rough cheeks and drawn features. His eyes were two dark marbles, sunk into bottomless sockets, as if they had already seen enough of this world. His right leg was wrapped in a white bandage, stained yellow and brown.

Under the doctor's strict gaze, Lena slowly unwound the bandage, and a pungent smell filled her nostrils. She stepped back. Far from healing, some skin had come off with the dressing, and amid the hair and pus protruded the opaline whiteness of a shinbone.

"Well, well," said Dr. Weiss. "My dear man, this is not getting better. I'm afraid we'll have to amputate . . . yes, as we had discussed.

What will you do with only one leg? I don't know, my dear man, I don't know . . . perhaps they will leave you in peace? Medically, it's the only sensible solution. Nurse, you will come back to redo the dressing after the rounds. Bed number 2, please!"

The morning flew by as usual, and before Lena knew it, it was lunch. The cafeteria offered three meals a day—a luxury during wartime—and Lena shared soup and a piece of bread with Sophie. They had thirty minutes of break left and used the remaining time to go back to the dormitory. There, facing the window overlooking the park, they shared Stefan's sandwich.

"Hmm, it's been months since I've tasted strawberry jam! Saint Stefan, I pray for you! May you never run out of lipstick!"

"Oh!" said Lena. "You know he doesn't like being made fun of!"

"But he loves it. He's not as delicate as you think." Sophie flopped down on her bed. "Come on, we still have some time. Let's rest a bit!"

Lena followed suit and lay down on her bed.

"Wake me up in ten minutes!" Sophie said as she turned on her side and closed her eyes.

Lying on the camp bed, Lena couldn't help but let her mind drift off.

No, she wouldn't ever forget that day. Ever since 1933, the Jews had learned to dread November 9—the marches of the SA and the Hitler Youth always carried their truckload of fear. But in 1938, hatred had finally boiled over. All over Ansbach, the rugged bodies of the SA and the Hitler Youth hadn't simply paraded through the otherwise picturesque streets of her village. That day, rage and hatred had unleashed themselves against the Jews.

She would never forget the sight—the sounds—of the village youth, strapped into their pristine uniforms, shattering the windows of her apartment. Their eyes full of rage and glee, they had forced their way through the door, wrecking the furniture, screaming with delight. Her mother had curled up in a corner of the living room, clinging to her daughter. Lena could still feel the imprint of her mother's fingers pressed into her forearm.

She could still hear her shallow gasps of terror. Neither one of them had dared move a muscle through the entire ordeal. Not when the Hitler Youth had destroyed their home, not when—amidst the chaos of it all—her father had come home, only to be immediately arrested by the SA men—men he knew, men he'd perhaps chatted with about the weather, maybe even shared a glass of beer with.

When they had finally left, she and her mother had cried for what seemed like hours. And when they were out of tears, her mother had said, "Don't worry, *schätzchen*. I'm sure this is all part of God's plan. We will see your Papi again, I am sure of it. Go to bed now."

Reluctantly, Lena had gone to her room—miraculously spared from the rampant savagery—and had spent one of her last nights in her childhood bed.

Sophie opened her eyes and stretched.

"Oh, I slept like a log. Didn't you? No, I can tell. You really ought to master the art of the nap, my dear. I feel like a new day is about to start!"

At 2 p.m. sharp, they were back in their respective departments. All the patients were Jews, their bodies bearing the marks of the deprivations imposed by the new German order.

"The hospital used to treat Jews and non-Jews alike, of course," Sophie had explained. "But that ended a year ago. No Jewish doctor is allowed near a non-Jew anymore. Well, too bad for them. We've got some *bona fide* geniuses working here! Let them be treated by their Nazi physicians if that's what they prefer."

Out of discretion—and perhaps because she wasn't sure she wanted to know—Lena rarely questioned her patients about the origins of their injuries. But faced with fractured jaws, giant hematomas, and lacerated skin, she couldn't help but wonder . . . Still, she had enough to do and clung to the doctor's words as to a lifeline—clear, short-term goals, that's all she really needed.

In the evening, she met Sophie in the cafeteria. The two friends exchanged little; each seemed lost in the day's events. Around them, conversations buzzed; the tinkle and scratch of cutlery on plates echoed the relief of another day coming to a close.

"Shall we go, Lena? My feet are killing me. All I can think of is lying down."

"Of course! I'm exhausted too. What a day. I don't think I'll ever get used to seeing all that pain. And those blood-soaked bandages! Sometimes I'm afraid I'll throw up!"

"Don't worry, you'll get used to all of it, eventually. But tell me, did you finally manage all your blood draws on the first try? After all, we've been practicing for weeks."

"I did! The doctor was really pleased with me!"

"That's good, my dear. Believe me, keeping your doctor happy is a bigger part of your job than you might think."

They stood up, ready to head to the dormitory, when they noticed a crowd forming near the large corkboard used for public announcements.

"Oh no, what's this about now," Sophie wondered.

They moved closer, gently elbowing their way through. The closer they got to the board, the more the bodies around them stiffened, the more eyes tightened.

They finally got close enough to read the message, simply typed in black ink on a large white sheet, pinned to the wall:

ALL HOSPITAL STAFF ARE REQUIRED TO BE IN THE MAIN COURTYARD TOMORROW MORNING AT 6 AM SHARP, IN UNIFORM. NO EXCEPTIONS, NO DELAYS, WILL BE TOLERATED.
—DR. WALTER LUSTIG, DIRECTOR

"All I hope for now is a dreamless night," said Sophie through closed lips.

3

• • •

Tuesday, September 29, 1942, 6 a.m.

In a matter of minutes, nearly two hundred people filled the courtyard. With arms crossed and shoulders hunched, the employees of the Jewish hospital shifted from foot to foot, exchanging worried glances. Their breath created cottony clouds that floated for a few seconds in the frosty air before melting away.

At six o'clock sharp, a man appeared before them. Standing very straight in his gray overcoat, wearing a wide-brimmed hat, Dr. Walter Lustig announced in an authoritative voice, which contrasted with his diminutive five-foot-five frame and his cherubic face, that he was pleased with his troops' punctuality. He had received orders, he said. Their group was expected an hour later in the center of Berlin. They had to leave immediately. The journey, obviously, would be on foot.

"Onward!" he said.

"So that's the famous 'Doctor Doctor'?" Lena whispered.

"You've never seen him?" said Sophie. "Not surprising. He rarely leaves his office. Anyway, you're well-informed. He insists that we use his two doctor titles when addressing him. But between us, we call him *the double doctor*, it's simpler . . . or sometimes *the pervert*, but that's another story."

"The pervert?"

"Don't worry about it. If you ask me, we have bigger problems to deal with today than our director's rampant libido."

"Oh," said Lena, not fully understanding.

The group had started moving, passing through the iron gates that partially shielded their cocoon from the madness of men. They emerged into an oily darkness, highlighted here and there by phosphorescent paint. Sidewalks and signposts took on a ghostly appearance in the ink of the night.

"Why aren't any streetlights on, Sophie?" Lena asked.

"Ever since the first bombings two years ago, the government adopted this technique to avoid marking easy targets for enemy planes. Didn't you have that in your village?"

"Oh, you know, it was a very small village . . ."

Lena realized that despite their closeness, she had told precious little to Sophie about her village. She'd had to leave it so abruptly. After that night of terror, she'd woken up, checked on her mother—fast asleep on what remained of the sofa—and hesitantly set foot into the neighborhood streets.

Calm had returned to Ansbach—a strange calm, strewn with shards of glass, shattered mirrors, and families now missing their men. A village whose heart had been torn apart by hatred—sudden, fierce, and, worst of all, inflicted by their own neighbors.

She had ventured as far as the synagogue—her synagogue—where, every Shabbat, she would sit beside her mother in the women's section upstairs. From there, she could follow the service while discreetly glancing at the young boys praying on the ground floor, later giggling with her friends about their various charms.

Lena had slowed her pace, her shoes coming to a stop on the cobblestones of Rosenbadstrasse. The synagogue had not been spared. Every window was shattered. She tried calling out her rabbi's name, but no sound had come out of her throat.

Stunned, she had quickly retraced her steps and pushed open the splintered door of their apartment. Inside, a man was standing over her mother. Frail, slight, almost a shadow of herself, she was bent over a piece of paper at the kitchen table—Lena's beloved table, now missing a leg and awkwardly pushed against the wall to keep it balanced. Her mother's hands were shaking, and tiny beads of sweat were dripping beneath her *sheitel*.

"*Ja*! Sign here! *Schnell*! You have until tomorrow to get out of here."

The officer snatched the paper with a rough gesture and left without another word. "Who was he, Mama?"

"He was . . . nobody, *schätzchen*," her mother whispered.

"Nobody? But what did he want? What did you sign?"

"I . . . we must leave. The house. I sold it, it's gone. Gone, *schätzchen*, gone."

The memory dissolved, cold gnawing at her fingertips. Lena glanced around nervously. So this was Berlin. A few cars glided on the asphalt, headlights turned off, requiring constant vigilance to avoid getting run over. Two cyclists nearly collided, dodging each other at the last moment like agile boxers, muttering insults before moving apart.

They had only covered a few hundred meters when Sophie clung to Lena's arm.

"Wait for me a second." She crouched down, repositioned the bunched-up newspaper stuffed into her heel, and repeated the operation on the opposite side. "Damn it! I'm sure to have blisters by the end of this little journey. If only we could still take our shoes to be repaired!"

A tramway screeched around a corner, under the walkers' envious gaze. Inside, a few Berliners watched them with a distant eye.

For seven years now, each new law had escalated in inhumanity, as if incrementally increasing the pain made it acceptable to the half-closed eyes of the populace. One day, Jews had to give up their radios, depriving them of a precious source of information. The next, telephones and cameras were confiscated by the Reich. But they were a resilient people, standing tall, and so, they moved forward, one foot in front of the other, again and again.

The immediate goal of the walkers was simple: they needed to be present an hour later at a specific address. They were aware of being a most privileged bunch—Jews working for Jews, in the middle of Berlin, during the war! Each carried in their heart the example of a relative who hadn't been this lucky. None of them, except the youngest or most adventurous, seriously considered the possibility of fleeing, where the group, driven by a madness as sudden as it was communicative, would suddenly disperse to the four corners of the city, shouting to the others, *Good luck! Let's meet up when everything calms down! Try to avoid cafés and train stations!*

No, because where would they have gone? No, because they were Germans first and foremost, and centuries of obedience to the Kaiser had made them a docile people, generally disinclined to revolt. It wasn't just that they didn't want to rebel or venture out; in the vast majority of cases, they just wouldn't have known where to start.

They headed straight south. Lena and Sophie walked in the middle of the group; unconsciously, everyone avoided being too exposed. They seldom left the hospital, and there was a certain comfort in the warmth of the group.

They passed a group walking heavily in the opposite direction. Women with dark complexions, their heads wrapped in shawls, holding the hands of children. A man in rags coughed violently, spat several times, caught his breath, and hurried to rejoin his group.

"Who are those people?" Lena asked.

"Hard to say. Probably forced laborers. Berlin is full of them these days."

"But where are they going, so early in the morning?"

"To the factories, Lena! What do you think? Off they go, building weapons the German army will use to destroy them."

"No . . . I don't think the state would force women and children to work. There must be another explanation," Lena said.

"Lena, grow up! Sometimes I wonder what goes on in your mind," Sophie said, a bit brusquely.

In the dawning day, the ominous crests of massive concrete buildings slowly came into view. Among the more informed employees, some scrutinized the plaques hung on street corners, on the lookout for certain addresses—Prinz Albrecht Strasse, Burg Strasse—streets already tinged with the acrid scent of violence.

After an hour, the group stopped in front of an old building along Oranienburger Strasse.

"I know this place," Sophie whispered.

The two women looked up at a massive red brick construction, whose main dome, topped with a Star of David, rose proudly in the Berlin skyline. "The Great Synagogue!" Lena said a bit too loudly. "I've always wanted to visit it!"

But Sophie wasn't listening. Her gaze had returned to the building's entrance, and when Lena did the same, what she saw froze her heart. Flanked by two German Shepherds as thick-set as they were ferocious, two SS soldiers were standing at attention, utterly motionless and armed with extremely well-polished rifles.

4

• • •

Tuesday, September 29, 1942, 7 a.m.

"FOLLOW ME," SAID DR. LUSTIG.

The elderly doctor usually exuded clear authority, but as soon as they had crossed the massive wooden doors, it was easy to see that power had shifted out of his hands.

"Move, Jews! And silently!" barked an officer. Instinctively, Lena touched Sophie's arm, providing her with a bit of reassurance. She glanced at the ceiling, noticing the gildings and intricate woodwork, remnants of an era that seemed so distant. The air was cold and curiously odorless. Surrounded by soldiers, they moved forward until they found themselves in a large, bare room. A petty officer's voice cut through the air like a poorly sharpened knife.

"Jews! Arrange yourselves in rows of twenty throughout the room! Find your spots, and don't move. Do not test our patience!"

The space gradually filled with bodies already heavy with fatigue. Lena and Sophie settled somewhere in the middle of the room and exchanged worried looks. The air echoed with terse commands. SS officers paced around, fingers light on their triggers. Others moved between the rows, eyes askew, pulling on leashes that seemed ready to snap. A dog, panting and drooling heavily, brushed against Lena's leg, causing her to startle and suppress a scream. Behind her, a man asked to go to the bathroom; he was rewarded with a punch to the sternum. "Piss in your pants, Jew!" yelled a soldier, young enough to be his son.

In the former meeting room, which in better times had hosted the celebration of numerous Bar Mitzvahs (Sophie wondered how many pre-teens had kissed their first girlfriend within these walls), one could still discern the spots where chairs and lecterns had been recently ripped from their moorings. Someone had clearly organized this meeting with a specific purpose in mind, Sophie thought. She knew Lena and her unwavering faith in God, but if her friend still hoped for a mere administrative announcement, Sophie saw nothing but the makings of a catastrophe. Her gaze shifted to the back of the room. There, a podium stood with a desk and three solitary chairs.

Hours passed, white, empty. A pale light filtered through the windows. From outside, you could make out the sounds of a waking city. A dull sound resonated at the back of the room.

"Don't turn around!" Sophie said a bit too late. Through a forest of legs, Lena glimpsed Ingrid, the head nurse, lying on her back; she had likely fainted. An officer pounced on her, slapping her with a gloved hand. "Get up, Jew, or it's immediate deportation for you!" The silence thickened further, weighing down on their shoulders, pinning them to the ground.

Somewhere, a clock announced noon. Sophie's back was starting to hurt terribly. Simple things—a chair, a glass of water—suddenly seemed like exquisite treasures. She imagined herself running toward the bathroom, pushing past one of the uniformed thugs who, in another reality, would have easily succumbed to her charms. Yes, a few years earlier, she could have turned his world upside down with a flutter of her eyelashes. She would have led him to perform feats for the promise of a kiss, she was certain of it, and that only added to her pain. For the situation had overtaken souls, and intuitively she knew that today, the young soldier would not hesitate to use his weapon.

Finally, a side door opened.

Three austere figures advanced toward the podium, their boots echoing in the silence. Behind them, slightly stooped, was a tall, thin man dressed in a gray suit. He wore a red armband, strapped tight on his upper arm.

"Adolph Eichmann and Rolf Günther!" Sophie hissed through her teeth. "And a new one, whom I don't recognize."

The third man, dressed entirely in black, allowed his colleagues to settle in before sitting down himself. He smoothed his jet-black hair, rotated his wedding band three times on his right hand, and took out a metal case from his inner pocket. He handed out cigarettes to his colleagues, placed one between his narrow lips, and struck a match. The act of exhaling white smoke, alternately through his mouth and nostrils, seemed to bring him intense pleasure. The three men appeared very comfortable, and from afar, one might have mistaken them for old friends catching up after the summer, eager to share stories of fishing trips or seductive conquests. They often laughed. After half an hour, they seemed to finally remember they were not alone. Ah, yes, humans. Or rather, Jews.

The man in the black suit crushed his cigarette butt, looked up at the room, and any trace of a smile vanished instantly. He looked like a predator ready to pounce, yet his gaze lacked a beast's elegance and nobility. Behind the ironed clothes, freshly shaved skin, and mineral-like pupils—he seemed never to blink—lay an empty and lonely soul. To his right, Eichmann watched him with what looked like pride.

"I am Alois Brunner, from Vienna! You don't know me yet. But the Jews of Vienna are not likely to forget me." He chuckled to himself, coughed several times. "I've come to show these Prussians"—he made a barely concealed sneer of disdain—"how to deal with their Jews!"

How to deal with their Jews . . . the words slowly penetrated Sophie's brain. It seemed to her the Prussians were already doing quite well in that regard. What new torments did this small bow-legged man have in store for them?

He went on in the same vein. "Let the hospital director show himself!"

The double doctor, who had lost all his grandeur on the streets of Berlin, slowly stepped forward.

"Is it you, Jew? Point out the heads of all hospital departments to me. Right now, I don't have all day."

With his head bowed, as if defeated by the situation—and especially, Sophie thought, ashamed to reveal his weakness to his troops—Lustig complied. One by one, he called out the names of the doctors who ran his hospital. He knew each of them personally; he even considered one or two as close friends. Ten men stepped away from the crowd.

"Good, good . . . each of you will now write on a piece of paper—give them paper and pencils, *schnell!*—the names of one third of your employees. One third, do you hear me? You have ten minutes." He struck a match, creating a brief orange spark, and lit another cigarette.

Initially, no one understood. Given the hunger and fatigue, some might have thought they were dreaming—a hideous and despicable dream, but a dream, nonetheless. In recent years, the idea of lists had taken on a terrifying significance. Gone were the days when lists conjured thoughts of wedding plans or ingredients for an apple strudel; now, they were lists of names, and everyone understood that at any moment, a Gestapo officer could appear in all his might, backed by the law, capable of smashing furniture if he wished, terrifying children if it suited his fancy, and one would have to follow him, often to disappear. The exact fate of the prisoners—forced labor, ghettos—was unknown but feared by all. People had adapted to this calamity as much as they could. But until then, it was about following orders and obeying the law, however unjust. No one had yet taken the cynicism to the level of asking Jews to be the architects of their own destruction. Until this man, perched on his small wooden chair, thinking the sooner he finished here, the sooner he could return to the comfort of his young bride. He, of course, would father a true Aryan, not one of these sub-humans struggling before him with their pencils.

"*Schnell!* Two minutes left . . . Very good. Give me that." He turned to the man wearing the red armband. "You there, count!" he snapped. "There should be a total of 166 names. All must be present here in two days at eight in the morning for transportation to the east." The air thinned in the room; a chill spread like a cold shadow. "Some of you might think of not showing up. I would advise against it. I have another list, which my assistant will read to you."

The man with the red armband began to call out the names of twenty hospital doctors.

Brunner squinted, pleased with himself. "My assistant Hans is a Jew! I grew tired of using good Aryans for these tedious tasks. I call them *ordners*; we'll be setting this up quickly in Berlin." He snorted loudly. "From now on, it'll be your job to arrest Jews directly at their homes and bring them to me for transport. Of course, you will be supervised by the Gestapo. This way, you will be somewhat useful! You should thank me." Eichmann and Gunther, who had been silent, looked at him with admiration. His upper lip curled. "I warn you: if in two days, a single one of the selected is missing, these twenty Jews will be executed. You may now return to the hospital.

Those among you who will have the honor of assisting the Gestapo will be notified this evening."

He exhaled a last puff of acrid smoke before turning to his mentor. Eichmann, eyes gleaming, uncrossed his arms and began to slowly clap his hands.

5

• • •

Tuesday, September 29, afternoon

THEY HAD TO HEAD BACK. BERLIN, WHICH ON THEIR WAY TO THE meeting had been cloaked in darkness, now lay exposed in a harsh, cold light, boldly revealing its scarred face. Lena matched her pace with Sophie's and let her gaze wander over the city she had once dreamed of. But instead of the refinement she had anticipated, what she discovered was a sickly landscape, adorned with posters warning Berliners against the *long-nosed Jew*. Yet, the city had only been grazed by bombs, and scenes akin to a normal life persisted. Through a café window, Lena caught the gaze of a well-dressed blonde lifting a porcelain cup. Startled by the passing group, the woman paused, the cup hanging in midair, barely touching her perfectly made-up lips.

"That bitch," Sophie said. "She's lucky to be on the right side of the fence. She looks at us but doesn't see us. To her, we're already nothing more than ghosts from the past."

Lena wanted to answer, but Sophie had already looked away. They walked past some soldiers, lowering their gaze, and the woman with her cup became just another memory. After an hour's walk, as one would return to a mother's loving arms, they reached the hospital gates. Before releasing them, Dr. Lustig, who had regained some of his composure, announced in a strong voice that by evening, two lists would be posted in the cafeteria: one would bear the names of those to be deported; the other, those selected to assist the Gestapo, what Brunner had called the *ordners*.

"You have an hour's rest before returning to your patients," he said. With a bowed back, he swept his gaze over his employees, wanting to add a reassuring word then thought better of it, turned on his heels, and disappeared.

The group dispersed in silence. Lena and Sophie walked through the large park, flanked on both sides by the hospital's various buildings. Lena breathed in the smell of dry grass and found it soothing. Sophie seemed consumed with a quiet, violent rage. They found an isolated bench and finally sat down. "Those bastards!" said Sophie. Her deep blue eyes had taken on grayish hues. "Can you believe it? They want us to do their dirty work. What if we refuse? I refuse. I won't do it. I won't be their puppet! If they want to deport us, if they want to kill us, let them do it themselves!"

"Kill us? Sophie, don't talk like that!" Lena said softly. "I think it's just a work transport. The Nazis probably need labor for their factories. So, some of us are going to work, that's all! Or maybe it's a relocation. I've heard they've created ghettos, little towns where we'd be amongst our own. Maybe it's not so bad, right? Since apparently, we're in the way here, it's almost logical if you think about it . . ."

"Of course!" Sophie turned to her. "So, according to you, Mr. Brunner, with his sadistic killer's face, came all the way from Vienna to organize a summer camp? According to you, it's *God's* will? I know your rhetoric, we must trust HIM, HE knows everything . . . well, my dear, if HE's organizing everything, you can tell him that instead of this morning's little excursion, I would have preferred a day by the lake sipping *schnaps*!"

On paper, Sophie was indeed a Jewish Berliner, thus an enemy of the Reich. But prior to the Nazis' rise to power, she had never truly felt Jewish. First and foremost, she was a proud German citizen, and the transformation of her identity was yet another blow added to the injustice engulfing her world. So, after the hours spent waiting, walking in the cold, she wanted to finally express to Lena that there was no all-powerful God to be found, except in the imaginations of the devout, that all of this was just fanciful stories meant to comfort the weak, and that the Nazis surely had plans for them that extended beyond factory labor. But seeing such misunderstanding in her friend's eyes, such hope in the quiver of her lips, Sophie was suddenly overcome by a profound weariness.

She reached out to Lena's face and, with a precise movement, tucked a stray lock of hair back into her cap. "Let's forget it," she said. "You know I tend to get carried away. Who knows, maybe you're right. For now, let's get to the cafeteria. I'm starving."

Lena smiled timidly, and the two friends stood up. They skirted around a massive weeping willow which, bereft of leaves, was bracing itself for the harshness of winter. The park's pathways were eerily empty. They were nearly at the main building when a voice called out from behind them.

"Hey there, my little lovelies! How beautiful you both look today! Oh, I've missed you . . . come here, let me take a look at you!"

They turned, having already recognized Stefan's voice. Dr. Elken allowed him an hour of freedom each day to relieve the pressure of hospital life. He enveloped them in his hairy arms and kissed them vigorously, leaving a wet purple mark on each cheek. "Have you noticed my lipstick? Isn't it fabulous? Look, it matches my dress!"

"Stefan, I think you've finally found your color," Sophie said. "And your dress, such style!"

"Oh, you flatterer, you. But yes, it's new! Don't tell anyone, but last night, I helped Nurse Klara with her blood draws—there are real sick people here, you wouldn't believe!—and she gave me one of her old dresses as a thank you. You have to admit, it's stunning! You can't find this quality of fabric even in the best shops in Prague. I've always said that Berlin was the place to be!"

Stefan's powerful body, squeezed into a dress many sizes too small, moved animatedly as he spoke; his Adam's apple bobbed quickly up and down his neck. Aside from the fact that he was born in Prague, no one truly knew his story, but legend had it that he'd always managed to escape from the clinics where he was committed. When found, he would simply explain to the exasperated caregivers that he would only accept treatment from Jewish doctors. Everyone knew they were the best, right? Though not Jewish himself, when the Nazis, nearly as frightened of mental illness as they were of *impure* blood, decided to shut down most of the country's psychiatric hospitals, they probably took sadistic pleasure in sending the poor soul to be treated in one of the last Jewish hospitals still functioning in their twisted world.

"You're not arguing, I hope? You know I have an eye for these things. Come on, tell Uncle Stefan what's bothering you."

"It's nothing, Stefan. Just Lena . . . still believing in an ideal world. She prefers to close her eyes, while mine are wide open."

"An ideological quarrel! I love it! It reminds me of the joke about the priest and the rabbi who walk into a gay bar, have you heard it?"

"Not in front of Lena, Stefan! You know her innocent ears couldn't bear it!"

Lena blushed, not quite understanding.

"Oh, my little lovelies. You're so sweet. Are you heading to the cafeteria? I'll walk you there. You need a bodyguard, and I'm your man," he said, draping his arms over their shoulders. "You know, there are some odd fellows lurking around."

"Yes," Sophie said. "Even Lena has noticed that."

•

The afternoon passed like a dream. The medical teams expended all their energy to make up for the morning's absences. There were wounds to clean, IVs to change, and by the time Lena finished her handover with the night shift, it was already late. She barely had time to gulp down a bowl of soup in the half-empty cafeteria before heading to the dormitory. There, she found Sophie lying on her bed, her gaze oddly fixed.

"What a day. I thought we'd never get through it! At last, we can rest; we've certainly earned it." Lena removed her shoes, slid them under the bed, and started unbuttoning her uniform. "Are you okay, Sophie? You're not feverish, I hope? With our morning march, anything's possible!"

Sophie turned toward Lena. Her eyes seemed to burn with a strange glow; her lips trembled slightly. "Feverish . . . that's what I thought. Your blind faith in your God is making you lose your mind. You didn't even go look, did you? No, your shocked expression confirms it: you're so sure of your fate that you don't feel concerned by our plight, us poor sinners. Well, then: you're neither on the list of those to be deported nor on Brunner's list of *ordners* for tomorrow night. Congratulations. But me . . ." Her voice cracked, like crystal shattered by a vicious blow. "I am on the list of *ordners*."

She turned away and buried her head in the pillow. Lena first had to decipher her words (the *ordners*? Ah yes, that Brunner's invention!) before letting out an ineffectual gasp. Sophie seemed shaken by the news. True, Lena had forgotten to check. But she had been so busy . . . and it wasn't the first time they had been selected for odd tasks. Only a week ago, in the middle of rounds, they had been requisitioned to work in the kitchen. After a few hours of slicing bread and tomatoes, they had been able to return to their usual duties. So why was Sophie in such a state of turmoil?

If Lena had listened a bit more carefully, she might have heard, hidden behind her deep faith, the embryo of doubt, the shadow of unease. But she was still so young, her spirit so thoroughly imbued with twenty years of Orthodox upbringing, that no troubling sign managed to penetrate her heart. All she could do to help her friend was to extend a hesitant hand toward her shoulder—a gesture that felt unnatural and awkward. Her hand remained among the blonde curls for a few seconds, then retracted. She wanted to speak but found nothing to say, murmured a platitude about the importance of restorative sleep, and thought that by the next day, all would be forgotten.

Slowly, she removed the rest of her clothes, recited a prayer, and slipped under her sheets.

6

• • •

Wednesday, September 30, 1942

The next day, Lena woke to find Sophie's bed already made. She must have risen early for a longer shower and a few minutes of peace and quiet; she did that sometimes. Yawning and stretching, Lena navigated the busy corridor to the bathroom, waiting for her turn. She quickly looked at her reflection in the stained mirror, smoothing her black eyebrows—she'd always found them too thick—before splashing water on her opal-white skin, her finely shaped lips. She'd often been told she was beautiful but never paid much attention to that sort of thing. Shrugging, she untangled her hair with an old metal comb, adjusted her cap, and deemed herself presentable.

The cafeteria was bustling with the usual morning activity. She scanned the room for Sophie but saw no sign of her; most likely, she had already gone up to the prison ward, a strange place where the patients were also prisoners. She quickly swallowed her breakfast before heading to the general surgery department. Adjusting from her hastily eaten slice of bread to the stark reality of bodily smells, to the rawness of humanity laid bare, was a daily struggle she still had not mastered. She spotted the night nurse, who was eagerly waiting for her before slipping away to the dormitory. But Ingrid, the head nurse, called her across the treatment room before she could get to her. "*Schwester* Lena! Come here, my dear."

Approaching her superior, Lena tried hard not to stare at her cheek, still bearing the mark of German violence.

"Yes, head nurse?"

"*Schwester* Lena. Don't worry, it's nothing serious. We're just short one nurse in the prison ward. Apparently, one of the girls simply didn't show up this morning. *Schwester* Rosa, you might know her? Rumor has it she often talked about escaping to Switzerland. Whatever she did, all I know is if the number of nurses in the prison ward isn't correct, Dr. Lustig will have trouble with the Gestapo. And if the doctor has trouble, it'll trickle down to me, and then to you. So, let's go."

Lena followed her superior up the stairs, feeling a knot of anxiety tighten in her stomach. During her three months at the hospital, she'd never ventured beyond the second floor.

Soon, they reached the fourth floor. "Welcome to the prison ward," Ingrid announced. "As you might know, this ward operates differently from the rest of the hospital. Our patients are unique because they are prisoners on reprieve. For reasons unknown to me, the Nazis sometimes decide that their prisoners—whether from labor camps, collection centers, or just regular prisons—are too fatigued for whatever awaits them, so they send them to us for a bit of a tune-up before taking them back. The irony of the situation does not escape me, of course. But what can you do? We have to do our job."

"Yes, my friend Sophie works in this ward; she's explained it to me . . ."

"Then you already know everything! But here's a detail Sophie might not have mentioned: we often get unexpected visits from the Gestapo, whose agents are eager to reclaim their prey. They're not doctors, but if they were to discover a healed patient that hadn't been reported to them, you can imagine the consequences for the ward.

So, no overachieving, no sparks! Follow Dr. Kreindl's instructions precisely, and all will be well. You'll see, he's a fair and experienced doctor. Come, I'll introduce you."

They crossed a vestibule into a long, wide room. At first glance, the treatment room looked no different from those in other wards. Beds were lined up on both sides, spaced a meter apart—an insular world governed by the informal ballet of nurses and nursing aides. However, upon closer inspection of each bed, Lena noticed small iron circles around the patients' emaciated wrists. "Yes, the patients are handcuffed to the beds," the head nurse said, preempting Lena's question. "Ah, there's Dr. Kreindl."

A man approached them, his hands buried in the side pockets of his buttoned-up lab coat. He had a friendly, wrinkled face. A cigarette dangled from his lips, bobbing slowly up and down as he walked.

"Good morning, doctor. Here's your new nurse, *schwester* Lena. General surgery is lending her to you. She promised me she'd be up to the task."

The old man took a puff and glanced at his new recruit as a grandfather might scrutinize the soul of a newborn. "Welcome, Nurse Lena. You'll see," he said with a gravelly voice, "once you get used to the handcuffs and the Gestapo visits, it almost feels like a normal ward." He hiccupped, a sound that might have been mistaken for laughter. "You'll be in charge of beds 1 through 5. These are fairly simple cases, some minor trauma. Our patients will tell you their stories; like in any ward, part of your work will be to listen to them." He leaned forward, and Lena felt the warmth of his breath on her forehead. "Of course, we're as concerned about their mental state as we are about their physical condition. They know their stay here is only a temporary reprieve, that sooner or later, we'll have to hand them back to the Nazis. But I don't want to dampen your spirits on your first day. Get going! Check their vitals and introduce yourself. I need to sign some papers, and I'll join you in a bit."

His cigarette was almost fully burnt; he took one last puff with a half-smile, turned on his heels, and disappeared into a cloud of smoke.

Lena moved slowly from beds 1 to 4, relieved to find that checking vitals wasn't all that different from one ward to another. She diligently recorded temperatures and blood pressures, inspected dressings and casts, immersing herself in the familiar routine amidst an unfamiliar setting.

At bed number 5, the patient was asleep. No matter, rounds would start soon; she would leave it to the doctor to wake him. His temperature was good, blood pressure stable . . . what did his chart say? *Crushed right hand, multiple rib fractures, ankle fracture.* Lena looked at his face. A thin mustache outlined his upper lip. He had a high forehead topped with thick, wavy hair, and even in sleep, he seemed to be smiling. Lena checked the IV bag. It was almost empty; she'd need to mention it to the doctor. A soft rustling made her turn: the sheet, which seconds earlier had covered her patient, had slid down to his navel, revealing a man's torso, covered in black hair. The young nurse let her pen drop; it rolled under the bed. She hesitated a second before getting on all fours on the gray linoleum. Raising her head, she saw Sophie watching her with a mix of amusement and distress. She was still in this slightly awkward position when she heard a moan.

"Room service? Did you bring me my breakfast?" Lena stood up quickly—dropping her pen again—and leaned toward her patient with all the commitment of a devoted nurse.

"No, sir . . . you're in the hospital, don't you remember?"

After a brief silence, the man opened his eyes and burst out laughing.

"Oh, you should see your face! Of course, I know where I am. But who are you? You don't look like my usual nurse."

Lena felt a flush of warmth cross her face—a strange, fleeting sensation. She adjusted her cap and quickly composed a professional look. "Ah, I see you're a comedian. Nice to meet you, Mr. Comedian. I'm your new nurse, *schwester* Lena."

"A thousand apologies, dear Lena. You'll understand that in here, humor is all we have left. I would shake your hand, but as you can see, some of our comrades were keen to test the resistance of metal against human bone, and it seems they've found their answer."

He contemplated the bandage wrapping his hand; a shadow passed over his green eyes. With his strong jaw, his face could belong to a twenty-year-old as much as to a seasoned forty-year-old, but upon closer inspection, a few lines crossed his forehead, and his gaze was that of a man who knew life. "I'm Arthur. Don't worry, I promise to behave if you ask the doctor to increase my doses of painkillers."

He gave a mysterious smile, pulled the sheet up to his chest, and closed his eyes.

•

There were many moments throughout the day when Lena had wanted to talk to her friend. They were going to work in the same ward! The patients were handcuffed to their beds, and one of them was quite the joker! But Sophie was always busy with a blood draw or a dressing to change and generally seemed to be doing everything to avoid communicating. At dinner time, her friend seemed so pensive that Lena decided not to push any further; they ate in silence. Sophie left the table before Lena was done. "See you later," Lena said softly.

Minutes later, Lena got up and started up the central staircase, already dreaming of a good night's sleep. How fortunate she had been to meet Sophie! In that vast dormitory, where nurses slept on camp beds only a few centimeters apart, she could have ended up next to anyone. But on the evening of her arrival, the head nurse had pointed to a bed, and said, "This is your spot for now; try not to get too attached to it." It was already late, and the dorm buzzed with the girls' snoring. Lena had placed her rucksack on the brown blanket and looked around, feeling completely lost. But Sophie had propped herself up on an elbow and given her one of her trademark looks. "Welcome to our establishment, miss; I hope the bedding will be to your liking!" There had been a moment of hesitation, a discreet imbalance, and then they had laughed, without quite knowing why. Sophie had taken her under her wing, and since then, they had been all but inseparable.

Through a window, Lena noticed a group of about ten people crossing the park. But her fatigue was such that the information passed through her mind without lingering. She splashed some water on her face—the bathroom was strangely quiet—and entered what was whimsically referred to as "the stable," thinking it a curious nickname for a dormitory. She removed her clothes, lay down, and closed her eyes.

She was sound asleep when the women cut across the darkness with muffled steps and, like soft shadows, spread out across the beds. If one could have seen their faces, it would have been clear that war had once again played its role as a catalyst for infinity, a compressor of time. These young girls, barely out of adolescence, bore the marks of a fractured world, a humanity adrift. Lena heard the squeak of springs, but she merely stirred in her sleep, murmured something, clung to her pillow, and returned to the boundless sanctuary of her dreams.

7

• • •

Thursday, October 1, 1942, 1 p.m.

At lunchtime, Lena hurried to find a seat near Sophie. She was eager to talk to her, having missed her again at breakfast. Oh, wasn't it grand that they'd ended up in the same ward? And what about that patient in bed number 5 . . . all the nurses found him devilishly charming. So, what did she think? Lena knew about her friend's reputation. Rumor had it that Sophie had extensive experience with men. While still in high school, she had reportedly seduced one of the Berlin orchestra's top musicians, and none other than maestro Karajan himself had walked in on them sharing a passionate moment in an empty room of the *Konzerthaus*. One evening, Lena had timidly asked her about the truth in these stories, and Sophie had just tilted her head back and laughed with that warm, velvety laugh Lena had learned to love.

"Sophie?"

Sophie hadn't touched her plate. She had a distant, fixed gaze. Her whole body was contracted—neck, shoulders, hands—giving her the air of a card castle ready to collapse at the slightest gust. Slowly, she turned toward Lena, who finally saw the violet circles under her eyes, the red conjunctivis, and the pallor in her cheeks. Sophie stared at her for a few seconds, her jaw clenched, then she suddenly pushed her plate away. Her chair scraped the floor as she stood up. Leaning forward, she whispered in a cold breath, "If you really want to know if your *God* is all-powerful and everything is for the best, then join us in Hilde's room. Those of us who were lucky enough to take a little moonlight excursion last night will be glad to enlighten you."

Several nurses stood up, following her lead. Lena wanted to speak, but the words got stuck in her throat. How foolish of her! She had forgotten about that *ordner* affair. Sophie must have gone through a disturbing experience, and Lena hadn't even been there to support her. Well, she would talk to her; things would work out. They had to. But first, to finish her lunch. She went back to her soup, letting her mind wander. Oh, how lucky she was with this new position! And the patients seemed so interesting. She drank a large glass of water. Still, it was troubling to see how Sophie reacted; what could have been so terrible last night? She looked up, noticing the scattered tables across the large hall, and the strange unease that had been twisting in her stomach for the last few minutes finally made sense: the hall did seem emptier than usual. About a third emptier. She swallowed the last sip of soup and got up.

She headed toward the "stable," wondering about the best way to appease Sophie. No doubt, she would be in Hilde's room. Some of the more senior nurses had the privilege of living in private quarters. Hilde, a pediatric nurse, had gathered around her a clique of followers, a sort of inner circle everyone called Lustig's girls. It was no secret that Dr. Lustig, though married to an Aryan woman—which afforded him a certain peace of mind, as did his conversion to Catholicism—couldn't resist plunging knee-deep into the fountain of youth offered by his subordinates. In the minds of these women, getting close to the hospital director was, in turn, one of the best ways to avoid disappearing without notice from the face of the earth, leaving behind nothing but an empty seat in the cafeteria.

Sophie had managed to be accepted by this exclusive group, even while claiming to still be resisting Dr. Lustig's advances. The young women would meet in Hilde's room after meals, smoke some contraband cigarettes, and relish the latest hospital gossip. After all, they lived in a closed space, and despite the war, couples formed and broke up, hearts melted, and jealousy and love were running everywhere. Sophie had often invited her, but Lena had never been able to bring herself to join them. She wasn't ready to hear those stories of liaisons, to inhale cigarette smoke while pretending to find no fault in it, and above all, she feared being questioned about her tastes or, worse, her lack of experience with men. And deep down in her heart, she considered her discretion, almost secretly, as a strength.

A few more steps and she would reach Hilde's door. Seeing her reflection in a glass pane, she suddenly thought of her mother. Toward the end of her life, her mind had lost some of its sharpness. But one evening, cancer had given her a brief respite, and a peculiar light had animated her eyes. She had grabbed Lena's hand and said, "My daughter. How beautiful you are. Look at me. How have I created such a magnificent soul? Here's yet another reason to believe in our Creator. You know, I've had a good life . . ."

Lena had wanted to object, but her mother had raised her hand. "Let me finish, while I still have the strength. Yes, I was fortunate to be happy, to live sheltered from the world. Your father knew my limits and loved me for my flaws. But in you, I see a spark, an intelligence I never possessed. One day, you might be tempted to stand out, but let me warn you: standing out comes with a price. So, if I can give you one piece of advice in these uncertain times, it's to keep your head down; let the wave pass. It isn't the first time our people have been threatened, nor will it be the last. Fear not, God will protect us. He has a plan, and we must honor it. Now come over here and give your old mother a kiss." Lena had hugged her mother one last time before going to bed.

Now she knocked on Hilde's door, emboldened by her friendship with Sophie, by her desire to make amends—for what, she wasn't entirely sure—and, she had to admit it to herself, by a certain form of curiosity. But when the door opened, instead of the conspiratorial wink she'd hoped for, which would have confirmed that this was all just a misunderstanding, a triviality of no importance, all she found in Sophie's eyes was a dark anger that chilled her to the bone.

So, she stepped back, muttering silent words, turned on her heels, and went back up to the prison ward.

No doubt, up there, someone would need her help.

8

• • •

Thursday, October 15, 1942, 10 a.m.

DAYS TURNED INTO WEEKS, AND SOON, IT BECAME ALMOST POSsible to think of the events of the community center as belonging to a distant past. The cafeteria's empty chairs welcomed new recruits, and there was work to be done, always more work; it became clear to all staff that their salvation lay—at least in part—in their utility, that the moment they became a bit less useful, a bit less efficient, their likelihood of disappearing eastward increased accordingly.

In the prison ward, Lena was slowly finding her footing. She had just opened a blood-soaked dressing when the head nurse called her over from across the ward. "*Schwester* Lena, come here," she said. The stigma of the German slap had vanished from her cheek, and she had regained all her natural authority. Sophie was standing by her side. "You are both requisitioned to help in the emergency ward. It's madness over there. As you may know, the number of suicides is increasing daily in the city . . . go! Dr. Kreindl is already there; he asked for you himself."

The two women looked at each other in silence. Since the tension of the scene in Hilde's room, their relationship had indeed softened; perhaps they needed each other more than they realized. After a few awkward days, through tentative steps, they had found each other again. They'd begun with mundane conversations about the quality of the soup or the temperature in the dormitory. And then one day, over some trivial misunderstanding—neither could recall exactly what—they had both burst out laughing, and after that, they'd simply fallen into each other's arms, suddenly understanding the futility of their quarrel. But each also felt that a bit of the original purity of their friendship had been lost and replaced with something less extraordinary, and this realization brought immense sadness to them both.

The two women followed their chief through the labyrinth of underground corridors that, like hollow roots, interconnected the various buildings. Besides their obvious practical role—allowing stretcher-bearers to transport patients from one ward to another without crossing the park—the basements had lately transformed into makeshift air-raid shelters, for lack of a better option. A few months earlier, the entire staff had experienced this first-hand when Royal Air Force planes had flown over Berlin, marking the dawn of a military reaction to the enemy and warming many hearts in the process.

They emerged from these depths to an apocalyptic scene. The corridor outside the emergency ward was lined with stretchers. On each stretcher, an ailing body. It was as if the treatment room, filled to the brim and unable to defend itself better, had regurgitated the overflow of patients all the way to the stairs. Despite the cramped space, doctors and nurses bustled between the beds, administering IVs, examining, speaking, encouraging. Hovering over them, and marring the whiteness with their dark presence, were dry souls with eyes like pebbles.

Gestapo agents were shouting absurd orders at the medical professionals, the wise healers trying to do their jobs. "You better revive that one! He needs to be ready for his transport to the east tomorrow morning!"

Lena spotted Dr. Kreindl, who without his cigarette, seemed a bit lost. But he knew better than to light up: the Gestapo would have never tolerated such an act of freedom, coming from a Jew.

"Ah, there you are," he said. "Listen, it's quite simple. Most of these patients have ingested large doses of Veronal. Do you know this drug? It's a highly powerful sedative. Anyway, many of these people were selected for transport, you understand . . . well, we need to revive them, that's what we're here for. You know the Nazis. They don't want to let a single life slip away from their grip." His thick eyebrows furrowed together. "We must do our job. Start with the patients at the end of the hallway; they're the latest arrivals."

"Yes, doctor!"

He looked exhausted, in his beautiful white coat. A blue bow tie peeked out from his collar, supporting his head with its curved wings.

The corridor was lined with about thirty stretchers, gathering individuals of all ages—from a teenager whose eyes had seen too much to a cachectic old man who, in a moment of defiance, had sought to maintain some control over his destiny.

"Come on, beautiful," Sophie said. "Let's split the work: I'll take those on the right, you take the left. Can you handle it? Don't hesitate to call me if you need anything." She lowered her voice and gripped Lena's elbow. "Let's not let them intimidate us, okay? Be strong, focused, and try to forget about them," she said, nodding toward the men in leather coats.

They set to work, moving from bed to bed with dexterity, performing blood draws, checking blood pressure. When possible, a brief interrogation revealed the nature and dose of the ingested medication. They enjoyed working together; they were still young nurses with so much to learn, and it was easier to do so in pairs. They had spent many evenings revising procedures, memorizing movements. One night—late, with the dormitory already asleep—Lena had wanted to show Sophie her vein visualization technique that made blood draws easier. Lying on her friend's bed, holding her arm, she had explained her trick. *"See, you have to imagine it parting in two, like a blue river . . . the gesture must be firm, yet supple." "Yes, it's always better if it's firm . . ." "What?" "Never mind, Lena!"* Exhausted, they had fallen asleep tangled in each other's arms. The next morning, an outraged head nurse had dragged them into her office to explain that *strange and unnatural relations* were completely prohibited in her establishment; no further tolerance would be accepted. Lena had wanted to intervene—what could she possibly be talking about?—but Sophie had stopped her. Once outside, she had said, "You didn't get it, did you?" and explained to her friend—whose Orthodox upbringing had skipped the chapter on lesbian loves—the meaning of the reprimand they had just faced. They had laughed until their stomachs hurt. The story, of course, had made its way around the hospital and prompted Stefan to start calling them his *lovely mouths.*

The two women worked fiercely, setting up IVs designed to flush out the poison from every patient's blood. But it was overwhelming work. After an hour, the confined workspace, compared to their usual treatment rooms, the heat, noise, and overpowering smells of urine and gastric content took their toll on Lena. She looked for Sophie and approached her unsteadily. Sophie, always the stronger one, was moving from one patient to the next without showing any signs of fatigue.

"Sophie, I'm feeling dizzy . . . could you finish setting up this IV, please? I need to rest for a minute."

"Of course, my dear. I've got you. Those Gestapo bastards are busy at the other end of the corridor."

Lena approached the window and pressed her forehead against the cold glass. Outside, autumn was quietly exhaling. "Air . . ." she thought. She opened the window and filled up her lungs. Beneath her, the weeping willow stretched its thin arms. Her vision blurred, and she thought she saw her mother's face in the intertwining of bare branches. "If only I could touch her," she thought, leaning forward as if in a dream.

"Miss . . . miss!" a voice said behind her. She startled and caught herself on the windowsill. "Miss, be careful. You almost fell!"

Lena turned around, her heart racing.

"Ah, you're awake! I'm glad. How are you feeling?"

"Were you going to jump?" asked the young girl, who couldn't have been older than sixteen.

"Jump? Oh no, not at all. I just had a moment of weakness. The fresh air is doing me good."

"Are you my nurse?" She wore a blue blouse with faded linear patterns. Her long, black lashes shielded an ageless sadness.

"Yes, I'm the one who gave you the IV. You took a lot of medication, didn't you?" The girl averted her eyes and clenched her jaw.

"Please, miss . . . could you close the window? I'm afraid I'll catch pneumonia with this draft."

Lena paused for a moment, then simply stood up, closed the window, and returned to place her hand on the girl's forearm. They remained like that for a while. Then, Lena pulled the blanket up over her shoulders and moved on to the next patient.

An hour remained before lunch break. Gone were the early days, when every patient was an opportunity for joyous discovery. She had always dreamed of becoming a nurse. But as a country girl, the path leading to the hospital wasn't an obvious one. Her father was a butcher, and so was his father before him. One of the joys of her childhood was digging her fingers into the henhouse straw, feeling around for the warmth of a freshly laid egg. Life had been simple, and beautiful. There was home, school, and the rabbi's lessons. Sometimes, she earned some pocket money by watching over the neighbor's children, and during one of those mornings, she'd stumbled upon a photograph of a nurse in a newspaper. Oh, what elegance she'd seen in the white uniform, the rolled-up sleeves, the pristine cap! Her destiny had suddenly became clear. That very evening, still exhilarated, she'd announced to her parents: she would be a nurse. They were used to her bursts of enthusiasm, usually short-lived—just days earlier, she had imagined herself an explorer in Africa—but that time, the whim had turned into a lasting passion.

Lena was busy setting up an IV for an elderly man with veins as thin as a child's hair. After two attempts at the wrist and one at the elbow fold, she had only managed to create rapidly spreading purple bruises. She sensed Dr. Kreindl standing behind her.

"So, *schwester* Lena, are you planning to place that IV in this lifetime or the next?"

Dr. Kreindl's exasperated tone took Lena by surprise. Was it the pressure from the Gestapo that had been harassing him for hours, the unbearable heat in the corridor, the relentless stream of patients? The doctor was undoubtedly under immense pressure. Lena didn't have time to ponder further and was already looking for a vein on the other arm. But Dr. Kreindl grumbled behind her, his heavy breathing distracting her.

"What's taking so long? Six more patients have just arrived."

"Just a moment, doctor, I'm almost there . . ."

Then, the doctor made a strange noise with his mouth, a kind of dry click, followed by a long sigh. He sunk his head into his bow tie and said, in a barely audible voice, "Anyway, it's pointless. All these people will be gassed, no matter what."

Those words traveled through the air, surpassing Lena's inner ear, the three small bones and all the usual machinery, and made their way to her brain, where they encountered a significant obstacle: nowhere in her vocabulary or experience did Lena have the means to connect those two words, *humans* and *gassed*. How does one gas a human? It made no sense. She blinked, continued to search under the old man's skin, and finally, the purple liquid flowed back into the needle. Pleased with herself, she loosened the tourniquet, filled three tubes which she gently placed on her tray, connected the saline bag, and crafted a smooth and clean dressing, applying exactly enough pressure to prevent bleeding. Then, she moved on to the next patient.

Dr. Kreindl, for his part, had already moved away. He would have given anything for a cigarette.

9

• • •

Friday, October 16, 1942, 7 a.m.

LENA RETURNED TO THE PRISON WARD WITH A SENSE OF RELIEF. How fortunate she was to have been transferred there! She could never have endured the pace of the emergency room on a daily basis. She hadn't told anyone about Dr. Kreindl's words—not even Sophie—and awaited his arrival with a touch of apprehension. Hopefully, he wouldn't revisit his crazy talk of gas.

The elderly doctor entered the ward. He had swapped his bow tie for a striking red tie and wore a crisply ironed lab coat. Smiling, he walked over to Lena and leaned toward her. "Good morning, Lena. Did you manage to get some rest? Thank you for helping us out yesterday . . . yes, a nasty business. But you and Sophie were perfect. Let's try to forget that day—and everything that may have been said—and focus on our regular patients. Agreed? As a start, please arrange a chest X-ray for the patient in bed number 2."

Overjoyed to see the conversation moving definitively away from the subject of gas and humans—it had already dropped several notches in her mind, and was making the turn toward her repressed unconscious—Lena began to search her cart for the X-ray request form.

"Did you know," Dr. Kreindl continued, "that I was trained right here, in Professor Krause's ward? Does that name mean anything to you? No, of course, you're much too young. He was a brilliant man who developed, as early as 1903, the sigmoidoscope still used worldwide today! The mind will always conquer brute strength. Remember that, my dear: the mind will always conquer brute strength . . ."

His body was suddenly racked with a violent coughing fit. He removed his glasses, wiped them with an embroidered handkerchief, and rubbed his chest.

"Doctor . . . are you okay?"

"Certainly, certainly . . ." he said, putting his glasses back on his crooked nose. "At my age, nothing more natural than a little dry cough as winter approaches. Now, I have some papers to sign. We start rounds in five minutes. Be ready!"

With a spring in her walk, Lena went to check an IV at bed number 1, passing by Arthur's bed. As usual, he had taken his shirt off, and his sheet was draped around his hips.

"*Schwester* Lena! My favorite nurse," he said as he saw her walk by. "Yesterday, I really thought you had abandoned me! Despite your colleagues' vehement protests, I insisted that my dressing not be changed in your absence. I can't do without your magic touch anymore."

Lena stepped back and nearly bumped into Sophie, who was passing behind her with a dressing tray.

"Watch out, Lena! You'll make me trip!" she said, strangely tense.

Lena regained her balance, crossed her arms over her uniform, and frowned slightly.

"He's something, isn't he?" she murmured to Klara, as they moved away toward the next bed. "I'm his nurse, nothing more. I'm not sure he's supposed to talk to me that way!"

"He just fancies you, that's all," said the night nurse, who had just finished her morning handover and was dreaming of a few hours of sleep. "Don't you complain. Do you know how many of the girls would like to be in your shoes? It's not every day we welcome such a celebrity to the ward!"

Lena wanted to know more, but Dr. Kreindl was back. "Rounds, *schwester* Lena!"

Over the weeks, it had become one of her favorite moments. With Dr. Kreindl, medicine suddenly became clear: traumatology, toxicology, plaster casting, and blood drawing—he explained everything with the ease of someone who understood the essential primary mechanics of it all. He got the nurses and the patients involved in his decision-making, explaining the medical options and his logical reasoning. And above all, he glowed with such humanity. Never would he hesitate to place a hand on a shoulder or whisper a few encouraging words to his most seriously ill patients.

"*Schwester* Lena, increase the aspirin dosage for the patient in bed number 4. He complained of intense abdominal pains last night." His voice deepened. "As you know, it's nearly impossible for us to influence the fate of our patients after they leave us. But as long as they are under our care, it's our duty to speak to them, to soothe their pain as much as we can. Can you take care of that? Go on, my dear, I trust you. If you need me, I'll be in the break room."

Lena began her rounds. Arriving at bed number 4, she searched her cart for aspirin.

"Sophie!" she called out, seeing her friend pass by. "Could you lend me a packet or two of aspirin? My cart is empty."

Sophie was oddly stiff that morning. "Impossible. The night team used up the last doses."

Yet, fulfilling Dr. Kreindl's prescription and alleviating her patient's pain was essential. The option of consulting Dr. Guber was there; his beautiful pharmacy, hidden in the basement and always tinged with a scent of camphor, was filled with odd vials of all shapes and sizes. But Lena could already imagine his answer, having heard it many times: "My dear child, we are at war. I'll do my best, but you must understand it's already a miracle this hospital functions at all!" This pleasant man was unique in being their only Christian colleague. When the Nazis had decided, a few months prior, to dismiss all non-Jewish employees from the hospital, he had been the only one granted an exemption. He drew no pride from it, though. According to him, the Nazis simply couldn't bear the thought of entrusting such a significant stock of medicines to a Jew.

Arthur's voice pulled her from her thoughts. "*Schwester* Lena, come here." He had propped himself up on an elbow and was looking at her intently. "I overheard, unwillingly of course, your little aspirin supply issue. Come, I might have a solution for you."

Lena hesitated, looked for Sophie—who was busy preparing a pill organizer—finally decided, and walked over to Arthur.

"I'm listening," she said.

"Well, *schwester* Lena, believe it or not, I haven't always spent the majority of my time handcuffed to a hospital bed, calmly waiting to heal before being shipped off to a labor camp."

Lena swallowed and moved her arms around, unsure where to place them.

"What I mean is, before all this, I was lucky enough to study chemistry, and as it turns out, one of my research areas was aspirin. It's a field that . . . let's just say I know it quite well. So, I want you to do something for me. When I first got here, I noticed a weeping willow in the garden. Do you know which tree I'm talking about?"

"Yes, Arthur. It's one of my favorites."

"Good, good. Here's what you're going to do: as soon as you have the chance, go down to the park and tear off about ten pieces of bark from that tree. Boil them in water for twenty minutes. Then, strain the liquid and hand over the magic potion to my charming neighbor in bed number 4."

His voice had taken on a dense, almost authoritative tone that Lena had never heard before. But she knew Arthur and simply waited for the moment he would burst out laughing and admit he was just teasing her, as usual. However, he continued to gaze at her with a strange calm, waiting for her reply.

"Give tree bark to my patients? You must be joking!" Lena finally exclaimed. "Why am I even listening to you? Are you trying to get me fired?"

She realized she had almost shouted. There was a moment of silence during which Arthur watched her with an amused look. Then, she shook her head, let out an incredulous grunt, and turned away, avoiding him for the rest of the day.

•

Lena and Sophie had a few minutes to spare before dinner and decided to go for a quick walk in the park. Soon, it would be too cold for these breaths of fresh air. They walked in silence, accompanied only by a few sparse birds hopping from branch to branch. Stefan's usual call pulled them away from their thoughts. "Yoohoo! My lovely mouths!"

He was wearing men's trousers, but his lips shone with a vermilion color. "So, what's new with you, my beauties?"

The two friends mumbled some trivialities.

"Oh, you seem pensive tonight. Did something happen?"

Their unspoken ritual dictated that Sophie would answer, but that evening, her mind was elsewhere.

"Well, yes, Stefan," Lena said. "This afternoon, a patient tried to play a trick on me. We were out of aspirin, and he seriously suggested—of all things—that I give tree bark tea to a patient. Can you believe it? Was he trying to poison him? And the worst part is, I almost believed him!"

"Tree bark tea? How curious . . . I've always believed trees held magical powers. In fact, I love wrapping my arms around their trunks, it calms me. But to drink a bark infusion, that's something else altogether. Tell me, who is this patient?"

"It's my patient in bed 5. His name is Arthur."

"Arthur? That's a fine name. Let me guess: extremely handsome, broad-chested, thick- haired man? Sophie, do you know who he is?"

"Not really . . ." said Sophie, absent-mindedly.

"Not really? Well, my little mouths, you're way off the mark here! Haven't you heard of the famous Dr. Eichenberg?"

He burst into hysterical, uncontrollable laughter. "Oh, you girls are really something! Fortunately for you, Uncle Stefan keeps up with the news. Lena, unbeknownst to you, you're treating the inventor of aspirin!"

Lena stopped and turned toward Stefan. Sophie had still said nothing.

"Sophie, you little sneak, you knew, I'm sure! Oh, you're incorrigible, girlfriends." His laughter finally subsided. He wiped away the tears running down his mascara, took a deep breath, and hiccupped one last time. "Well, since I must be the one to enlighten you: the good doctor worked at Bayer before the war. Actually, he led a whole research laboratory. He had already made a name for himself by discovering the treatment for gonorrhea, and just for that, I'd erect a statue in his honor—but, on my right, we've already lost Lena, who doesn't know about gonorrhea. Never mind, that's for another time, moving on!—as I was saying, he led a research laboratory, and as you keep searching, eventually, you find. His team was the first in the world to discover a pure and stable form of aspirin. But his timing was terrible. Jews were gradually being excluded from all professions, and quite quickly, he found himself out of a job. It's also said—and this is top secret, my little mouths!—that Bayer's CEO took the precaution of gathering all his top scientist's research documents before firing him. Then, he calmly patented the molecule in his own name. Now, every time an aspirin box is sold, that sneaky old man's bank account gets heavier with gold coins, while dear old Arthur, he gets only Lena's gentle care. Which is worth all the gold coins in the world, if you ask me, *meine liebe!*" he said, pinching her cheek.

Lena sat on an old bench. "Well, then! But why didn't he tell me! So, the weeping willow bark is related to aspirin? Is that it, Stefan? And you, Sophie, did you know?"

"Me? No, I'm just finding out. Besides, he's not my patient. I don't know him."

"Ah, Uncle Stefan has surprised you tonight, hasn't he? But let's get back to more serious matters. It's dinner time; I'll walk you to the cafeteria." As usual, he placed himself between the two women. "Want to be in on another secret? Nurse Klara promised to lend me her tweezers after dinner. Look," he said, pulling up his trousers to his knee, "my legs are so hairy! It's damn right terrifying!"

The three friends, who in another life would never have crossed paths, thus entered the cafeteria, under the amused gaze of their peers. Stefan left them to join the table reserved for psychiatric patients. Lena and Sophie lined up for dinner, but an odd silence had set in between them. Lena, dreamy-eyed, was already wondering about the best time to collect the bark. Sophie, for her part, whispered something ("I'm not very hungry, I'm going to bed") before slipping away, but her words were lost in the dining room's clatter, and when Lena turned around to tell her friend she was saving her a seat at the table, she realized Sophie had vanished.

10

• • •

Saturday, October 17, 1942, 8:30 p.m.

DRENCHED IN SWEAT, THE TWO BODIES FINALLY DISENTANGLED from an age-old struggle. Sophie laid back, swiftly pulling the white sheet over her chest. The man, still panting, lay on his back, boldly presenting his protruding belly to the room's humid air.

Dr. Lustig reached for the nightstand and grabbed a cigarette. "Want one?" he asked as he struck a match. "Here, take this one." He took one puff before passing it to Sophie.

"Ah . . . nothing like a cigarette after sex. Don't you think?" he said, lighting up another for himself.

"That's exactly what I was thinking, Doctor Doctor," Sophie said, exhaling a cottony cloud that floated, weightless, in the semi-darkness.

"Oh, none of that between us, my dear. In public, of course, we must maintain appearances, but in here, you can call me Walter. Or even Walt, if you like."

Sophie sat up against the headboard, drawing her knees close to her, struggling to conceal her grimace; she would never call him Walt. The cover slipped momentarily, and the double doctor devoured her with his gaze. What a beast of a man! She'd been with him for over an hour. Never would she have imagined such ardor in a man of his age, stocky and bald as a billiard ball. But there was no denying it: the doctor's appetite was indeed insatiable.

It had been a week since Sophie first shared his bed. For months, Lustig had courted her, both discreetly and clumsily. She had resisted at first, feeling only distrust and aversion toward this severe man and his ridiculous mustache, clipped tightly over his small lips. But her friends from the Lustig girls—those who had already consented to exchange favors with the director—kept encouraging her to accept even his most intimate propositions.

"Come on, old girl, what's the risk?" Hilde, one of Lustig's long-standing mistresses, had told her. The young women were sharing a cigarette, sitting on the edge of a bed. "Sure, he's no fashion model, but in these times, I don't see a better insurance against a trip to the east. And after all, our dear doctor isn't so bad-looking . . . if you see him from the right angle, that is!"

"Yes, in the dark, he's almost handsome!" said Leslie, a fierce little brunette.

"That's it," said Ella, the third of the group. "He has an inner beauty. His beauty is his ability to erase you from the lists. Isn't that enough for you?" Her thick black eyebrows and serious demeanor contrasted with the other two's gentleness—a dominatrix, thought Sophie.

"Yes, you know what they say about him," Leslie resumed cheerfully, "*if you keep his balls light, stay off the lists you might!*"

"I've heard it more like: *focus on suction, to avoid deportation!*" added Ella, her eyes sparkling.

The girls erupted into a fit of laughter. It was the kind of sound that's precious during times of war, carefree and youthful—a laughter that makes your stomach hurt and your face wet with tears. Once calm had returned, Hilde told Sophie: "Go on, my dear. If you know what's good for you, don't miss this opportunity. At worst, you'll just have to close your eyes and think of someone else."

"What are you talking about?" she replied, trying in vain not to blush. "I have no ties, you know that. Love is for fools and children. Especially in these times."

"I'm not talking about anything! Sensitive one here, girls . . ."

Thus, week after week, the possibility took root in Sophie's mind. But she never mentioned it to Lena. She already knew what her reaction might be. She would have talked about principles and honor before retreating into a finely accusatory silence. But Lena didn't know life. It wasn't her God who wrote down the names on the lists. In their reality, God was named Lustig, and everything had to be done to be in his good graces. So, when night fell, she imagined the director's body against hers. She felt his breath against her skin, his mouth over her breasts, and ultimately didn't feel as disgusted as she had imagined. And above all else she couldn't help noticing, day after day, the slow disappearance of many friendly faces.

They were in a small room on the second floor that the director kept for his personal use. "Do you know, Sophie, that you're my favorite? At least with you, I can talk freely."

"Me, your favorite? I thought that was Hilde. Everyone knows she's your oldest mistress."

"Ah yes, everyone knows? Well, I guess I shouldn't be surprised. You know, with the others, it's purely sexual. Even with Hilde—and yet, I adore that dear child. Don't get me wrong; they're all absolutely charming. They come in, undress, laugh at my jokes, and accept my gifts, but after that, it's a quickie, and as soon as they feel they can leave without offending me, they do."

"A *quickie . . .*"

"Ha! You're amused by my expression. Well, it's always nice to make a woman laugh. Anyway, you get it. They're nice, but a bit foolish. Whereas you, I've always felt you knew life."

"Doctor, you're going to make me blush," Sophie said, throwing her blonde hair back.

"You know what I mean. No one else would dare talk to me that way. They're all about obedience and respect, despite our frolics. Can you imagine my situation? On the one hand, I know they're only here to please me and hopefully stay off the lists; I accept that, it doesn't make for a dire existential problem for me. What bothers me, ultimately, is this deep, cold, unspoken fear they all have of saying the wrong thing, expressing something that would displease me, subsequently ending their contract with me. But really, do they take me for such a monster? Whereas you, Sophie, I can sense that I don't scare you."

"I suppose I'm just too impressed by your aura, professor."

"Yes, I see, you continue to mock me. I like that. It's a nice change for me. For the last few years, I've oscillated between two positions: I terrify some, while others treat me like their puppet."

"Their puppet . . . are you talking about the Nazis?"

"Well, yes, the Nazis," Lustig said, suddenly sitting up straight. "You know, I'm not naive. I'm well aware that the staff fear me. And for the hospital to function, they must fear me. I must show myself to be uncompromising, hard, strict, even unreachable."

"Unreachable—not for everyone," Sophie said, winking and caressing his thigh.

"God is great, as the religious would say," Lustig mused, admiring the perfect body outlined by the white sheet. "The Nazis, on the other hand . . . well, I think you've already understood. I actually have no leeway. If they ask me for a list, I must provide it. If I don't, they'll kill me and my family and replace me with someone else, someone for whom the hospital's survival is not of the utmost importance. In reality"—his eyes took on a dark, almost black shade—"what I'm living through is hell. Writing down the names of my nurses, my doctors—people I respect and know well—on those lists, knowing full well what will happen to them, it's enough to finish a man. Peaceful sleep is but a memory for me. I already know their names will haunt me forever. If, by some odd chance, my life lasts long enough to afford the luxury of regret."

Sophie was caught off guard by the suddenness of these confessions. Since she had been sharing his bed, it was the first time Lustig had opened up like this. It was as if, physically emptied of an internal tension that had accumulated too long, his insides relaxed, his muscles finally freed, he could finally reveal a piece of his soul. She couldn't help but be fascinated.

"Go on, Walter," she said.

"Yes, call me Walter," Lustig said, smiling. "You know, my wife has nothing but harsh words for me; in order to please me, the staff call me 'double doctor' in my presence, undoubtedly using less flattering names behind my back. But you . . ." he turned toward her, and his hand slid the sheet down a few centimeters, revealing a heavy, joyful breast. "You understand me. You know what I'm trying to do. Because you're made of the same metal as I am."

"Survive, Walter?" Sophie said, looking him in the eye.

He drew his flushed face closer to her chest, and his hand was now moving under the sheet.

"Yes, my dear . . ." he said breathlessly. "Survive. Trust me, if the Nazis let me go on like this, then I will survive this war. Even if each name I write down takes a little bit of life from me, even if my soul frays with every filled-out form, I will do it. Anything for the hospital to stay open." His breathing shortened, and with an authoritative gesture, he vanquished the sheet's remaining resistance. "If some doctors, nurses, or patients have to leave, then so be it. I will remove two or three per department. Anyone who is not indispensable will be eliminated, but always, yes always, I will keep the hospital open, because if the hospital lives, then I live, and if you allow me, then you will live too . . ."

Sophie closed her eyes. Lustig drew closer and kissed her warm, lively body. And Sophie—who throughout the conversation had maintained a cool, calculating mind, thinking that the more information she gleaned, the greater her chances of survival would be—bit her lower lip, let go, and accepted Walter's kisses in a strange, primal, unpredictable surge of vitality. Thus, when he shifted his body onto hers, she offered no resistance, slowly moving her hands over his bald head, and when he said *oh, Sophie, that's why I love you*, she thought she had misheard and closed her eyes even tighter, and in the end, it was all just words because he was quickly inside her, and both were able, just for a moment, to escape from a world that had become too cruel.

11

• • •

Tuesday, October 20, 6 a.m.

HE TWITCHED HIS NOSTRILS AND CAUGHT THE FAINT SCENT OF warm coffee. A smile tugged at his lips. His dear Elsa was no doubt preparing one of her famous breakfasts in bed that had added a welcome touch of whimsy to their marriage over the years.

Truly, they had much to celebrate. After all, wasn't it he—the celebrated Dr. Arthur Eichenberg—who, after countless failed experiments, had finally unraveled one of modern science's most tantalizing questions? A stable form of aspirin. His discovery, the one that ought to have etched his name into the pantheon of great minds.

He shivered. The apartment was a nest of drafts; he really would have to speak to the housekeeper. He kept his eyelids shut, clinging to the illusion just long enough to nearly fool himself. He yawned, stretched—and the icy grip of the handcuff bit into his wrist, dragging his entire being back into the present.

The ward lay in a dim hush, broken only by the faint murmuring of the night nurses sipping their dreadful ersatz coffee in the break room near his bed. *Let them enjoy it,* he thought; moments of respite were rare enough to be cherished. He wiggled his toes, took stock of his pains, and admitted that—compared to some of the men that surrounded him—he was indeed fortunate.

His right hand had been crushed; his body was swollen with bruises, his bones likely cracked. But he was alive, tended by skilled physicians—Jews, of course, for who else would treat him?—and by tireless, kind nurses. Each day, three meals appeared before him. He had never asked where they came from, no doubt afraid that naming this small wonder might make it disappear.

Yet he was also a perceptive man, one who could not ignore the absurdity of his situation. He knew he was living on borrowed time, spared a prison cell—or worse—by no more than the Nazis' own contradictions. The same madness that had led them to arrest him had also prevented them from keeping him: they would not jail or deport (that hated, baffling word) anyone whose body was not "presentable." His own still hovered in a strange in-between, suspended in thin air between darkness and light. But he had seen many men, some in worse shape than he was, dragged away from their bed by Gestapo officers, armed with laws as new as their pistols were plentiful. As soon as they deemed him healed, his fate would be sealed. He understood that perfectly.

He took a deep breath, and a stab of pain shot through his ribcage.

Could he have avoided any of this? He would never forget his last conversation with the laboratory director. "*Eichenberg, you're a fortunate man. Thanks to your connections, the Gestapo will let you be. Stay home, work if you wish, but don't set foot here again.*"

Only later did he learn that the man who had dismissed him had already invited Elsa to live with him in a mountain chalet—seizing in one swift gesture the work of a lifetime and the woman he loved.

Weeks had passed. From the lonely comfort of his apartment, he could see the desolation descending upon Berlin. Should he have felt grateful? He did not know. He was alone, forgotten, betrayed.

He had given his life to science, contributing to the betterment of men. All for this to be his fate? Ah well. What use was aspirin—what use was relief—to men intent on destroying one another?

So came the evening when he opened one of his last bottles of cognac. He poured himself a glass. The poetic movement of the golden liquid leaving the bottle and blooming inside the glass stirred something in him. He drained it quickly, eager to repeat the experience. The warm blades of alcohol slid down his throat, rekindling a few dim internal lights. He felt a little less alone—and he needed to speak.

He found a blank sheet of paper, uncapped his fountain pen, kept the bottle close.

"Dear Laboratory Director . . ."

Ah, how sweet it was to let his bitterness spill onto the page: had he not given humanity a generous push forward? Not only through his work with aspirin, he reminded the man who had humiliated him, but through dozens of patents throughout a life's work. Did he not deserve better?

He continued in this spirit, lifting his fountain pen and quietly chuckling at the best parts, until he was satisfied. He inhaled, breathed out, and signed: *Dr. Arthur Eichenberg.* No—he struck out the "Dr." He had retained just enough lucidity to remember that titles were forbidden to him.

Satisfied, still faintly amused, he slipped the letter into an envelope, sealed it, and ran downstairs to drop it into the nearest mailbox. Then he returned to his apartment and fell asleep instantly.

Two days later, around six a.m., someone knocked. Three sharp blows—for three hulking silhouettes.

"Arthur Israel Eichenberg?"

Fear shot through his legs. *Why? Why now?* Then he pictured himself, half-drunk, signing the letter. Had he gone too far with his superior? In his mind, his tone had stayed acceptable; curteous, even. Sure, he'd had a bit to drink, but he'd been sober enough to remember not to sign *Doctor*—he was sure of it. A cold sweat ran down his spine. Could he have forgotten the second given name the Reich forced upon every German Jew? He couldn't have. But that was precisely what the half-shaven brute with hands like mallets was now announcing.

". . . for this serious offense, you are under arrest. Come with us, and don't make trouble."

He tried to resist—one last time. Too much injustice can break a man. But nature had placed more skill in his mind than in his fists, and it took the officers barely three minutes to turn his body into a canvas of red and blue.

At the police station, the head jailer—renowned for his perverse brutality—deemed the "package" too damaged for his cells.

"Take him to the Jewish hospital. They'll patch him up for us."

Yes, he was fortunate indeed.

He was surrounded by kindness, by his own people. The nurses were gentle and, some of them at least, still graced with a touch of innocence. Ah, innocence. To him it smelled of honey, wrapping itself around the bruised edges of his soul. Yet whenever his gaze met that of the older physicians, a quiet, shared worry passed between them.

And speaking of innocence—there was young Lena, entering the ward. Up early today.

12

• • •

Tuesday, October 20, 6:30 a.m.

That morning, Lena had woken up early. Quietly, she slid out of bed, slipped into her uniform, and headed toward the prison ward. The ward was calm. She cherished these rare moments of stillness when the night team was finishing up their duties while the sun revealed its first silvery rays. In those suspended moments, the days felt ripe with opportunities. She walked over to the break room, boiled some water, and fixed herself a cup of ersatz coffee.

Holding the hot mug close to her chest, she walked to the window. The true nature of the grains dissolving in the hot water mattered little to her—in her opinion, a barley grain was as good as any other, and truth be told, she had never tasted real coffee before setting foot at the hospital—and so, the smell of roasted grain, the sight of the park gently awakening before her, all of it was enough for her to feel content.

The night team joined her shortly, their bodies weary, dark purple circles painted under their eyes. "You're up early, Lena! Too eager to see your dear Arthur?" said one of the nursing assistants, sitting down abruptly.

"Arthur? I don't know what you're talking about . . . Did the night go well? Are there any patients that need close monitoring?"

"Sorry, Lena, we didn't mean to shock you," said Klara. "You know us, we enjoy teasing you." She leaned against the wall and slid her thick glasses up over her forehead. The two women got along well. They had realized that they had grown up in neighboring villages and under certain circumstances, that was enough to forge a quiet bond.

Klara tapped the bottom of her pack of cigarettes, grabbed a white stick, and delicately placed it between her lips; then she struck a match, protecting the flame with a skilled movement of her hand, before taking a first puff. The ritual never ceased to fascinate Lena.

"Want one?" she said, exhaling with delight. "No? As you wish. So, regarding monitoring, since that's what interests you: you've got the patient in bed 4. The bark teas are doing wonders for him, that's for sure—Dr. Kreindl was very impressed—but the current problem is that he's starting to show blood in his stools."

The patient in bed number 4. Lena knew him well. This man had been selected for a departure to the east, but severe abdominal pains had brought him to them. Wasn't that proof enough that these men and women were indeed destined to work for the war effort? Why would the Nazis go to so much trouble to nurse these prisoners back to health, only to kill them the moment they became operational again? They undoubtedly needed labor too much to do without these cheap workers. Lena was certain of it, but she made sure to keep her mouth shut. She took particular care not to share her convictions with Sophie, now that their relationship had returned to a semblance of normalcy. Work, work, and wait. That was all she could think about.

"Sit down, you must be tired," she told Klara. She got up, rinsed her cup, and headed to the treatment room.

It was precisely seven o'clock, and as every day, Dr. Kreindl's footsteps echoed down the hallway. He walked with a slight limp—a reminder of an old war injury. During the first world war, his bravery had been awarded with a first-class Iron Cross. Averse to honors, he had never worn the decoration in public, even when he was still allowed to do so.

By a common reflex, the young women stood up and walked in his direction. But was it the lack of enthusiasm in his step, the paleness of his features? When she saw him, Lena immediately noticed that something was off. Behind him, other footsteps resonated. It was no longer the sound of old shoes, but that of freshly oiled boots, with full and hard soles, clacking on the floor. Emerging from the shadows, SS Obersturmbannführer Adolf Eichmann appeared, his cap adorned with a skull and crossbones slightly tilted over his right eye. The folds of the uniform were perfect, the belt was greased, and the buckles shone. Two broad-handed brutes escorted him.

Eichmann. Even if no one knew his precise role in the Nazi destruction machine, the staff had learned to fear his name. They knew he could appear at any time in the hospital corridors. He chose a ward, prowled around with the air of a slicked-back feline, looking for the smallest fault—invented or observed—in the countless rules created by his regime. He never left without prisoners. This miniature tyrant, this small man who had been told that his blood made him superior, and who'd had the weakness to believe it, did not yet know that his life as a free man would end with him lying in the back of a car, his wrists bound together, his mouth crushed by the gloved hand of a Mossad agent, somewhere in Argentina, in 1960.

Knowing the rule—Dr. Kreindl had explained the attitude to observe in such a situation—all the staff stood at attention. Eichmann stopped, pretended to listen, and seemed satisfied with the silence. He raised an eyebrow and began to walk among the rows of caregivers. Hands clasped behind his back, his gaze scanned the room, sniffing, feeling, nodding slightly; his lips moved in silence, as if he were having a long dialogue with himself. Suddenly, he stopped in front of Klara. He noticed the thick glasses, the slightly round hips. Then, he moved his face closer until his nose almost touched the young woman's lips. He sniffed once, loudly, grimaced. "*Tabak*!"

he said in a dry voice. With a nod of his head, he signaled to his guards, who grabbed the nurse by the arms.

In a tense silence, he continued his inspection, showing no more excitement than a Berliner choosing his vegetables at the Sunday market. Lena stood perfectly still, feet joined. Behind her, Arthur had half-risen in his bed. Eichmann chose another nurse and the patient from bed number 4 with the same discreet movement; his soldiers placed them next to Klara, whose knees wouldn't stop trembling. Passing by Sophie, Eichmann's body leaned slightly forward. He ran a hand through her blonde hair, observed her tall stature and turquoise eyes, made a strange noise with his mouth, and continued. Finally, he stopped in front of Lena. He let his eyes wander from her feet to her head. Lena barely dared to breathe, let alone make any movement, so she looked straight ahead and saw the closely shaved skin, the dimple delicately carving his chin, and without knowing why, she imagined the man in a bathrobe, barefoot on a thick carpet, delightedly dreaming about his morning outing. A whiff of cologne filled her lungs, and she nearly gagged. Finally, to hold onto something—Eichmann still had not moved and continued his unashamed up-and-down, back-and-forth inspection—she locked eyes with him. To her surprise, she detected no emotion there. All she saw were two black discs, surrounded by green circles, drowned in the void of a dead soul. Suddenly, Eichmann's hand plunged into his right pocket. He pulled out an extremely well-sharpened pencil. Moving slowly, he brought its tip close to Lena's body. *Sophie was right,* she thought, clenching her teeth until they grated. *They're all mad, this man is going to stab me in the heart with his pencil in front of all my colleagues!* She closed her eyes, felt a pressure on her chest, and it was as if the whole universe screamed at her, *don't move, Lena, remember the rabbi's words, God is all-powerful, He will protect us!* But another voice, deeper and full of doubt, whispered in her ear, *then why has He left, why has He abandoned us? God? Our beloved rabbi?* Everything blurred in her mind, time lost its substance, and then the pressure was released, and the footsteps receded. When she opened her eyes, she saw Eichmann's back, flanked by his brutes, taking away his morning loot.

She remained immobile, petrified. Every fiber of her being vibrated with a new tone, a dissonant harmony, as if the gates of hell had cracked open and its master had made her a terrible promise: *not yet, little one, not yet . . . but now, we know each other.* She heard sounds, and above a dull humming, a voice.

"Lena! Lena! Answer me, you're scaring me!"

Finally, she came out of her trance and recognized Sophie's face. But why was she shaking her so?

"Lena! Oh, my dear. This time, I really thought it was over!" said Sophie, unable to choose between laughter and tears. She took Lena in her arms and whispered in her ear. "You know you're going to make a believer out of me! When I saw him stop in front of you, I was terrified. It looks like your God does protect you, after all!"

"Sophie . . . I . . . what happened? I felt his pencil against my heart. And then, nothing!"

"I think he was trying to slide the tip of his pencil between your uniform and your star. I've heard about his technique. If he succeeds, he pretexts a sloppy job and bam, he takes you away. Luckily, we made sure to sew it on nice and tight, right?"

Lena finally breathed, half understanding, not wanting to understand. And then, the two friends looked around and realized what Eichmann had left behind. Desolation. Everywhere, young women were crying. Dr. Kreindl had sat down and was staring at the ground, his head buried in his hands. And Klara, sweet Klara, had been taken, and no one could say what would happen to her. Then, without even thinking about it, they turned to Arthur. He had sat up on the edge of his bed and was watching them with an intensity, a confusion, that neither of them could fully decipher. Embarrassed—without really knowing why—they looked at each other one last time before returning to their respective carts.

Work had to be done. What else could they do?

13

• • •

Monday, October 26, 6:30 p.m.

Ever since Eichmann's visit, Lena had felt a deep sense of fatigue seeping into her bones.

Never had the reality of the war brushed so closely against her. Never had she felt so scared. Sometimes, she did feel the urge to tell Sophie that she wasn't as naïve as she might let on—that she too had noticed the rate at which their friends and colleagues were going missing. But each time she wanted to say something, she lacked the energy to do so. In any case, experience had taught her to keep her most intimate convictions to herself. Nevertheless, she remained determined to believe in a brighter future.

The disappearances left vacancies, and so the landscape of the hospital, its very DNA, was in constant mutation. The new faces were most often those of half-Jews—*Mischlinge*, according to Nazi terminology. These well-integrated Germans, who quite often had received a Christian education, were sometimes surprised to discover their Jewishness when the Nazis, who had in some cases managed to dig up their names on an old community register, showed up at their doors to handcuff them. The Mischlinge posed a thorny problem for the Nazis: many had a brother or a son serving in the Wehrmacht, bleeding for the fatherland; it would therefore have been seen as quite indelicate to kill them outright. So, in the meantime, a number of them were filling the positions left vacant by the deportation of those Jews whose genealogy posed no such ethical dilemma for the Nazis.

In the break room, two of these new recruits were enthralling a group of adventure-crazed young women with tales of their exploits. These blonde twins had managed to maintain a nonchalance akin to blindness in the face of danger. They had just explained to their captive audience how, after carving a piece of wood into the appropriate shape, they had managed to attach their star to it, fixing a safety pin on the opposite side. Thus, they could pin or remove it quickly depending on the urgency of the situation, which allowed them to easily organize little excursions into town during their afternoons off.

"Tell us again what you found at Café Kranzler! My mother always talked about that place, but I've never had the chance to go!"

"Coffee, ladies! Real coffee!" said one of the twins, her eyes shining. "Oh, you can't imagine the difference with what we're served here . . . and cakes! Well, to be honest, they taste a bit like cardboard, but if you close your eyes, you can imagine yourself biting into the best *Linzertorte* in Berlin!" The audience drew closer, their pupils dilated.

"Tell us the story of the Kaiserhof: is it true that you dined at a table next to Eichmann?"

Lena and Sophie were sitting a short distance away from the group, only half-listening.

"I need to talk to you," Sophie said softly.

"Yes, Sophie?" said Lena, who despite herself wanted to hear more about the Kaiserhof.

"You know, I've been thinking. With every passing day, I feel we are a little less safe here. Moreover, you've surely noticed that the Gestapo visits are getting more frequent."

"Well . . . this might surprise you, but I quite agree with you," said Lena, turning toward her.

"I'm glad. You're starting to understand. Listen, what I'm about to confide in you is very delicate. First, you must swear to me that you won't tell anyone."

Lena felt a warmth fill her chest. At last, she was back in Sophie's most intimate sphere. She had regained her place as confidante, relegating Lustig's girls to the background.

"Of course! You know you can trust me."

"I know, my dear. I just wanted to hear you say it." Her voice was now but a whisper. "So here it is: my parents are living underground in Berlin. In hiding," she explained, seeing Lena's perplexed look. "The pressure was getting too great, and they found a reliable hideout. As for me, initially, they were happy to find me this position. The hospital seemed safe enough. But things can change quickly, and I'm starting to believe that nowhere is safe anymore. I've been told about how Lustig chooses names for the Nazi lists: those least useful to the hospital's functioning will be the first to go. At the slightest weakness, the slightest misstep, our position here hangs by a thread. Do you understand what I'm telling you?" Her mouth was now inches from Lena's ear. "Lena, I'm going to join them in hiding. And I want you to come with me."

The warmth that had been radiating in Lena's chest gave way to an abyssal void.

"You want to join them? But have you really thought this through? It's a life full of risks, isn't it? And we'd be abandoning our posts, our patients, the hospital?"

"Lower your voice . . . others will take care of our patients. Of course, living in hiding is not ideal, but working here waiting for the day Lustig decides he's seen enough of me doesn't exactly appeal to me either. You know, my parents aren't doing so badly. Their landlady is a Christian they've known for years, a trustworthy woman whom my father helped during a difficult time. Sure, it's dangerous; they rarely leave the apartment. But my father is incorrigible. Believe it or not, every Saturday night, he drags my mother to the opera! You see, with finesse and a bit of madness, one can manage to live."

"They go to the opera? Without their stars? But that's an enormous risk!"

Sophie smiled; her eyes softened. "So, are you coming with me? I've already asked them. They've agreed to take you in."

Lena felt her skin tighten, her heart contract. Suddenly, she was short of saliva. To flee her cocoon for the dangers of a life underground? To trust a non-Jew who could change her mind and denounce them at any moment, rather than to trust in God? She wasn't sure she felt ready. "Let me think about it, okay?"

"Give me a quick answer, Lena. I might act in the next few days.

"I promise. The opera . . . Incredible!"

Sophie winked, placed her index finger on her lips, and left.

Lena sat for a moment. Life in hiding, what an adventure that would be! Surely, Sophie knew what she was doing. And this way, they would stay together. But the hospital? Her colleagues, her responsibilities? Her patients?

The twins' voices grew louder and tinged with fear. ". . . and in other news, it seems the Gestapo has managed to get some Jews to work for them as spies, in exchange for immunity. I'm telling you, girls, we're not out of the woods just yet."

A clock chimed, and the break room emptied. It was time to head to the dormitory, undress, sleep, and then start all over again the next day. Lena took to the stairs, stepping over them one by one. She tried to imagine herself, spending her days in a cramped apartment, sharing food rations with Sophie, waiting . . . for what, exactly? The end of the war? It all seemed so unclear to her. An unknown feeling took root in the pit of her stomach. It wasn't hunger—she had dined well—but something else, more ancient, like a primal urge, a violent desire finally emerging from the shadows: she wanted to see Arthur. And when she realized this, her first reaction was to feel ashamed. Visiting a bed-ridden man after hours? How utterly unacceptable. She continued toward the dormitory, but her pace had slowed, become less assured; eventually, she stopped and leaned against the wall. She felt so tired. Yes, she was tired of denying her desires, exhausted by the weight of doing exactly what was expected of her. Indeed, she had desires—even the word made her blush—what of it? Was she not human, after all?

So, she turned around, her small shoes clicking on the stairs, and soon, with her heart tender and racing—how pleasant that was!—she reached the fourth floor. She entered the corridor, then the treatment room. Only a few night lights were on. She slowed down, adjusted her cap, suppressed a smile when the night nurse gave her a surprised look, and headed toward Arthur's bed. Would he be happy to see her? Yes, of course he would! Her heart, in reality, asked none of these questions, driven only by a youthful, pure, and sincere impulse. So, when she got closer and saw the blonde hair, let loose, flowing freely on the white gown, when she heard the deep, throaty laughter faintly echoing in the silence of the ward—when, finally, she recognized Sophie's generous body sitting on the edge of Arthur's bed—her legs suddenly seemed very frail, her heart very heavy, the world dark and violent.

14

• • •

Tuesday, October 27, 6:30 a.m.

LENA WAS ONE OF THE FIRST TO SLIP OUT OF BED. SHE HEADED to the bathroom and checked her reflection in the mirror. Was that her first wrinkle? What was happening to her? Her short-lived happiness of having regained her complicity with Sophie couldn't compete with the image of her friend sitting on Arthur's bed. She felt a slight dizziness and clung to the sink.

While brushing her teeth, she decided she would be direct with Arthur, even provocative. Since when was it acceptable for a patient to receive visits at such late hours? Besides, he needed his rest. She spat, rinsed her mouth, and started brushing her hair with unusual vigor. *Yes, Lena, you are right, he would say, but I was thinking only of you. There's nothing between me and Sophie, you know that!* Similarly, as she put on her tunic, she imagined herself in turn frivolous, conquering, sad, indifferent. But once in the ward, the morning flew by as it usually did, and all she could do was to steal glances at Arthur while a mix of new feelings troubled her heart. When he winked at her during the rounds, she felt her face flush and nearly dropped the dressing tray.

Noon finally arrived. She was waiting in line at the kosher buffet when Sophie leaned in to whisper, "So, have you thought about my proposal? We'll talk tonight." She stuttered a response while noticing that Moshe, the kitchen attendant, was casting not-so-discreet glances in her direction. "He fancies you, old girl," said Sophie, pinching her cheek. "Why don't you talk to him? Come on, live a little! I'll save you a spot!" Lena shrugged and took the plate Moshe handed her, offering nothing but a shy smile in return. Once seated, she chewed in silence. After a few minutes, no longer able to bear her inner tension, she claimed sudden fatigue and rose from the table.

The park was almost deserted. Lena took a few steps on the dry grass, inhaling sharply. The cold air stung her lungs. She walked around the weeping willow, absent-mindedly caressing its trunk, and suddenly, her internal monologue overflowed, became whispers, then fully formed words. "Oh, my beautiful tree . . . what's happening to me? Yesterday, I wanted to tell him everything, tell him about my lovely village, my house, the violet flowers that grow at the back of the yard. I wanted to tell him about my father! I'm sure they would have liked each other. How proud I was to be the butcher's daughter! Did you know I could watch him work for hours, my beautiful tree, hours! With his muscular arm stretched out, he was a real chopper virtuoso. He fed the entire community with that arm! And I never saw him think twice about giving some sausages to the village kids who came begging at our door . . . yes, those very same kids who a few months later, hiding behind the dark leather of their Hitler Youth uniforms, came back to confiscate his knives. Because the Führer had decided that being a butcher was a job too cruel toward animals. Too cruel, can you believe that! My father couldn't believe it. He kept repeating it over and over, *too cruel, too cruel,* even as we were being thrown out of the house, tossed onto the street . . ."

She circled the trunk, dizzy with the frosty air and the sound of her voice. "Yes, my beautiful tree, I would have told him all that, but he'd rather spend his evenings with her!" She finally stopped, her gaze fixed on the frozen bark. "You know, my childhood was a happy one. Despite Mama's illness, my father always remained joyful. And he always thought of me first and foremost. Even when he managed to get to England, it was with the certainty of being able to bring me over there quickly; in fact, he was almost able to obtain a visa for me before the borders were closed. Imagine that! I could be English now. High tea! Scones for breakfast!"

She laughed tenderly at herself, murmured something.

•

For several minutes, he had been watching her. Stefan spent so much time roaming the park that he knew every tree, every blade of grass. Thus, he could move among the trunks, glide over the lawn with the silent elegance of the morning mist. So, he watched her, but he did not understand. Oh, he was no stranger to such sights. He had known other hospitals before ending up in Berlin, and the spectacle of worn-out patients, nerves frayed, bodies squeezed into straitjackets had been his daily load. But not his Lena, not his little lovely mouth . . .

He leaned against a trunk, closed his eyes. God, how distant normal life seemed now. He had been shoved into a dirty room. *Clack!* went the latch hitting against the concrete wall. The nights were scary and lonely. But the mornings . . . the memory of the nurse's fingers pushing tablets deep into his mouth made him gag.

Everything had happened so fast. For a long time, he had been a respectable member of German society. But he had erred. How he had loved his work as a watchmaker! The precision of these small machines had always fascinated him. As a child, he could spend hours watching the family kitchen clock, hypnotized by the regular sound of the hands, his gaze swinging with the pendulum from left to right. So when, as a young graduate, he had discovered the existence of a watchmaking school located less than a hundred kilometers north of Prague, his destiny had seemed clear. Those were blessed years. The shimmering hills of Saxony gave Glashütte the appearance of an enchanted village; the charming cobblestone streets, the centuries-old St. Wolfgang's church standing vigil to his beloved school . . . there, he learned his craft among cheerful comrades and strict, demanding professors, yet infused with a mischievousness Stefan came to understand was essential to the spirit of discovery of these master artisans.

A brilliant student, he became a serious professional, until one day, as he was screwing on a crown, he felt a burning desire to put on makeup. *Curious*, he thought. He chalked it up to his whimsy. During his studies, he had been known as the class clown, an unfailing spirit-lifter. The desire passed like a cloud, and he almost managed to forget it.

Years flew by, and while most of his colleagues had started families, he remained a bachelor. He was quite content with the state of his life; he'd saved up to buy a small apartment in the heart of the village. Every Thursday evening, he would drink beers with Daniel, his best friend.

Alas, the hills of Saxony didn't prove a sufficient barrier against the fury that had seized the country. The Nazis had been in power for less than a year when a delegation entered his workshop. They exchanged a few heated words with his team leader, before heading toward Daniel. They had a heavy step and smelled of leather and sweat. "You, the Jew! You're coming with us!"

In the workshop, no one moved. Who were these men, and what did they want with their colleague? But, as often happens, fear had overtaken curiosity, and everyone remained glued to their seat, hands frozen over the tiny cogs of time.

Stefan had never had to fight—the last few years had been gentle—but he was of ample build. Daniel was his friend. For years, they had studied the principles of watchmaking together, dreaming of the day when they would construct a watch of revolutionary beauty and ingenuity. That dream still remained a dream, but every day they worked side by side, their eyes fixed on the infinitely small, reassured by each other's presence. Just a few days earlier, Daniel had told him of his wife's pregnancy.

He stood up, noting that the top of the head of the Reich's envoy barely reached his chest. He adopted the friendliest tone possible.

"Gentlemen, good morning! Do you know that this man is an excellent citizen, an impeccable worker, and a faithful friend? There must certainly be a mistake, don't you think?"

The violence of the soldier's shout was confirmed by a rifle butt to the sternum, and Stefan felt his breath leave him. A burning pain shot through his body, as if a red-hot iron had been applied directly to his skin.

"Silence! Who else has something to say?" said the small soldier, bolstered by the presence of his cronies.

The world froze. Daniel, his face chalk-white, stood up and followed the armed men.

For Stefan, it was as if his belly had been sliced open and his insides scooped out with a teaspoon. As soon as the Nazis left, the team leader insisted that everyone resume their work where they had left off ten minutes earlier. In the evening, Stefan packed up his things, put on his coat and hat, and started for his apartment. With trembling legs, he took a few steps before collapsing onto the cobblestones.

He had only vague memories of the following days. He had to stay in bed—a stubborn fever prevented any sudden movement—and only a friend from work came to visit. *No*, she said, *no news of Daniel.* He closed his eyes, a meager barrier against his tears.

One day, his friend was making tea in the kitchen. Stefan lay on his bed, crushed by a viscous sadness. Summer had finally arrived, and with it, flies had invaded the valley. For several minutes, a hairy specimen had been buzzing around Stefan's face. *Enough!* he said, trying to swat it mid-flight. He merely managed to knock over his friend's handbag, perched on a chair near the bed.

"Stefan, are you okay? Did you hurt yourself?" his friend asked, worried.

"It's nothing! Just a chair that tipped over!"

The contents of the bag had spilled out onto the wooden floor. Stefan slowly got up to pick everything up. His gaze fell on a small stick of lipstick. Without thinking, he grabbed it, tucked it under his pillow, and smiled for the first time in weeks. Two days later, he was back at work.

He first confined his new habit to the privacy of his apartment; in the evening, he closed the shutters, applied the lipstick, and admired himself in the mirror. He didn't know what to think, but he felt a new warmth, a calmness in his chest, and that was enough for him. At work, no one spoke of Daniel.

Emboldened by his initial successes, he took more liberties. At first, he ventured only to the end of his street. Then, he pushed on to adjacent streets, eventually circling the neighborhood, his face shielded by the night. Beneath the brim of his hat, he laughed. Oh, how good it felt! He wanted to dance. But one evening, his mind was wandering—perhaps surprised by the sight of forced laborers, who were gradually invading the city, or maybe he was simply thinking of Daniel. He entered a café. A gray cloud hovered around the cigarette smokers; beer flowed freely. He leaned on the bar, observed his reflection in the mirror, and realized his mistake. Fortunately, no one seemed to have seen him. He was almost out of the bar when he ran into one of his old professors. The two men knew each other well—Stefan had been one of his best students—and their eyes met. "Professor," he said, feeling his heart rate double as he thought of all the components of a watch—springs, barrels, and balances—that would suddenly race, before derailing in a fatal cacophony. He had liked the professor very much but wasn't sure about the man behind the science. He reached his apartment in record time.

The next day, he was summoned by the administration. His professor was present, but his body had shrunk, and he kept sadly shaking his head while staring at the floor. The hearing was brief. Stefan was immediately dismissed, with the obligation to be at a certain address, at a certain time. The next day, a car was waiting in front of the psychiatrist's office.

"Get in," said one of the minions in a white coat.

•

The tree bark was starting to hurt his back; a birdsong, light and beautiful, brought him back to the present. *Come on, that's all in the past. Pull yourself together, old man, your friend needs you!*

With somewhat weak legs, he approached Lena, close enough to distinguish her words. "At school, you know, I had managed to fit in. I even had non-Jewish friends! We all got along very well. And my group of friends from Hebrew class! We were inseparable! How I loved our good Rabbi Munk. He always had answers to my questions. And believe me, I had many. In fact, when things started to get complicated at school—in 1933, you know, when they hung Hitler's picture in the classroom and classes started with the Nazi salute—I had even more questions. I asked him, 'My dear rabbi, do you think we should leave? Leave Germany? Because I feel like they don't want us here anymore . . . my teacher told me Einstein was a fool, and I have to spend the day sitting at the back of the class, forbidden to ask any questions!' Do you know what he told me? 'It's not that serious, Lena. We must stay, of course, we must stay. This Hitler character won't last long. Soon, he will lose the people's support, and then everything will be back to normal.' Well, my beautiful tree, can you believe it? One day, my rabbi left town with his whole family, without telling anyone. I try to tell myself he had his reasons, but it's hard . . ."

Lena was vaguely aware of her madness, but it was so pleasant to talk, to finally say out loud what she would have liked to tell Arthur—Arthur, and his human weakness—that she had almost forgotten where she was.

A hand rested on her shoulder. "Lena! What are you doing here?"

She jumped, turned around, unable to utter a sound.

"I've been watching you for a few minutes. You're telling your life story to a tree? Are you sure you're okay?"

"Oh, Stefan . . ." She fell into his arms, pressed her head against his chest.

"There, there, it'll be alright, my little mouth."

Silence engulfed them; a few birds sang.

It would have been sweet for them to stay like this, to sit on a bench, to take a little time, but reality forced itself upon them once again. The park gradually filled with nurses and doctors. Silence was broken by the powerful voice of the head nurse:

"*Schwester* Lena, what are you doing there? Haven't you heard? Dr. Lustig summoned everyone to the central courtyard. Hurry up, he doesn't like to wait!"

"Right away, madam."

She stepped away from Stefan and wiped her face with the back of her hand. Then, she adjusted her cap, turned on her heels, and followed her superior.

15

• • •

Tuesday, October 27, the afternoon

AMONG THE HUNDRED NURSES AND DOCTORS GATHERED IN THE central courtyard, Lena quickly spotted Sophie and—out of habit—positioned herself beside her. They exchanged a look too laden with emotions to describe here. Dr. Lustig spread his arms as if to calm his troops, furrowed his brows, and announced in a powerful voice, "Is everyone here? Good. There's an update. Brunner is summoning you—he didn't tell me why, no point in asking me—to the old community center on Oranienburger Strasse." A shiver ran through the group. "You are to leave immediately! I'm placing you under the responsibility of Dr. Kreindl, whom you all know."

As soon as he finished speaking, the austere doctor turned on his heels and disappeared, followed by his loyal secretary. Clearly, this time, the skilled strategist had managed to avoid the trip.

"We have one hour," Dr. Kreindl said between coughing fits. "So, let's maintain a steady pace, and we'll make it there on time." A few nurses from his department were tempted to take his arm, but none found the courage.

They passed through the hospital gates into a heavy silence, and just like that, they were back on the streets. Passersby stopped to observe this curious vision of caregivers marked by the Jewish star, walking through the city. Shivering in their white coats and uniforms, they had covered only a few hundred meters when, on the opposite sidewalk, a boy picked up a stone and threw it in their direction. The stone, propelled only by eight-year-old arms, fell in the middle of the road and rolled foolishly on the cobblestones.

"Juden! Juden!" he yelled.

"Come now, Fritz, don't waste your time," his mother said. "We'll be late for the cinema."

They followed the same path again, brushing past ordinary Berliners, whose only concern seemed to be to live as normally as possible, even if that meant turning a blind eye to the sufferings endured by their fellow humans. A few soldiers looked at them and laughed, and soon, almost relieved to withdraw from the public eye, they arrived.

SS officers led them to the large hall they already knew. It too seemed to have lived a thousand lives. During their first visit, some remnants of Jewish life were still visible to a keen eye—an old prayer book, a poster announcing a literary evening. By now, the building had been stripped of its soul, leaving only sad, bare walls to bear witness to it all.

The soldiers gave short, confident orders. They knew these weary bodies would not rebel. So they paraded, chests high and eyebrows arched, always flanked by their heavy-footed German shepherds. Lena and Sophie, as if to afford themselves a semblance of logic in this recurring nightmare, positioned themselves in the same spot as a month earlier. But they quickly sensed that everything would be different. Brunner was already there, seated on his platform, watching them with a skewed eye while twirling his wedding ring in a mechanical gesture. A tense silence settled in the room, suddenly broken by the small man's voice.

"Jews! After our last meeting, I managed, despite some reluctance, to trim your group by a third of its mass. Some of the selected found it wise to go into hiding, while others committed suicide before their departure to the east. But one does not idly steal a life from the Reich! We will find these fugitives," he said with a sadistic smile. "We have the means."

Behind Lena, a woman sobbed.

"Today, we will proceed differently. Let your leader step forward; he will be my assistant." Dr. Kreindl limped forward. That very morning, with a mischievous smile, he had explained to Lena that to adapt to the scarcity of contraband cigarettes, he had resigned himself to smoking tea leaves. *What do you want, my little one, one gets used to everything . . .*

The doctor took a few steps; his face turned a pale shade of green. Despite the cold, drops of sweat ran down his forehead. He slowed down a bit. From behind, Lena thought, he seemed to carry the entire weight of a sacrificed people on his shoulders. Slowly, he brought his hand to his chest, then he stopped. His head went back, his whole body tensed, and he fell, stiff, onto the cold, bare slabs.

No one dared to move. Lena tried to breathe, but the air remained locked outside her mouth. The thought came to her that she might have made everything up, so she closed her eyes and finally swallowed a gulp of air. But when she reopened them, nothing had changed.

"*Ach*, a sensitive one! Get this Jew out of here," said Brunner in a neutral voice. "He's going to catch a cold, lying on the ground like that."

And then it was like a dream. Lena perceived sounds, her body obeyed the commands spat in her direction, but her mind was elsewhere. Like all the others, she heard the metallic voice say that he would do everything himself since these Jews refused to cooperate. Another list was placed before him, and like a vicious robot, he began to call out names, and seeing him comfortably seated in his chair, one could easily understand that he would not stop until he had extracted from that list the last drop of soul, the very last breath of life.

Guided by Sophie's hand, Lena stepped forward at the sound of her name. In a semi-fog, she saw an arm pointing toward the group on her left. Her legs carried her to the designated spot. Outside, the night had long fallen; in the room, silence was broken only by Brunner's voice, reading, and reading again the names of these humans whom a bit of politics and a lot of sadism had placed under his command that day.

Finally—it could have been two hours later, she had long since lost such benchmarks—the macabre roll call ended. Two groups of equal sizes stood on either side of Brunner. With a sharp gesture, he pointed to a doctor near him: "You, Jew, you will repeat my orders word for word!"

Then, through the monotone and terrified voice of Dr. Elken, who over the course of his career had dealt with many schizophrenic patients plagued with megalomaniacal delusions, the employees of the Jewish hospital of Berlin heard the verdict of their day, like an echo from the gates of hell:

"All Jews placed to my left must report here in three days, on October 30th, at precisely eight o'clock in the morning, for transport to the east. They will all be collected by the Gestapo on the evening of October 29th and taken to a collection center. For this task, the Gestapo will be assisted by certain Jews from the group on the right, who will be notified tonight. For each Jew who fails to show up or who tries to flee, a head of department from the hospital will be executed."

Satisfied, the small man lit a cigarette, jumped off the platform, and disappeared into a corridor.

•

Two hours later, Lena lay on her bed, her gaze vacant. She felt Sophie's hand stroking her hair, and when her friend finally spoke, her voice had never been so gentle.

"Oh, Lena, my Lena. I'm sorry to tell you this, but you need to know." She closed her eyes, took a deep breath. "You're on the list to assist the Gestapo on the evening of the 29th."

PART 2

1

• • •

Thursday, October 29, 1942, 9 p.m.

IN HAPPIER TIMES, THOSE TRUCKS HAD BEEN USED TO TRANSPORT furniture. Standing on sidewalks, starry-eyed Berlin couples had awaited them eagerly, already picturing the placement of the sofa, the space reserved for their unborn child, dreaming of Sunday naps and brunches with friends. But those days were long gone. Now parked in front of the hospital in the freezing fog, the former moving trucks were being filled with terrified employees, closely guarded by Gestapo agents.

Lena had barely had the strength to swallow a bit of soup before heading down. For two days, the sight of poor old Dr. Kreindl being carelessly carried away by thugs kept circling in her mind. She had barely been able to perform at work; everything else was still a blur.

Sophie had walked her down her to the courtyard. "Come on, don't worry. Everything will be fine," she said, touching her friend's shoulder.

"Are you sure?"

Without waiting for an answer, Lena crossed the hospital gates with the group of nurses and doctors selected for the *special mission*. Suddenly, she felt terribly alone. But everything happened quickly, with typical German efficiency, and immediately a soldier threw a red armband at her. "On your arm, Jew!" he shouted. "And then, get in there." She slipped the armband over her white tunic and climbed into the back of the truck.

A shadow moved in the darkness. Lena froze, imagining the worst—a killer lurking in the shadows? Was it her time to join Dr. Kreindl?—but the seated figure opposite her remained strangely calm. She heard a throat being cleared, and the sound of legs leisurely crossing and uncrossing.

She made out an aquiline nose, a confident jawline. And finally, a voice, clear as a razor blade. "So, you're Lena? My name is Hans. I believe this is your first experience with this kind of work. The Gestapo has asked me to assist you, to ensure everything goes smoothly." He placed his bony hands on his knees and leaned toward her, revealing white teeth in a half-smile. "I trust that reassures you?"

She jumped at the sound of a door slamming shut. A Gestapo agent, thick and hairy, grumbled as he settled into the driver's seat and started the engine. The tires screeched as they pulled out onto Iranische Strasse, and the hospital's reassuring cocoon vanished in the mist.

Lena positioned herself as far away from Hans as possible, looking down at her tired old shoes. The random bumps in the road jostled the two bodies. The silence thickened; the roads were all but deserted at that late hour. Five minutes passed.

"So, Lena," said Hans. "Do you have any idea of what's going to happen tonight? Surely, your colleagues from the hospital who have already been on these outings must have told you something."

"No, I mean . . . no, sir."

"Hans! Call me Hans. You're not from Berlin, are you?"

"No, that's true."

"I can tell by your accent. Bavaria, isn't it? Yes, I was sure of it. Well, you see, I am a pure-blooded Berliner."

Lena shrugged, almost without realizing it.

"That bothers you, I see. And yet, yes, a pure Berliner, that's exactly what I am. But back to our mission: everything must proceed in the most perfect order. Do you understand? No heroics, no zeal. But you're no heroine, Lena. No, I can see that you're not. Maybe you would make a good *ordner*, who knows. Look at me! I'm an *ordner*, and I'm not ashamed of it! I help maintain some semblance of order in this chaos. And I'm not less of a Jew because of it!"

He hadn't raised his voice, but it had hardened. Lena felt the thread of the conversation slipping away; her usual reaction would have been to remain silent, but everything seemed different in this dark, damp truck.

"Did you grow up in Berlin?" she said.

"Ah, she speaks! Well, do you know the Alexanderplatz area? I grew up in those streets. Back then, all the kids played together. Jews, non-Jews, the religious and the atheists . . . I even had a friend whose father hosted tea dances on Sundays. Those were the good old days! Hard to imagine now."

Finally, a thread to cling to.

"I have a friend named Sophie! She also grew up near the Alexanderplatz."

"Sophie . . . a pretty blonde with turquoise eyes? Yes? It can only be her. Incredible! You know, she was the first girl I ever danced with: to be honest, she was the only reason I ever went to those little parties. Oh, this brings back memories . . . one afternoon, after much hesitation—she was already quite beautiful—I asked her for a dance. And I got three minutes of a waltz that haunts me to this day."

"Yes, she's told me about those parties! What a coincidence."

"Her parents were lovely. Her father called me 'my little Hans.' Truthfully, my growth spurt came a bit late . . . I hope they're doing well. By the way, do you know if they're still in Berlin?"

The truck took a tight turn, and Lena was thrown against the tarp. For a moment, she thought she was going to crash onto the asphalt of the Berlin night, leaving the truck to continue without her. But Hans's hand caught her in time.

"Oh . . . thank you," she said a bit hastily, pulling her arm back. But Hans hadn't let go of her wrist. He moved closer, and Lena felt his gaze deepen, his eyes take on a glassy hue. With his free hand, he caressed her face, and at the touch of the dry, cold, almost reptilian skin, a shiver ran down her spine.

"You're quite the pretty one, you know. I'm sure we could get along just fine. I could make your life easier, if you relaxed just a bit." His voice was but a whisper, but each syllable he pronounced had the clarity of a well-sharpened axe. His hand moved to Lena's mouth, sliding his thumb across the edge of her lower lip.

Something revolted deep within her chest—survival instinct, the energy of despair?—and without even realizing what she was doing, she opened her mouth and sharply clamped her jaw down on the intrusive thumb, feeling the bitter taste of the nail crunch under her teeth. She didn't see the hand pull back, stiffen, and return, firm and vengeful, to strike her cheek. There was a suspended moment, and then warmth spread across her face.

"Oh, you little bitch! You bit me? Really?"

Lena shielded herself, suddenly aware of her action, the man's strength, her own helplessness. But Hans's body relaxed as quickly as the slap had come.

"Ha! Well, I must admit you surprised me there. This little one's got spirit!"

He sucked loudly on his thumb before crossing his legs again, returning to the darkness.

"Alright, alright, let's calm down, shall we? We are not savages. Anyway, I was joking. The frightened little virgin type is not my thing. I've always preferred more experienced women."

Lena curled up in a corner of the truck, trying in vain to control her heartbeat. Her cheek hurt terribly, but her instincts told her that if she started crying, things would only get worse.

"Besides, you were about to tell me what you knew about Sophie's parents. As I was saying, I was very fond of her father, and I'd be delighted to see him again." He leaned forward. His voice had regained that reassuring, warm, and smooth quality that seemed to come naturally to him. "If you know something, I advise you to tell me now. There are others who dream of questioning you, and they will undoubtedly be less gentle than me."

Sophie's parents? Why did these maniacs want information about them? No, she would never betray her friend. Anyway, what did she really know, apart from the fact that they were hiding in Berlin? What had Sophie called it? Living underground? Thankfully, she had no idea of the address. Oh, this was all so foreign to her . . . but she had to say something, anything. Otherwise, Hans would beat her again, or worse, hand her over to the Gestapo, and then, who knows what would become of her.

"I don't know anything, sir. I'm really sorry. I wish I could help."

"Last warning, little virgin. Have you seen our driver? His reputation precedes him; he's a major sadist, a virtuoso with the whip. I guarantee it's better to confide in me than in him. In his world, a little slap like the one you just received is the equivalent of a love tap."

"No, I swear to you . . . all she told me was that her father loves the opera . . . I mean, he loves opera music! Yes, that's it, she told me *oh, he's a true music lover! He composes music, and one day, he's sure to be a famous musician!* That's all, Mr. Hans, that's everything, I swear! I don't know where they are. And I'm sorry for biting you . . ."

Hans looked at Lena, listened to her breathing, saw the moisture in her eyes, and understood he would get nothing more from her. Not right now, at least.

"Well, you might find this surprising, but I believe you. Come now, let's remain good friends, shall we? My advice is to swallow your tears, forget all this, and focus on the present. Don't you feel the truck slowing down?"

The truck left Unter den Linden to turn onto a parallel street, lined with trees exhausted by the cold. The downshifting made the old engine roar, and it finally sputtered to a stop.

The driver got down from the truck and lifted the tarp. "It's your first time, Jew, so I'll show you. Observe and learn!" A vein traced a dark river on his left temple, where, despite the cold, several drops of sweat ran down.

With trembling legs, she followed the man across the deserted street, leaving Hans in the truck. "This neighborhood needs a good cleaning. I can't believe Jews are still allowed to live here, among respectable Aryans!" His gait was heavy in his leather shoes. An old Luger hung limply at his hip; in his right hand, he held a brown leather whip.

They climbed to the second floor of a brick building. The man, already out of breath, spotted the Star of David, painted in black ink near the front door, and spat on the ground. "Gestapo! Open up, *schnell!*" he yelled, pounding on the door.

The door opened to reveal an elderly man. Lena remembered seeing him in the hospital garden—he pruned the hedges once a week, she was suddenly sure of it—and at that moment, she regretted never having greeted him. He stood there almost at attention—only a massive lumbago prevented this posture—surrounded by two worn suitcases. "Yes, captain. I am ready, I do not want to cause any trouble," he said with a calm, polite voice.

"*Nein*! Jew! You won't need all that, where you're going! Didn't you read the instructions, idiot? Only a small rucksack is allowed for transport! Get ready, you have one minute and not a second more, *schnell*!"

The old man, who in his youth had been a badminton champion (muscles tight and nimble, his body agile, he had been quite the lady's man and had only lost his Gloria a year earlier) struggled to understand. He had done everything to make this go smoothly. And now this terrible man was yelling at him? His limbs refused to move and he remained still, unsure what to do. "So, Jew, resisting? Want to feel my whip?" His arm retracted and his wrist made a small sharp movement. A few bright red drops flowed down the old man's cheek. His face contorted in a sort of painful incomprehension; perhaps was he thinking about the slow descent of humanity into the depths of a bottomless abyss, perhaps even telling himself it would be good to leave now, before knowing where all this would lead. He dropped the handles of his leather suitcases and left his home without a backward glance.

"Do you understand the method, Jew?" said the brute, with a satisfied look. "If you want to avoid more whipping, you'll go get your kind yourself, at the next stops."

And so it was. Instinctively, she knew she had no other choice. The driver would give her a name, and she would jump down from the truck, followed by Hans. She knocked on apartment doors, sought the most reassuring tone, the most accurate words. Anything to avoid the whip, the violence. *No,* she said, *you cannot take this lamp. It was your grandmother's? I understand, it's sad, but believe me, they will not let you keep it.* She drove back the images of her mother repeating endlessly *let the wave pass, God will watch over you . . .* So where was HE, and why was HE forcing her to gather her brothers and sisters on behalf of the Nazis?

Everything was mixed up in her head, everything was happening too fast.

A few hours passed and soon, the truck was nearly full. Around Lena were men and women uprooted, torn from their houses, betrayed by a homeland gone mad. *And gathered by a Jew,* Lena thought, without even comprehending what that implied. A cold scent of fear hovered. Lena avoided making eye contact with the other prisoners and looked at her shoes. When her father had gifted them to her, they were still free citizens. She had walked lightly in these shoes, never thinking they would accompany her in this horror. Only Hans seemed serene. He sat close to Lena—almost pressed against her thigh—and leaned toward her.

"This is the last stop. I'm tired, I'll let you go alone. Be quick; I'd prefer our driver took us back soon, before he starts weaving down the road."

Lena glanced and saw that the driver's head, heavy from drink, was leaning forward significantly.

The truck stopped along a sidewalk. "The house across the street! *Schnell!*" said the driver, without even turning around.

"Alright, Hans. I'm going." She jumped from the truck, crossed the street, spotted the small, isolated house, and knocked on the door, which opened to a familiar face.

"Moshe!" For months he had been serving her kosher meals at the cafeteria; they had never exchanged more than a few simple words.

"Oh, Lena… come in for a minute, if you can. It's a sign from God that you are the one to come and fetch me. I will follow you, of course—look, I've already prepared my rucksack—but . . ." He lowered his voice, and it was but a whisper. "Something must be done for my little sister."

Lena looked up and saw, surrounded by shadows, a frail figure, holding a small oval shape in her arms. "She lost her husband a month ago. I've done my best to take care of her and her baby. But if I go, what will she do? I beg of you, Lena, can you think of a solution?"

It was warm in the house, so warm that Lena dreamt for a moment she could lie down on the couch, cuddle the baby, maybe even drink some tea. Suddenly, she felt drops of sweat run down her back. The room began to spin, her legs gave in, and she collapsed onto the wooden floor.

"Lena!" said Moshe. He tapped her cheeks, checked her pulse—it was the first time he had touched her diaphanous skin, which he had dreamed about so many times—and lifted her legs onto a small stool.

He turned to his sister, who hadn't moved. "She can't help us now . . . no matter. Look, the truck is parked on the other side of the street. But if Lena takes too long to get back, they will lose patience and send someone else. So, go now: you remember our cousin's address? Run there right now. Yes, I'm sure."

He got up, kissed his sister, placed a hand on the warm little skull, and murmured a prayer. "Go now, it's your only chance."

Lena slowly opened an eye, hoping to wake up in her childhood bed; maybe her mother had prepared her a cup of hot chocolate? But reality gripped her throat. She stood up abruptly.

"Moshe, what's happened? I think I fainted. Where are your sister and her baby?" she said, looking around for them. "Of course, we'll try to find a solution; just let me think."

"They've left, Lena. God will watch over them. Now, I'll follow you."

In the truck, the Gestapo agent began to find the wait tedious. What a pain, these nighttime outings playing babysitter! Ah, when he was still a police inspector, his job was far more exciting. But times had changed; one had to adapt. Still, this regime sure had its perks. Soon, they would be rid of these Jews, and for his part, he had never been blessed with so much prestige, alcohol, and women. In less than an hour's time, he would have returned the truck to that wretched hospital and could meet up with one of his mistresses, whom the story of the whip would surely excite in exactly the right ways. Aryan women loved power and authority, and he had plenty of that to offer.

He finished his beer, threw the empty can out the window, and felt his bladder stretch. *Damn*, he thought. *To pee outside in this weather.*

He jumped off the truck and nearly sprawled out on the sidewalk. He took a few steps to the side, confident that none of the prisoners would dare to attempt anything, and found a bush to his liking. He slid down his zipper and began to water the dry grass with a strong and steady stream. White smoke burst from the bowels of the earth. *Heh*, he chuckled, for he had a sense of humor.

What was that Jew doing, anyway? He'd have to go see. He turned his head toward the house and in a half fog, he perceived movement. Someone was slipping along the wall, trying to escape. He zipped up his fly with a clumsy motion—it got stuck halfway—and shouted "*Haaalt!*" in a rough and powerful voice. He saw the figure freeze for a second and then speed up. He started to run, his pants poorly pulled up and impeding his steps. He realized that with his weight and his alcohol level, he would never catch up with the figure now maneuvering through the bushes. There would be paperwork, maybe he'd even lose some of his privileges, and he was not ready to accept that. He knew he had the law behind him, and so, the decision was simple. He stopped, pulled out from its holster the beautiful Luger his father had given him for his twentieth birthday, aimed as well as the alcohol running through his veins would allow, and fired three successive shots.

In the silence that followed, he advanced with a heavy step through the bushes. When his shoe encountered an obstacle, he kneeled and placed his hand on a still-warm body from which life was draining onto the Berlin soil. Then, he zipped up his fly, buckled his belt, put the Luger back in its holster, and headed toward the house.

2

• • •

Saturday, November 7, 1942, 8:15 p.m.

FOR OVER AN HOUR, A SMALL CROWD HAD BEEN GATHERING AT the foot of the opera house; all of them longing for a semblance of normality amid chaos, a temporary breath of fresh air. Unter den Linden, the historic avenue that once teemed with life and energy, was now mainly populated by soldiers, forced laborers, and the occasional "outlaw" keeping his head low while looking over his shoulder. Nearby, the Spree River carried its muddy waters toward the distant Elbe. To the east, the Alexanderplatz police station loomed over the city, and even further east, where the transportation lines ended, horrors were unfolding—horrors that the mature couple, mixed among the crowd of music enthusiasts, preferred not to think about. They had already lost so many friends there.

The man, wearing a felt hat with worn edges, was well aware of the risks. He knew full well that any sensible person would have immediately rejected the idea of gambling with his life for an hour of music. But he had become an expert at rationalizing, playing with facts and probabilities as if this were a mere game of chance rather than a deadly race. They were so careful, no one would recognize them . . . for months, they had only left the apartment on weekends, and even so, never going anywhere beyond Madame Grosz's block. Either way, for the man, it was a matter of pride. Life *underground* was, at its best, nothing more than a half-life, a muted life, with little flavor to it; it needed a little spice from time to time to maintain its *raison d'être.*

He had always believed in his lucky star, and for a long time, the world seemed to prove him right: a wife he loved, an adorable daughter, a stable job, and financial tranquility—at least until this new regime confiscated all his belongings. A few years earlier, he had managed to extricate his gardener's wife from an uncomfortable debt. And while her husband had since passed away, she had never forgotten his kindness. When the wind turned, she had opened her door to her benefactor, and when he asked if her new status as enemy of the Reich and protector of illegals didn't worry her, she would softly laugh and shrug. The man would then smile and understand. But that didn't stop them from taking all the necessary precautions.

So yes, he needed to go out, to feel the worn leather of his shoes pounding his city's pavement. If everything else had changed, that, at least, remained immutable. This crack in the sidewalk was there before Hitler; it would remain thereafter. Nothing lasts forever; reason always prevails.

A man is not meant to live in socks, he would say to his wife. He understood the risk of being denounced by an overzealous neighbor—*since when does Madame Grosz have guests? I've counted two extra pairs of steps, officer, two! Wouldn't you have an extra ration card, say, for my efforts in the Reich's favor?*—yes, he knew and accepted these risks and adhered to the discipline of gliding like a specter across the apartment's wooden floorboards. But an old maxim from his late father had stirred his heart: *living in socks in one's house is a sign of mourning, my son!* Well, if there was one mourning he was not ready for, it was that of life. Not yet—never, perhaps.

The crowd still wasn't moving much. Standing in front of them, a woman wrapped in fur held a cigarette with an aristocrat's gesture.

The man wondered how many Berliners saw the war as an aberration, a temporary inconvenience, while their neighbors perished by the dozens.

He wiped the lenses of his small, wire-rimmed spectacles, took a deep breath, and risked a glance at the city. A few years earlier, he could well imagine himself headlining. A composer whose work was performed at the opera . . . why not? He knew he was talented. His job as a notary was just a temporary way to earn a living. After the war, perhaps? He squeezed his wife's hand. God, was he a lucky one. Tall, gentle, with a mind as sharp as they come, she was everything he had dreamed of. He remembered the night they'd met. They had both attended an evening of Wagner, right here in the opera house. She was there with friends, he was alone, but their eyes had met, and somehow, they had recognized each other. After their wedding, they had nurtured their common passion for the arts by hosting social salons where painters, writers, and musicians mingled and exchanged ideas in a festive atmosphere. A full, wholesome life that Sophie's birth had only made more beautiful.

The man's gaze drifted to a tall figure wrapped in a wool overcoat. His eyes lingered on the sharp face, drawn by some familiar air, but couldn't make out the features precisely. Better anyway, to avoid staring at people. After all, he was on the run. *On the run!* The words amused him and reminded him of the spy movies he used to watch with his daughter. He missed her so much . . . but they would see each other soon, she had promised him that. He turned to his wife, caressed her cheek.

On the opposite corner of the square, the man in the overcoat had a moment of doubt. Had the old man recognized him? Would the couple disappear into the crowd? No, they lacked the imagination for that. After all, they hadn't seen him for years, and he had changed a lot.

He rubbed his hands. His intuition had been correct. What fools, queuing in front of the opera! In the weeks he had been assigned to this new job, he had built a solid reputation as a physiognomist for himself. He could recognize a Jew on the run in a crowd, sitting in an opera box or at a café terrace. His fellow Jews were so brazen. Who did they think they were? One had to either hide—but then hide properly, without parading on terraces in broad daylight—or do what he was doing, finding the best possible compromise between a questionable sense of morality and a much safer life. Anyway, subtlety had never been their thing.

He took another moment to observe them. How they had aged since those Sunday dance parties. They had probably only invited him out of obligation; *little Hans*, the neighbor's son. He had always sensed a polite mistrust toward him. Was it because, even at a young age, he was already hanging out with the neighborhood's most crafty, most roguish kids? At the time, he's never stopped to wonder. He willingly attended those little parties, fascinated as he was by young Sophie's budding anatomy. Sophie the unattainable—blonde, perfect, towering over him by a head. He never dared speak to her. Until one day when, gathering all his courage, he had dared ask her for a dance. As a well-bred little girl, she had accepted—he still remembered her slightly awkward curtsy—and there they were dancing, she the pride of a well-to-do family, he the rebel with the unruly hair. They had swayed to a waltz's rhythm; for a minute, he'd almost felt like he belonged. But was it her floral perfume, the intoxication of discovery? He had grown bold, sensing an opportunity for a feat, a story to tell, and suddenly he had let his hand slip from Sophie's shoulder blades down to the blossoming undulations of her young woman's body.

What followed had been quick—a body stiffening, a little girl's screech, strident, unexpected. Her father stepped in, demanding explanations and not finding any that suited him, letting his hand fly. To this day, he still felt the burning on his cheek. Amid the other kids' snickers and Sophie's satisfied look, he had somehow managed not to cry.

Suddenly, like a predator tired of waiting, he was on the move.

He signaled the Gestapo agents waiting in the crowd and crossed the square, his eyes fixed on the unsuspecting couple, as if possessed by his hunt. His steps quickened, his well-polished shoes hammering the ground like the sound of a machine gun. A few raindrops began to fall.

The queue had finally begun to move, and the man was already savoring the evening's program. Furtwängler conducting Mozart! Two masters united for sixty minutes of beauty. He turned to his wife, saw a blonde curl bouncing on her forehead, and with a tender gesture, gently pushed it under her hat. He was about to kiss the corner of her mouth—he knew her aversion to public displays of affection, but he couldn't help himself—when he noticed a change in the depth of her eyes. From a dilated pupil full of love, he followed, as if in slow motion, the contraction of the black sphere surrounded by turquoise, the vertiginous and immediate fall from surprise to fear, from dread to panic.

The next thing he felt was hands gripping his arm, and the cold barrel of an automatic pistol pressing against his back.

3

• • •

Tuesday, November 10, 1942, 2 p.m.

Two weeks had passed since Lena's trip in the truck. And every night, the nightmares returned, subtle variations of hell.

Days were hardly easier. Despite her habit of walking with her head down, Lena couldn't ignore the corridor rumors, the words whispered as she passed by: *Have you heard? Because of her, Moshe's sister was killed! And her baby too!* And each word burned her eardrums a thousand times deeper.

So, she worked. Maintaining a certain routine, focusing on her job, that's what her instinct dictated. *A blood draw for bed number 2? Right away, doctor. Change this dressing? Nothing could please me more.* But instead of the caring nurse, whose visits they had come to anticipate eagerly, her patients were only treated to a specter, a shadow, the negative of the young woman they had learned to know.

Arthur often tried to make her smile. But his humor slid off her like water off the feathers of an indifferent swan. So, one day, he switched tactics.

"*Schwester* Lena! Come over, I have something to show you."

"Good morning, Arthur. How's your hand today?"

"My hand is fine, Lena . . . but there is something else I wanted to talk to you about. You know that our good Dr. Elken now allows me to stretch my legs in the park twice a day. Isn't he the best? And all that with the Gestapo's blessing."

"Yes, that's good, Arthur," said Lena, her eyes searching for the doctor, hoping for an IV to change.

"During one of my walks, I came across our old friend the weeping willow. It felt like revisiting an estranged relative."

He sat up a bit straighter on his bed.

"It has suffered from the cold, but it's a tough old tree. While passing my hand over its trunk, I came upon a piece of bark that was ready to fall; it made me think of you. You know that thanks to our stratagem, the doctor has been able to alleviate many patients' pains! You've been an excellent assistant, and I thank you for that. So here,"—he cleared his throat—"I wanted to give you this."

He reached under his pillow and took out a piece of bark. Lena noticed that it could, if looked at in a certain way, resemble a heart. In one of the wood's contortions, there was a hole in which Arthur had passed a piece of string, thus creating a rudimentary and, thought Lena, wildly beautiful pendant.

"So, what do you think? As a thank you for your consistently perfect dressings and your kindness."

He smiled, hoping to create a spark in this youthful body, hoping—did he even know it?—to bring a little joy to this strange world, where death lurked on every floor. Yes, he knew she was young, that he was divorced, but it sometimes happens that a man ignores reason and lets his soul speak out.

With an automatic gesture, Lena grabbed the pendant. Suddenly, she felt very warm, and the pain that had been tearing through her back for days awakened with a vengeance. Because it hadn't been enough for the Gestapo man to kill a woman and her child. With red eyes, a trembling jaw, he had grabbed Lena and Moshe and slammed them against a wall. Petrified, Lena had heard Moshe reciting a prayer. But no gunshot had been fired; instead, the man had lashed each of their backs with ten strikes of his whip. Then, he had only said, "Into the truck, Jews! Otherwise, we'll be late." She hadn't shown her scars to anyone, and she wouldn't, even if it could silence some of the rumors. Because deep down—and this was what scared her the most—she believed she'd deserved them.

She couldn't take her eyes off the pendant. Suddenly, she felt like crying, or laughing, or even jumping with joy. Was this what they called a gentleman's consideration, or better, a proof of love? She didn't know. She could only move her lips slightly and utter an inaudible *thank you*.

She took a few steps back and nearly bumped into Sophie. Sophie, who was always there for her when she woke up, in a cold sweat, in the middle of the night. "Lena, what's going on? You seem upset. Is it Arthur? Did he say something inappropriate?"

"No . . . it's nothing," she said in a breath. "He just gave me a pendant." Sophie eyed the piece of wood sticking out from Lena's hand.

"Come on, forget about it, my dear. Let's get back to work."

"*Schwester* Sophie, please come here," said the head nurse, from the other end of the treatment room.

"Excuse me, Lena, it looks like I'm needed over there. I'll see you tonight!"

"See you tonight, Sophie."

Yes, she still had Sophie. Everything wasn't perfect between them, but there was no more loyal friend. When the other girls looked at her sideways, Sophie was there to tell her to ignore them; in a few days there would be a new drama, and no one would remember that cursed truck anymore. Intuitively, Lena felt she should have asked her what had happened to her in that same truck, a few weeks earlier. But she also knew that the moment had passed, and she continued to keep silent, thus swallowing a vague, and bitter, feeling of guilt.

•

That evening, Lena decided to get some fresh air before going to bed. She caressed the trees with a light hand. A gust of wind made her shiver; winter promised to be harsh. In the distance, she could make out the city's muted rumble. Her excursions beyond the reassuring limits of the hospital walls hadn't made her want to see more of it. She knew it was filled with Nazis, Germans ready to betray their neighbor for a piece of dry bread, trains departing eastward . . . and yet, she would have to answer Sophie: was she going to join her in hiding? It might be a golden opportunity. If things got worse at the hospital, if outings with the Gestapo became her daily routine, she wouldn't be able to endure it for long. But the unknown frightened her; she was attached to her routines. The patients, the dormitory, the park. Arthur . . . All of this, although imperfect, structured her days. Without Sophie, what would her life at the hospital be like? They had been taking care of each other for months. Oh, how difficult it was! Alright, she would take another day or two before answering her. What difference could it possibly make?

She spotted Stefan sitting underneath a tree. Something about his posture made her uneasy. As she approached, her friend's features became more distinct: his arm was in a sling, and several bruises marred his face.

"Hello, my lovely mouth . . ." he said in a faint voice.

"Stefan! What happened to you?"

"Oh, my Lena . . . you won't believe it. I was walking in the garden when a uniformed man—very ugly, by the way—came my way. I was wearing my beautiful yellow dress; I looked like a little sun! When he saw me, his face changed: his eyes tightened. All I could see was pure hatred. He opened his mouth and started to yell, but I was so scared I couldn't bring myself to move. So, he pulled out his riding crop and starting beating me with it. I screamed for help, but that excited him even more. So, I curled up, protected my face, and waited. After a few minutes, he stopped and disappeared, after giving me one last kick. You see, Lena, what kind of world we're living in? Sometimes, I miss Prague so very much . . ."

Lena sat on the grass, took her friend's arm, and laid her face on his shoulder. "Stefan, don't worry . . . it will be okay, I promise."

"Oh, my little mouth. The hatred in that man's eyes . . . it's not the first time I've encountered it." He leaned back against the trunk, never letting go of his friend's hand, and his pupils dilated. For a long time, he said nothing. Then, in a voice that had taken on the consistency of the wind, he spoke.

"I was four years old when Mother lost the baby. Her *little princess*, she'd called it, without even knowing if it would be a girl. Even before its arrival, she had given it all her love. A name, a room, enough clothing to last five years—my cousins were already full-grown, and my mother's sisters had been happy to declutter their wardrobes. I had always felt, even as a child, that Mother wasn't completely at ease with me. So, every additional inch on the oval of her belly added a star to her gaze. And then, it was time. I can still picture my parents leaving for the hospital, Mother barely controlling the emotion of meeting her daughter. Alas, when two days later, they returned under a radiant and indifferent sun, I hardly recognized her. Her face had dried up, deep wrinkles had etched their furrows on her forehead. Her mouth especially, had become an immobile, stiff line. She sat down in her usual armchair and began rocking back and forth in silence. I quickly understood something had gone wrong: her belly had disappeared, sure, but then where was the baby?

"The following years were tough, so tough . . . I did my best to make Mother smile, but she was stricken with melancholy, and even though Father did his best to cheer her up, I also felt, deep down, his profound irritation. One day—it could have been two years later—my mother entered my room. *Come, my Stefan, we're going to play a game.* Play? Imagine my surprise, my excitement, my little mouth! It had been so long since she had played with me. In the evenings, she barely managed to prepare soulless meals before going to bed, often forgetting to come kiss me goodnight. So yes, Mama, let's play! I joined her in her deceased daughter's room (that was still how she referred to it) and she took out a stick of lipstick and a beautiful blue dress. *Put this on, my big boy,* she had told me. If it was a game, and what's more, one that made my mother laugh, what could be wrong? Surely, nothing. So, I put on the dress, let her apply the lipstick, it was fresh and quite pleasant, and we laughed. Oh, Lena, we laughed! *Dance, my Stefan, dance!* and I danced. Suddenly, my father appeared in the doorway—I will never forget that moment—with a look of stone-cold fury in his eyes, close to what I saw today in that uniformed man. He dragged me by the arm up to the bathroom to wash my face and ripped off my dress. Even after he'd let go of me, I still felt the pressure of his fingers on my arm, Lena, but the worst was seeing Mother curl up in a corner, her head hidden behind her trembling hands.

"After that, everything happened quickly. Father took me to live on my grandparents' farm while Mother was referred to a psychiatrist, who decided that her condition required continuous care. Poor Mama . . . from then on, I was only allowed to see her on weekends, and only under my father's supervision. This lasted a few years, and then one day, I was told the visits would no longer take place. No matter how much I insisted on being told the truth, I only found out many years later. Mother could no longer bear life; she had done what was necessary to never suffer again."

Lena was still firmly holding her friend's arm. A gust made them shiver; they got up.

"Great, my butt is frozen!" said Stefan. "Turn around, Lena. Oh, you've got a bit of dirt on your uniform, let me clean that for you!"

With his good hand, he patted her behind. "I hope that Mr. Gestapo isn't around anymore! Who knows how he'd react if he saw me touching your *tuches, meine liebe!*"

Despite herself, Lena burst into crystalline laughter. "Oh, Stefan . . ."

They parted ways, and Lena headed back toward the stable. The truth was hard to ignore: if even Stefan, whose greatest joy was wandering the park and talking to the trees, could see his life threatened at any moment, then maybe Sophie was right. Perhaps it was time to change perspective, to disappear until the storm had passed. Certainly, a life in hiding was full of dangers. She would have to take a thief's precautions, become an outlaw—in reality, she only had a vague idea of what that meant—but if Sophie was there to help her, then . . . Yes, she had made up her mind. It was time to leave. It was time to leave, and she had to tell Sophie right away before she changed her mind.

She crossed the corridor leading to the dormitory. Most of the young women were already preparing for the night. Sophie wasn't there yet. Yes, the more she thought about it, the more excited she became. Hiding from those Nazis, who thought they could do anything they wanted. Living underground like an adventurer, and with her best friend, no less . . . and who knows, maybe they could even bring Stefan along! Oh, how stylish that would be! As she undressed, she found Arthur's gift in her front pocket. She played with it for a while before putting it away. She donned her nightshirt and slipped under the covers. Sophie still wasn't there. She was probably spending the evening with Lustig's girls, gossiping and smoking those awful contraband cigarettes. No matter, she would wait for her. Sophie would be so happy.

Lena stayed that way, her gaze alternating between the wall clock and Sophie's bed. The lights went out, silence fell over the hospital. What could Sophie be doing? No outing with the Gestapo was scheduled, no secret romantic meeting in the garden, nothing. Come to think of it, she hadn't seen her since early afternoon.

An hour passed.

A painful ball of anguish formed in her chest. Small at first, it then expanded until it almost choked her. No, Sophie wouldn't have done that. Not after everything they had been through, after everything they had told each other . . . and yet. Did she really know her friend? Who, behind her back, would talk to Arthur, at nightfall? Oh . . . no, she shouldn't think like that. And yet, it seemed so obvious.

She stared at the wooden ceiling—impassively bearing witness to decades of petty human struggle—and a few tears ran down her cheeks, still flushed with the excitement of an adventure about to begin. Three o'clock in the morning.

Her eyes red, Lena buried her face under her blanket. The truth was hard to face: tired of waiting for an answer, Sophie had decided to take action. She had joined her parents in hiding.

Sophie had left her behind.

4

• • •

Tuesday, November 10, 1942, 4:30 p.m.

THEY HAD TAKEN HER SHOES.

For hours, Sophie had been hopelessly searching for an angle that didn't cause any part of her body to hurt. Finally, her hips bent, fingers stretched out over the slippery stones—almost convincing herself she could push them back a little—she thought she had found it. Yes, she could hold this position for a few minutes and not feel any pain. All the while, she couldn't keep her eyes off the long corridor that extended endlessly behind the rusted metal bars.

Cold, muddy water carpeted the cell's floor, just high enough to make dryness an impossible feat. As a child, only a few streets away, she had always eagerly awaited the end of thunderstorms. Once the skies would clear, she would run out of her apartment laughing and, along with her neighborhood friends, leap into the freshly formed puddles of the Alexanderplatz. Yes, when she was younger, the entire neighborhood had been her playground, her universe to discover and conquer. She closed her eyes and tried to focus her attention on happy memories, but the screams that regularly tore through the ever-present sound of an air duct prevented her from escaping, even for a moment.

She would have loved to sit down; but she refused to soil her beautiful white uniform. She caressed its grainy fabric, ran her hand over the yellow star, sewn with care in front of her heart. She tried to remember the last few days. Had there been any precursors to this disaster, any warning signs that might have alerted her to the impending catastrophe, that might have prompted her to flee while there still was time? She couldn't think of one.

The weeks and days blurred into one another. Since joining the hospital, she had to wake up at ungodly hours. How she missed her childhood! Raised to be a princess, her father always reminded her how special she was. "You can be whoever you want, *liebling*—an opera singer, a doctor, an actress in one of those American movies!" She believed him, dreaming of glamorous premieres and handsome leading men. But adolescence brought hormonal turmoil and shifting desires, causing her to abandon those childhood dreams. Instead, she became fierce and fearless, earning her friends' admiration and igniting the teenage lust of her masculine peers. Her father was surprised by this new Sophie, yet he never missed her goodnight kiss.

Then reality crept in with the regime change and new laws. She discovered, abruptly and painfully, that she was Jewish. Doors closed, faces turned cold, and Hollywood faded into a distant pipe dream. Survival demanded a practical path—especially with war looming. The Jewish hospital offered a short training program with a guaranteed position, an opportunity she couldn't ignore. And so, she found herself changing bandages and drawing blood, leaving behind the dreams of stardom for the stark reality of the present.

Lately, mornings were the hardest: once the head nurse had woken them up, she had to quickly make her way to the ward, tend to her patients, and mix with the doctors and her fellow nurses. To this routine, she had added a new task: since her outing with the Gestapo, Lena was but a shadow of herself, as if she had lost part of her illusions in that truck. And even if, in a way, Sophie was almost glad of this turn of events—it was about time, after all, that Lena understood the risks inherent to their new life—she nonetheless felt sorry for her friend and never shied away from waking up in the middle of the night to place a reassuring hand on her sweat-soaked shoulder.

No, nothing, she was sure of it, could have alerted her. Thus, when the head nurse had called her over to tell her that Dr. Lustig urgently requested her presence, her first thought had been that her dear Walter, suffocating under the Nazis' ever-present pressure, had decided to summon his favorite mistress in broad daylight, no longer caring about any discretion.

But upon entering his office, she'd realized her mistake. The face of the powerful Dr. Lustig had drained of color, and his entire body, strangely hunched, spoke of profound suffering. Facing him, two Gestapo officers stood upright in their black overcoats.

"*Schwester* Sophie," he had said in a hoarse voice. "Good, you're here. I don't have time to explain, but it turns out these gentlemen have received orders to . . . escort you to an undisclosed location. Only the urgency of the matter has been conveyed to me. You must accompany them immediately."

Sophie's breath was taken away, as if Dr. Lustig, without moving an inch, had found a way to deliver a serious sucker punch to her sternum.

"But . . ."

"*Nein*, Jew! You do not speak!" said one of the thugs, caressing his service weapon with a sweaty palm. "You're coming with us, right now!" They had grabbed her by the arm and pushed her out of the office. She had neither the reflex nor the strength to resist; everything was happening too fast. They had walked through deserted hallways, down the staircase, and across the garden. A large sedan was waiting for them alongside the hospital gates. Sophie, thrown into the back seat, had barely been able to twist her head to see the hospital vanish as they rounded the first corner.

Twenty minutes later, they stopped in front of a building that, as a Berliner, Sophie had no trouble recognizing; 26 Burg Strasse's infamous reputation was no secret to her. The car doors opened. A powerful instinct to flee had clenched her stomach. *Run, run, sprint away and disappear* . . . but where would she have gone? Would she have even made it ten meters before being shot down? The moment passed. Firmly held by the agents, she was escorted into the Gestapo headquarters. Only the monotonous sound of their steps echoed on the cold and dirty tiles. Through several corridors—all similar, all flooded with the same yellow light—they led her to the basement. Finally, they stopped in front of a miserable cell. "Get in! This is your new home." Her few seconds of hesitation had earned her the first slap.

Since then, there had been only silence, her thoughts, and the screams.

She extended a hesitant toe out of the cold water, transferred her weight onto her left leg, and observed her foot, leaning her back against the wall. Already, the skin had whitened, little wrinkles forming on the pads of her toes. She massaged, warmed, repeated the process on the opposite side. She focused on her breathing. It was still possible that all this was nothing more than a huge misunderstanding. They might have mistaken her for someone else, and she would soon be sent back to the hospital; because, in truth, what crime had she committed?

She put her foot back in the water, being careful not to slip. Suddenly, footsteps echoed down the corridor. They grew louder, and soon a huge man—a colossus, really—stopped in front of her cell. His face, covered in scars, housed tiny black eyes devoid of light. His large head was covered with freakishly boyish blond curls. He wore a short-sleeved white shirt. His hands, as wide as paddles, manipulated a small key. Sophie's cell door creaked open.

"Wait, sir . . ." said Sophie, who was accustomed to charming men of all shapes and sizes.

But the man had a job to do, and he would do it well. He took a step back, pulled back his leather boot like the football champion he might have dreamed of becoming, and delivered several formidable kicks toward Sophie. Petrified, she couldn't make a sound, and when the boot finally made contact with her shin, the colossus sniffled, ran a hand through his hair—he had worked up a bit of sweat—and receded like a bad wave.

Sophie felt her heart beat, flutter, pound against her chest. She thought of herself as someone who knew what violence was, what it was capable of; as a nurse, she'd had to tend to multiple wounds and fractures. But never had a man targeted her like this, inflicted such physical punishment, and it was as if her soul screamed, *See Sophie, this is the end . . . if you do nothing, he will return again and again until he no longer finds this amusing, and then he will use his handgun.* Instinctively, she ran her hands over her feet, her legs—avoiding the painful shin, where a bruise was almost visibly spreading under her skin—her pelvis, up to her stomach, her chest, her face, then back down to the yellow star. Her fingers clenched around it, and she suddenly wanted to rip it off, tear it apart, and another instinct emerged, amid the tears that had started to flow noiselessly down her cheeks, an instinct that told her to get a hold of herself, to puff out her chest, to call back the colossus and give him doe eyes, to touch the human part that surely still existed somewhere, to whisper sweet nothings in his ear and finally, when he was confident and at the right distance, to plunge a pointed piece of metal into his carotid artery.

Exhausted, she sat in the muddy water, buried her face in her hands, and soon, when the warm tears had finished expressing all their silent distress, she fell asleep.

5

• • •

Monday, November 16, 1942, 5 p.m.

After six days in her cell, Sophie's uniform was little more than a tattered collection of ragged brown fibers. For relief, all she had was a plastic bucket, the contents of which filled the air with an unbearable stench. Her shins showcased every color of a bruise; the silent colossus had done his work well. But to her great surprise, with each of his visits, Sophie found her apprehension diminishing. After the initial shock, she had found a way not just to get used to the pain but to anticipate it, to imagine it worse than it would actually be. She let her mind wander into horror, imagining herself already dismembered, lacerated, burned alive. She was being used as a human punching bag by a thick brute? *What of it?* she told herself while biting her cheeks as he beat her. The more the colossus hit, the more the inner voice—new, unexpected, foreign almost—whispered in her ear, *Enjoy this while you can, coward . . . one day, it will be my turn to repay you, you and all those who derailed my life. I shouldn't be here. No, I should be at the opera, at the cinema, being courted, flattered, maybe even married. Instead, I'm rotting in this hole, pissing myself and getting beaten, because this mad regime decided I was a Jew . . . me, who hasn't set foot in a synagogue for years!* She focused on the voice, letting the colossus wear out his boots on her strangely loose, curiously relaxed body.

Then, the colossus's visits became less frequent; after a while, they stopped entirely. The soup rations became more generous, her legs started to heal. Sophie caught herself thinking that, this way, life was almost bearable. But these were rare moments of happy confusion.

She had too much time to think. How had she ended up here? Ah, if only she had gone into hiding sooner! Her parents must be going out of their minds with worry. Yes, she remembered; she had promised Lena to wait for her decision before taking action. Lena, that foolish girl. What madness to have offered her to come along! With her frightened little ingenue's hesitations, she had wasted precious time, and now, who knew if she'd ever see her parents again?

Footsteps resonated down the corridor; lighter than the colossus's; they belonged to a mere soldier with a stiff forehead and a vacant gaze. He opened the cell and placed a towel on the floor. "Dry yourself, prisoner! You are expected," he said in a mechanical voice. Sophie unfolded her body with the caution of an older woman. Every joint in her body burned like it had been scorched by fire, compressed under the weight of a molten anvil. She ran a hesitant hand over her scalp and noted that her thick hair, which ever since her childhood had attracted the envy of women and the gaze of men, was now no more than a heap of dried-out straw, several strands remaining between her fingers. The towel's soft, silky texture, its lavender scent, seemed almost insane amidst this hell. Under the soldier's watch, she quickly dried her feet and face.

"*Schnell!* Prisoner! Dry yourself, you stink! You have one minute!"

After the allotted time, he pushed her ahead of him.

At first, her steps were awkward, and then her body remembered, and her muscles firmed up. They walked through a maze of corridors, she the twenty-one-year-old woman with turquoise eyes and only rags for clothes, he the brave soldier—barely older, whose homeland had claimed a piece of his soul. Their steps pounded the floor in unison, bare feet against leather soles, and Sophie glanced at her jailer. She was suddenly certain she had seen him before, certain that behind the helmet and uniform was an old classmate—a boy, really—who perhaps had watched her from afar, betting with his friends that before the year's end, he'd muster the energy to steal a kiss from the golden goddess.

They stopped in front of a wooden door. "In there, prisoner."

Sophie pushed the door open. A table, two chairs placed face to face. A bare room, smelling of death. A few brown stains dried on the floor. Sophie wanted to sit, hesitated, and finally decided that her legs could no longer carry her; if they wanted to beat her again, so be it. She knew now that she could endure the pain.

Minutes ticked away in heavy silence. Sophie naïvely thought that after the days she had just lived through, nothing worse could happen to her. What would they do: pull out her nails? Sever her fingers? Sure, they could always delve deeper into horror, but to what end? What did she possess that they could possibly desire? The things men typically coveted were of no interest to them. What, then?

The door opened. A short bow-legged man dressed in a black suit entered briskly. He sat down, adjusting the chair to find himself exactly opposite Sophie's face, and remained silent for a moment. With his left hand, he mechanically twirled his wedding ring a quarter turn one way, then reversed the movement. He clicked his tongue, swallowed.

"You recognize me, I believe." His voice was clear, cold, surgical.

"Yes, sir," said Sophie, breathlessly. She could never forget Brunner.

"Good. Then you know that my mission, ordered by the Führer himself"—he had a small spasm that resembled a smile—"is to complete the task he started. Namely, to make Berlin *judenrein*. I will not leave the city until I have succeeded. You have probably noticed that my methods are quite effective. But, like all great achievements, they can always be perfected, don't you agree?"

He took out a cigarette from a metal case, offered one to Sophie ("*nein*? as you wish"), lit it with a confident gesture, and took a long drag; its tip glowed like a miniature sun, the only spot of color in the gray and brown room.

"I have just created a new program of which I am quite proud. A program that, I hope, will address an unexpected problem." His jaw tightened suddenly, and he almost whispered. "Tell me, Nurse Sophie: are you familiar with rodents? Mice, hamsters . . . rats?"

"Uh . . . I mean, yes, sir. We occasionally had mice in our Berlin apartment."

"Fantastic. Then, you will understand. You see, it seems that a significant number of these Jews have hidden underground, like rats . . . what can you do, they do not want to face their natural fate. Fine! I can accept a minimum of resistance, even if it makes no sense. I would even find it amusing if I had enough time and energy to devote to them. A little Jew hunt, now there's something to invigorate a man! But the reality is that I lack agents to track down these vermin. So here is my theory: just like these noble rodents, it is almost certain that these Jews occasionally come up to the surface to breathe Berlin's air, and that's when I plan to capture them."

He was almost whispering, but his temples had swelled with a barely masked rage. "Nurse Sophie, so far, are you with me?"

"Yes."

"*Wunderbar*! You see, Sophie, I've found out all about you. You grew up in Berlin, is that correct?"

"Yes."

"And, according to all the interviewed witnesses, you had quite the active social life. With your face, your hair, your figure, men must have been at your feet! Ha! Even the true Germans, isn't that so?"

Sophie said nothing.

"No, no, there's no need to answer. I have no desire to imagine the coupling of a Jew and an Aryan." He crushed his cigarette, looked up. She searched his eyes for a trace of emotion, an unconscious sign that would guide her toward the best course of action. But all she saw was a vast black horizon.

"Listen well, Jew: I'm going to ask you a question, and you're going to think carefully before answering: do you want to be part of the Gestapo?" The words hung in the air for a moment; then, slowly, they penetrated Sophie's brain.

"Are you surprised? Yes, I understand. Here is what I offer: you won't have to wear the Jewish star anymore. We will provide you with official Gestapo documents; your name will be removed from the lists for the convoys to the east. Isn't that what you want? A smart girl like you . . . you must have understood that these are not pleasurable holiday trips. You'll get warm clothes, a private room, as much coffee as you want." The corner of his lips twitched imperceptibly. His eyelids came closer together, leaving only a thin black opening. "In return, I will ask only one thing of you: you will walk around the city, and if ever you recognize any of these clandestine Jews, you simply need to discreetly alert our agents so that they can carry out a little cleaning operation."

Sophie couldn't take her eyes off the man, who had straightened up and resumed his endless fidgeting with his wedding ring. She tried to ignore the beating of her heart, which suddenly sounded like a locomotive speeding between her temples, and forced herself to imagine this relentless killer as a good family man, who in the evening, after having washed his hands, would stroke the hair of a little Karl, the perfect dream of an invincible Germany. She felt a wave of nausea wash over her, clenched her jaw, swallowed some dry saliva.

"I see you've lost your voice. The amazement, no doubt, of learning that you can still be of some use to your country. Good! I'll give you until tomorrow to answer me. In the meantime, let me escort you back. I owe you that honor; after all, we're almost colleagues, aren't we? Guard!" The soldier opened the door and grabbed Sophie by the arm. "Let's walk," said Brunner.

They advanced slowly through the corridors, Sophie wedged between the adolescent guard and the bow-legged man, who, she couldn't help noticing—although he stood up as straight as he could—was truly a very short man. What had been his life before this? How did a man become so full of hate? She had no time to think about it. Emaciated limbs appeared from time to time, clinging to the cell bars as they passed in silence, making her flinch. Her heart couldn't seem to calm down. Finally, Brunner stopped; Sophie didn't recognize her cell. She had allowed herself to imagine that they would place her in a more comfortable room while waiting for her answer. Were they just going to push her into another filthy hole?

Brunner crouched down, lit a flashlight, and directed the beam inside the cell. Two exhausted bodies, ghosts of what they had once been, sat side by side, holding hands. The man protected the woman's face from the beam of light with a desperate, brave, futile gesture. Still kneeling, Brunner turned his face toward Sophie. He wore a devilish smile, and in the depths of his eyes burned an intense, profound, jubilant hatred.

"Well, Sophie, aren't you going to say hello to your parents? There's nothing like family, you know."

PART 3

1

• • •

Wednesday, February 10, 1943, 8 a.m.

WITH HER COFFEE CUP PRESSED AGAINST HER CHEST, LENA stared down at the snow-dusted trees. A few doctors crossed the park at a brisk pace. The sun pierced the clouds with a few white rays. She drank up, rinsed her cup, walked to the treatment room, and began to fill her pillboxes. Despite the repetitive nature of her work, she still found satisfaction in a job well done. During her first weeks at the hospital, her movements had been a bit awkward, almost clumsy; now they were regulated by an internal clock, an invisible compass smoothly navigating her hands through the motions. Every movement had a precise role, a semblance of order that soothed her. *Here, at least, I am useful,* she would tell herself on her good days. Those days—and they were becoming fewer and farther between—feeling that her morale could use a little boost, she would tell herself that if it came to that, she could navigate the ward in complete darkness, distributing tablets, changing IVs and dressings for her patients while frantic technicians would try to fix the outage. Her patients . . . so many of them had disappeared, snatched by Eichmann and his impromptu visits. Their names inscribed on those dreaded lists by Lustig's pencil. The Gestapo tore them from their beds, wounds still gaping and dressings wet with blood. When that happened, Lena looked away and tried to ignore their cries of agony. It wasn't that she had become desensitized, quite the contrary, but a feeling of uselessness, of guilt had crept under her skin. If she wasn't cut out to be a hero, then what was the point of looking on? Better, if possible, to hide in a corner—*to let the storm pass.*

With the pillboxes filled, she began her rounds. Her routine remained unchanged: beds 1 to 5, over and over again. Suddenly, she felt very old, even though in reality, less than a year had passed since her first day at the hospital. A lifetime . . . she approached bed number 5. Arthur's wounds were almost healed. For a moment, Lena wondered if his status as a famous scientist afforded him some kind of unofficial protection; such longevity in the ward was exceptional. But she remembered all the great men that were already gone, all those who had deemed themselves untouchable and were now no more than distant memories, and she shrugged the idea off.

"Good morning, Arthur. It's time to check your ankle. May I?"

"Of course, beautiful Lena," he said, smoothing his mustache.

He still allowed himself these familiar little jibes, all the while realizing they sorely missed their mark. At first, teasing Lena was one of his day's few pleasures. Her youth and shyness had made her blush so easily. But for the past few months, a discreet weariness had crept into her smile, her tone had gotten a bit harsher, and more importantly, the glint of innocence had left her eyes.

She unwound the bandage in silence, head bowed, lost in a reverie of which she alone held the key. Arthur watched her intently. She was so close he could smell her hair. He wanted to grab her hand, to tell her *Beautiful Lena, don't worry, I know this is scary but soon we will leave this place together. We will bathe in a sparkling river, just the two of us and the sun and our laughter, and all of this will be nothing but an ugly memory.* But he couldn't bring himself to say those words out loud, only half believing them himself, and he turned his gaze toward the treatment room.

He had become accustomed to his environment and expected nothing more from it than what he was already receiving. The care, the handcuffs, the two hours of freedom per day. The ever-present and indefinable smell of a hospital ward. While some details seemed immutable—the doctor always started his rounds at a fixed time, and no delay was tolerated—the hospital, like a giant snake, regularly shed its skin. More than half the nurses present upon his arrival had disappeared. Often, they were replaced with young faces, carefree bodies striding the halls without a worry in the world. Yes, he thought to himself, the Mischlinge were really something else.

The sound of laughter echoed from the break room. Three young women came out. They had only been at the hospital for a few weeks, but already they felt perfectly at home. They were now making their way between the beds; one of them was entertaining her enthralled colleagues with a lively story, regularly stopping to touch the back of their hands for dramatic effect. They soon reached bed number 5.

"Yesterday, Stella and I went to the hairdressers without our stars!" she said.

"And guess what, just as we sat down, two SS officers showed up. Damn! Apparently, a woman who had just left the salon had had her purse stolen. She sounded the alarm, and here they come, all huffy and puffy, looking very serious. *'Papiere!'* they say. Okay, I'll admit, at that moment, we were a bit scared. Luckily, our fake papers were neatly tucked into our bras; you should have seen their faces when we pulled them out. *'Jawohl, Herr Kommandant*, of course my papers are in order,' I told him! Ha! He was completely taken aback. He glanced over my papers with an absent look, never really taking his eyes off my chest. The other one was eyeing Stella, his tongue was practically touching the ground! And then, their colleague came in, running. Apparently, he had arrested a Jew two streets away. He was sure he had found the culprit; she didn't have the purse, but she had tried to flee. Anyway, they left without even turning back. We finished getting our hair cut, paid, and once we left the salon, we had one of the biggest fits of laughter I can remember. Oh my, what an adventure we had!"

Lena had not raised her head. After cleaning the wound, she wrapped a clean bandage around the ankle. Arthur noticed a slight tremor in her hand. The group of young women had moved on, but the astonished sighs could still be heard in the distance.

"Lena, forgive them. They are young. For them, the war has barely begun. They can't understand . . . not yet, at least."

Lena tried to smile, applied a piece of adhesive tape on the bandage, and left without a word.

•

Since Sophie's disappearance, Lena had grown even closer to Stefan. Once a day, they would meet by the weeping willow. She would take his arm, and they would walk. Sometimes, they would enjoy the jam sandwiches that Stefan religiously set aside from each of his repairs. But he had changed as well. It had become rare to see him wearing a dress, and his makeup had taken on darker shades. He looked like a sad old clown lost under his own big top. They walked, and sometimes he would tell Lena stories about his mother, how he'd always felt she had never loved him more than on the day they had played dress-up. He never spoke of his father, and Lena never asked. These were their only moments of respite. As she did every night, Lena struggled to fall asleep. Lying on her bed, she looked at her neighbor, a young girl who had recently arrived from the countryside. How could such a frail body produce such terrible snoring? A *bona fide* locomotive. Gone were the days of Sophie and the evening whispers.

She'd had to adapt to these new faces, to the changing texture of the hospital. Those new recruits all put on a good face . . . and yet. In their moments of doubt, they too confessed that the city was changing. They spoke of double agents, of Jews at work for the Nazis. They were seen sitting calmly at the most beautiful terraces, eyes alert under their felt hats. Others spotted them lurking around restaurants frequented by the underground. They would chat you up, put on a show of camaraderie, and a few minutes later, you would find yourself handcuffed by a Gestapo henchman. But among the mists of rumors, one was more persistent and chilling than any other: there was a woman of extreme beauty, her hands gloved in leather, who approached you with grace and intimations. She always found a way to gain your trust; maybe you attended the same school, or *Did you know Mrs. X? Oh, that's extraordinary, she was my nanny!* But beware, if you let yourself be fooled. A shared address, a nod in the direction of your favorite forger, and you would disappear without a trace. It was said she had already captured about twenty Jews. *The blonde poison . . . the angel of death . . .* said the young girls, without Lena being able to tell if it was fear, fascination, or a mix of both that sparked that strange glow in their eyes at the mention of this specter.

Sleep was but a dream. Outside, a snowstorm was cleansing Berlin of the previous day's filth. The wind howled through the trees. A noise loud enough to wake the dead, Lena thought.

She hugged her pillow to her chest, pulling the blanket over her shoulders.

"The *blonde poison*. What bullshit!" she thought, surprising herself with her own vulgarity. Somewhere, a window slammed shut, but Lena didn't flinch. Finally, she fell asleep.

2

• • •

Thursday, February 18, 1943, 5 p.m.

THE TIP OF THE LIPSTICK PRESSED SOFTLY AGAINST THE UPPER lip's cushion. Leaving behind a scarlet trail, it worked meticulously before repeating the operation on the lower lip. Then, a bare hand placed the lipstick on the table, maneuvering among the clutter of makeup and perfume bottles, until it reached a radio. The fingers twiddled a knob in search of some unexpected poetry, but it was Nazi songs that emerged from the static. They soon gave way to a stoic announcer's nasal voice: "And now, live from the Berlin Sportpalast, we now turn to Dr. Goebbels for his much-anticipated speech!" A thunder of applause signaled the arrival of the propaganda master.

Sitting in front of a large mirror, Sophie watched her reflection. With an affectionate gesture, as if greeting an old friend, she started brushing her voluptuous blonde curls. For the first time in years, a hairstylist had agreed to cut her hair; the old Frau had even complimented her on her golden highlights. She had always loved her long hair, but she'd needed a change and now sported a hairstyle fashionable among young German women, a sort of bob that danced joyfully on her shoulders. She admired the classic harmony between her mouth and her hair; only her eyes remained to be perfected.

On the radio, the man had begun his speech. True, the news from the front was not all excellent; he even went so far as to admit that the Wehrmacht had encountered *serious military difficulties* in the east. That was an understated way of saying that General Paulus had bent the knee at Stalingrad, Sophie thought. The three days of national mourning that had followed had done nothing to soothe Berliners' morale. But in truth, wasn't the population already mourning their pre-war lives? Water and food were terribly scarce, winter clawed at the city, and the promise of a short and glorious war was little more than an old memory. *An odd start for a motivational speech*, she thought. But she sensed in the furious energy of his voice that he would soon turn to more unifying, warlike, conquering themes.

She applied her mascara carefully, giving her lashes the curves of a prima ballerina, listening to the speech with only half an ear. How pleasant it was to take her time in front of the mirror, without a crowd of impatient nurses stomping at her back.

On the airwaves, the man had finally reached his favorite theme: The Jews and their total responsibility for the ills of the universe. "*. . . and if necessary, we will proceed to the erad . . . to the complete removal of Judaism!*" Sophie thought she had misheard. But after all, why wouldn't he own up to it? His desire for the complete eradication of the Jewish people was no longer a secret to anyone. Did he suddenly fear being judged too harshly by posterity? Did he still want to maintain a semblance of decency, avoid overly harsh words? It was quite unnecessary. Rumors circulated; last month, two thousand Jews had been sent to the east, swallowed by filthy wagons. The population knew it; the politicians knew it. Those who applauded, screaming their hysterical approval in the overheated atmosphere of the Sportpalast, knew it too, no doubt relished it.

Sophie closed her eyes. Now that she owned a radio, she spent hours each day going through the stations. She had listened to several speeches by Goebbels, and each time, she was struck by a sense of *déjà vu.* Finally, it came back to her: It was a Wednesday, in the early spring of 1933. With two of her friends, she was bicycling back home from her piano lesson. It was their custom to speed along Dorotheenstrasse before crossing the Spree and heading toward the Alexanderplatz. But that day, heavy rain had caught them midway, and Sophie had suggested they take shelter in a café on Unter den Linden, where she was a regular. For hours, the three girls indulged in hot chocolates and biscuits. "I must chase you out, my beauties," old Madame Roth finally said. "It's time to close the shop. A piece of advice: head straight home! This rain bodes ill."

"Yes, Madame Roth," they responded in unison.

They pedaled under the rain, laughing at the situation, when they heard them. At first, it seemed joyful, almost ludicrous—songs, percussion, a brass band. But the procession drew closer, and they saw them: students in their SA uniforms, chinstraps tightly bound, chanting warlike, patriotic, violent songs. Women and children, with a terrible glow in their eyes.

Trucks moved slowly through the crowd. Curiosity got the better of them, and the girls followed the strange procession. Finally, their destination seemed clear, as they all stopped on the large square facing Humboldt University, Berlin's oldest university.

They parked their bikes and took shelter under a tree. Slowly, the crowd got organized and almost naturally, human chains formed between the trucks and the center of the square. The trucks' precious cargo was finally revealed, passing quickly, feverishly from hand to hand: books. Dozens, hundreds of books, thrown onto the cobblestones like vulgar trash. Under the drums' haunting rhythm, the pile became a hill, then a mountain; the books were thrown with increasingly unrestrained fury. Some, among the most zealous, tore out pages, underlining their folly with guttural, primal screams.

A fire truck mixed into the crowd. *Finally,* Sophie thought. *Authority will put an end to this madness.* She thought of her father, whose book collection had always been a source of pride for him. A few days earlier, uniformed men had knocked on their door, barged in and shoved her father to the side. They had walked straight to his study and confiscated about twenty volumes from the shelves. After they'd left, he had locked himself in his office and when he finally came out, he refused to talk about it. But she had heard him mutter that the world was becoming a dark place for intellectuals, that the government was turning to obscurantism . . . but he was wrong, he had to be. The firefighters would send everyone home, Sophie was sure of it.

What followed, she would never forget. Before the madness of a cheering crowd, the firefighters doused the books with gasoline. Someone struck a match. Then, under a pouring rain, red and yellow flames licked the smoke-stained sky. Amongst the chaos, a man had climbed onto the stage and, in the same voice that still echoed on the radio ten years later, had launched into a venomous diatribe about the century of Jewish intellectualism. Sophie had forgotten the words, but the force, the power, the absence of doubt in his voice had both terrified and impressed her. Indeed, he was full of hate, but he was also possessed, consumed by his speech and in that matter, so different from her father and his tormented artist's eternal hesitations. Eventually, a policeman had asked them what they were doing out so late, and the girls, shivering and suddenly very tired, had stuttered an excuse before darting off.

Sophie stood up and opened a large wooden dresser. She had been able to choose her clothes, with an unlimited budget to boot. *Courtesy of the Gestapo.* She winced and took out a silk blouse and a long purple skirt. The blouse's fabric floated over her skin like an angel's caress. Looking at her bare legs, she tried to ignore the scars.

The pain was still there whenever she walked too fast, but she could afford no weakness. She quickly slipped into a pair of stockings and wiggled into the skirt, which perfectly hugged her newly rediscovered curves. *Not bad,* she thought.

On the radio, the speech was coming to an end. The man had started a series of questions, which he delivered to the white-hot crowd with furious energy. "*. . . and I ask you: do you want total war? If necessary, do you want a war even more total and radical than we could have imagined so far?"* Clearly, they wanted it. Yes, they were willing to become cannon fodder—or at least they were willing to send ever more young soldiers to the front. Yes, they were willing to give away their women and daughters to the Reich's factories, and yes, they agreed to close the last remaining places of leisure, because what was the point of entertainment before total victory?

A shiver ran down her spine. *Well, fine. If they want it, let them have their total war. But not for me. I won't work in a factory, paid a pittance and killing myself with hard work.* She slipped into high-heeled shoes and adjusted a green felt beret over her silky curls. No, she would no longer be a victim. From now on, she had other plans.

The speech was over; the radio resumed its usual programming. The nation had just tipped into total war.

No matter, Sophie thought. *For me, the dice are cast.*

She opened a drawer and took out a small black semi-automatic pistol—a woman's pistol, she had been told. She secured it to her thigh, well hidden under her skirt, and a pleasant shiver ran through her body. She checked her handbag's contents one last time—making it a point never to leave her room without her new identity card—put on a winter coat and a pair of leather gloves, and was out the door.

3

• • •

Saturday, February 27, 1943. 6 a.m.

EVERY MORNING, THEY WALKED. ONE FOOT IN FRONT OF THE other, with the absurd hope of surviving one more day through the war, the hunger, the freezing cold. They were Jews or half-Jews, and despite the terror in which they lived, they felt privileged. As employees of the Reich's factories, they contributed to the war effort and thus received a salary—50 *pfennigs* a day, half as much as an Aryan worker—which allowed them, in the evening, to feed their families. So yes, they walked. They would go tighten bolts, forge metal, because *those who remain useful stay alive*, they told themselves in a sort of protective mantra. *Those who remain useful, stay alive.*

•

At the same moment, a division of the Leibstandarte SS, Adolf Hitler's personal bodyguards, were preparing for a fine day. They adjusted their helmets, slipped on pristine white gloves, and checked the sharpness of their bayonets. They had left behind warm *fräuleins*, chubby babies, pampered mistresses. Comments flew in low voices among the clean-shaven faces, whose muscular jaws framed predatory smiles. Finally, orders that would allow them to vent, to put to good use their destructive capacities that had been wasted for months, standing on guard duty in front of the Führer's Eagle's Nest. Pacing in front of a mountain chalet, thanks for nothing. No, they needed action. Their nerves were stretched to the limit, vibrating in unison with a common excitement. They were on a sacred mission, coupled with an excuse to finally unleash their hatred. Today would not be boring; they would crush Jews for the grateful Fatherland! They were finally going to cleanse Berlin of all these intruders, Heil Hitler!

•

An hour later, three hundred trucks roamed the city. They parked in front of the Reich's factories and spilled their vomit of soldiers, policemen, and SS. Boots snapped sharply on the cobblestones, sometimes blending with the sound of sewing machines or the jittery rhythm of the workers' hearts. And everywhere the same scene unfolded: an officer—a former failed postman or a bitter unemployed man—foolishly stood in front of the factory manager and shouted, certain of his power: *We are here for your Jews! Schnell, unless you want to be taken away as well!* And the manager acquiesced. Caught in their work clothes, hands still full of parts meant for German tanks and Wehrmacht radios, these men and women were seized by brutes, beaten at the slightest resistance, and pushed into the trucks.

Some of the more vigorous tried to flee, but that was a true gift to the helmeted troops, and the sound of rifles echoed through the city, mixed with the deafening, viscous melody of chaos.

4

• • •

Saturday, February 27, 1943, 8 a.m.

It was but a whisper, but Lena felt it as soon as she walked into the cafeteria. An unusual tremor was sweeping through the room. These doctors walked a bit too briskly for such an early hour; those secretaries had left breakfast exchanging worried glances. And why was the head nurse walking from table to table? Lena was about to sit down when the latter grabbed her arm. "Good morning, Nurse Lena. Put down your coffee, there's news. Please follow me."

Almost paralyzed by anxiety, she followed her superior through the corridors to an office she had only heard tales about: the heavy wooden door, the vestibule—the loyal secretary's private domain—and then the holy of holies, the heart of the hospital's power: Dr. Lustig's office. A shiver ran down her spine. So, it was happening. She was going to be sent east.

"Enter, Nurse Lena. Everyone is waiting for you," said the secretary.

A dozen nurses stood upright, around the desk. Seated deep in his chair, Dr. Lustig sucked on his pipe, well nestled between his lower jaw and his mustache. "Ah, you're the last one?" he grumbled. "Good. Listen, it's quite simple: I've received instructions from Brunner. You have been divided into groups of two. You must go to the addresses indicated on this sheet. Here are special armbands, which will allow you to take the tramway. Immediate departure!"

Lena wanted to ask a question, but she joined the silence that hovered over the scene. If Brunner ordered and Lustig acquiesced, then none of the young women had a say. She grabbed an armband and leaned over the sheet of paper. With Ada, a newcomer, they were assigned to an address on Rathenhower Strasse. With no time to grab any bag or sweater, the two women crossed the garden. Lena caught sight of Stefan pacing around the weeping willow, looking very agitated, arms crossed behind his back. *Poor thing*, she thought. *What will become of him without me?*

They crossed the street and, after a few seconds of hesitation, boarded the tram. Their first reflex was to cross their arms, hiding their Stars of David and thus showing to anyone who cared to see, their protective armbands. This was Lena's first time on a Berlin tramway! But she could barely enjoy the excitement of this new experience the way she would have, had the circumstances been different. She clung to a metal bar (she didn't dare push the experience as far as sitting down) and ventured a circular glance. Fearing offensive sneers or hateful faces, she met only indifference instead. Some of the passengers had their eyes closed, snatching a few precious minutes of sleep, others absent-mindedly browsed the pages of a newspaper; all these bodies bore the marks of a long, hard winter. Sitting on a bench, a child chewed on the remnants of a lollipop, twisting the plastic stem to extract one last sweet drop of it. Their eyes met, exchanging everything that can be exchanged between a woman and a child.

"Rathenhower Strasse! That's our stop!" said Ada.

They jumped off the tram and found themselves in an unfamiliar neighborhood. Lena suddenly had a crazy idea: what if they tore off the star and the armband and just started to walk? Sure, their uniform made them recognizable as nurses, but really, what made them so terribly different from other Berliners? They had just spent thirty minutes on a crowded tramway, and not a single voice had risen against their presence. Without the star, they would be utterly invisible! They could spend the remainder of the war hiding in a cave, watching planes passing overhead . . . a soldier's voice brought her back to reality. "You there, the nurses! This way!"

They went through a metal gate and came upon what looked like an old circus tent. They had to dodge three moving trucks, which stopped in the center of a sand-covered courtyard. Soldiers uncovered the trucks' side tarps. "Get down, prisoners!" Unable to move or make a sound, Lena watched the scene unfold: rifle butts rained down on the slowest prisoners; many of them were already injured. A young woman with thin limbs limped forward. Her beige dress was stained with blood.

"You, nurses!" shouted an officer. "Report! You will set up the newcomers. A bit of straw, a space of twenty centimeters, more straw. You welcome, you treat if you can, and—" he had a malicious grin—"you reassure! We will take care of everyone! *Schnell*!"

Straw. Welcome, set up, reassure. Alright. She could do that. Without really admitting it to herself, Lena was relieved to have simple orders to obey. The most important thing, she thought, was to keep panic at bay. So, they were there to do their job. But what job? Without bandages, without equipment, without a doctor to assist, what could they possibly achieve? No matter. First, they would help those who could be helped.

She grabbed a few pieces of straw and entered the tent. Once inside, she was greeted by a new version of hell. Sticky mud sucked at her soles. The air was heavy with fear and sweat. There were about five hundred people already scattered throughout what looked like a former stable, and the space was still half empty. Guards paced everywhere, flanked by German shepherds. She looked around and was met with panicked glances; everyone was trying to make sense of it all, to carve out some semblance of a personal space, to find a logical explanation for this specific moment in their life, one minute at a time. Lena focused on her straw. First, she set up the injured, holding hands, whispering sweet nothings without believing them. She recognized a doctor from the hospital. He too wore an armband and appeared totally bewildered amidst the chaos. He was squatting next to a man, but without equipment, without an operating room, he was but a man of science, faced with the reality of an open wound.

The young girl in the blood-stained dress wandered like a ghost through the mud. Her cheeks had turned pale gray.

"Miss! What happened? What's your name?"

"Rita, my name is Rita . . . this morning, I went to work as usual. They told us that as long as we worked, we would be protected. But they came with their trucks, and they wanted to take everyone! So, you know how it is. I don't like to give in. There was a door that led to the backyard. I helped some of my older colleagues through it before following them. But I was too slow, the Nazis noticed me. One of them shot me; his colleagues found it very amusing."

"Oh, my poor thing . . . Lie down, I'll examine you."

Lena lifted the dress. At the top of the thigh, a crust had begun to form near the bullet's entry wound. A silent stream flowed from underneath. Lena looked around for the doctor; not finding him, instinct took over. She had to act quickly, or else young Rita would bleed out. It was already a miracle she was still alive; the bullet must have only grazed the artery. With a sharp tear, she ripped a five-centimeter-wide strip from her uniform's hem and used it as a tourniquet, strangling Rita's fortunately thin thigh. Gradually, the bleeding stopped.

"There, you'll feel better like this," said Lena, relieved and almost surprised by the effectiveness of her makeshift solution. "Rest now, I'll come back to check on you later."

"Thank you, you're an angel . . ."

Something swelled in Lena's throat, but she tried to ignore it. Out of straw, she walked back to the courtyard. The trucks were persisting in their relentless to and fro. In some places, the sand had taken on a scarlet hue. Off to the side, a few women squatted, attending to their natural needs. Leaning against the trucks, SS soldiers relished the spectacle, smoking cigarettes and occasionally throwing in lewd remarks. One of them was taking photos. Memories of Berlin.

The street bordering all this activity was reasonably busy on this Saturday morning. Across the sidewalk was a building that housed the offices of a famous newspaper. For nearly an hour, a woman had been leaning out her window, observing the cream of the crop of Germany's youth humiliate other human beings. This woman—awarded an obscure journalism prize for one of her articles on Hitler's "vision"—this woman suddenly felt a surge of humanity infiltrate her heart and her lungs. Having always considered herself a good person, she was not surprised by this emotion and wanted to share her noble feelings with the world. "Hey! You! Come on, leave them alone!" she shouted from the safety of her tower. "Why are you beating them? Can't you see they've already lost!"

After the relative astonishment of seeing a civilian question their methods, the Leibstandarte SS soldiers used their considerable voices to crush the insolent one. "Silence, spy! Do you want us to come and get you? You can join the prisoners if you're so concerned about their fate!"

The words crossed the street, dodged one or two pigeons, climbed the four floors before overwhelming the young daredevil. Reduced to silence, she closed the shutters and went back to hiding behind her typewriter. Thus ended the German people's revolt against the atrocities committed on Rathenhower Strasse.

Inside the tent, the air had taken on a thick consistency. An acrid smell, a mix of fear, sweat, and blood filled the atmosphere. The number of prisoners kept increasing; the youngest remained standing to avoid sitting on ground now defiled by human excretions. Lena noticed two young girls sitting on a tree trunk, covered with an overcoat. She approached, wanting to know where they could have found such a wonder, when what she had taken for a branch revealed itself to be a human arm, stiff and cold. She closed her eyes, controlled her nausea, moved along.

A row of tables had been set up in the center of the tent. Prisoners moved from one to the other, stating their identities, emptying their pockets down to the last pfennig ("you won't need those anymore!" Lena heard). When they got to the last table, a soldier hung a tag around their neck. *Like cattle,* thought Lena, petrified. She tried to make out the words written in black ink on the tags but was too far away. She had no time to dwell on it further. Always, she was asked for straw, water, and food. Her white uniform placed her at the center of all requests, all hopes. How long had she been there? It could have been an hour, or five or six. Hunger gnawed at her stomach; a tinge of dizziness forced her to sit down.

Time slipped by, unnoticed. She often crossed paths with Ada and the doctor, reading in their eyes the same helplessness, the same sadness. "Why are we here? Why?" Ada asked her. "I don't know . . . maybe they're counting on us to give this disaster a show of sanitation? All we can do is help as many people as possible. Remember, as soon as they find us no longer useful, they'll get rid of us. So, let's stay useful."

Finally, the trucks stopped their infernal ballet. *Even murderers rest sometimes,* Lena thought. She looked for a place to lie down, her gaze landing on Rita. She had been so busy that she'd forgotten to check on her. Oddly, she had already developed a sisterly affection for her. Perhaps was it due to the young woman's dark, deep gaze, which reminded her unconsciously of her mother's?

She came closer, squatted down, and placed her hand on her shoulder. But months of working at the hospital had given her a new and terrible ability: she knew the difference between the gentle warmth of living skin and the cold of eternal winter. Touching Rita's icy skin, Lena made a great effort to protect herself. She thought this was the nature of war, that Rita might have passed into a better world . . . that she had done her best, that her tourniquet had been good, yes, very good indeed . . . She wanted to scream, to tear out her hair, to spit out her misery. She wanted to run to the first soldier she saw, snatch his Luger, and riddle him with bullets. She wanted to lead an army and liberate her people. Instead, she could only squeeze Rita's hand while a few tears ran down her face. Then, she tried to get up, but her body had become extremely heavy. She felt a bony hand placed under her armpit, helping her regain her balance. An ancient-looking woman gazed at her, smiled a toothless smile, and caressed her cheek. Then, she took off her shawl, and together, they covered Rita's body.

Night had fallen over Berlin. A few employees of the Jewish community had been allowed to dig holes at the back of the yard, creating makeshift latrines. Soup was served to those who still had the strength to eat. Coffee, however, remained a hope, a promise.

Exhausted, Lena wanted to help further, but her body simply refused to budge. She collapsed onto a few strands of straw and closed her eyes.

5

• • •

Sunday, February 28, 10 a.m.

DAVID ROSEN HAD ALWAYS LOVED WOMEN.

His first stirrings of emotion traced back to kindergarten, when, with his scraped knees buried in the sand, he covertly admired his fellow schoolgirls' plump thighs and crystalline laughs. Childhood gave way to adolescence, and his boiling hormones intensified his desire, gripping his gut, tingling his stomach. For him, those were long years of eternal wonder. His days were spent floating amongst the curved bodies of uniformed young girls, and in the evenings, he almost confused the Liesels, Ruths, and Erikas, whose hair and lips intertwined in a maelstrom of emotions that disturbed his sleep and delighted his soul.

David Rosen was not of a shy nature; he readily spoke to the youthful beauties, wielding a humor that had always made his mother laugh. But he quickly understood that his mother was an easy audience; outside the family cocoon, his quips were most often met with cold, indifferent stares. Moreover, on other purely anatomical points, nature had been less generous with him than with some other boys. Despite his best efforts, his short, coarse hair seemed glued to his skull, earning him the worst mockery from the schoolyard's most dominant young males. His body was slow to fully develop. Even past the age of sixteen, he retained the somewhat chubby appearance he had as a child, as if his limbs refused to shed their protective fat, as if his back and shoulders preferred to stay hunched, rather than blossoming toward the heights frequented by his classmates. Adding to this picture was a visual weakness that required him to wear thick corrective lenses. David Rosen thus understood, through a series of failures and humiliations, that it was futile for him to seek the company of women any further. And so, faced with this dismal realization, he did what generations of frustrated teenagers had done before him: he threw himself into his studies. If women didn't want him, then he would excel elsewhere; if physical prowess was all but denied to him, then he would outshine those bullies on the report card.

Thus, David Rosen finished high school at the top of his class, and it was with high hopes that on an autumn day in 1926, he entered, head held high, the University of Berlin's lecture hall. There, at least, he told himself, he would meet sharp minds capable of seeing beyond mere physical considerations. There, he would finally touch a sort of infinity. And, he thought with feverish excitement, women.

For a few days, he believed he could start anew. He would gladly greet the female students, attempting to strike up conversations with the most beautiful among them. But the nightmare began again. Indifference, snickers—such were the responses to his friendly greetings, to his clumsy attempts at seduction. So, after a few weeks, he understood that the gaze of the female students overlaid seamlessly with that of the high school girls, and thus would his life be; he would be invisible to women, for whom only the reassuring shoulders, tanned foreheads, and massive jaws of wavy-haired boys seemed to matter. David Rosen thought he must be quite unattractive to provoke such reactions, and he was filled with a profound sadness. He thus immersed himself in work, asking professors ever more questions, leaving the library only to return to class, eventually delighting in this deep dive into the world of science. He specialized in the study of psychology.

The years passed quickly, and soon, he was crossing the university courtyard to present his thesis on depressive illness before a jury, his family, and a few friends. He was halfway across the courtyard when he saw her. And for David Rosen, it was one of those moments that would forever linger in his soul. For what he saw was an angel. An angel who had stumbled over a rug and had ended up, after a long fall, in the university courtyard. The angel had gotten up and, having lost her wings, decided to enroll in the first year, just to have a sense of what the world of men was like. She had blonde hair cut in a bob; her face seemed drawn by a child's hand, still untouched by the cynicism of men. They were walking in opposite directions, and their gazes met. The angel looked up at him, at his compact silhouette, his gentle features, and she smiled. They stopped, exchanged a few words—David Rosen struggled to calm his heart, which fluttered wildly inside his chest—promised to see each other again (*to see each other again!*). Then, he walked—floated, really—to the amphitheater. Of his presentation, he retained no memory, except for a sentence, uttered by his mother while tapping his cheek in front of his professors: "David, my son, when will you meet someone nice? A good Jewish girl to cook for you on Shabbat, and give us beautiful grandchildren?" He simply knew that afterward, he had roamed the campus, feverish, searching for the miracle.

He found her, sitting alone in the cafeteria. Dora came from a Catholic family in Bremen; she studied philosophy and loved ballet. Without knowing why—and he never asked her—she seemed happy to see him again. As for him, he was fascinated by the kindness he sensed in her eyes. Her soft voice flowed like honey over his heart. She radiated a kind of joyful calm, as if an inner force was propelling her toward a radiant future. They talked for hours; the cafeteria emptied around them. They saw each other the next day, then the day after that.

After a few weeks, with a trembling heart, he introduced her to his parents. He knew they would have preferred a Jewish woman, but he also believed, after all his misadventures, that they would be happy for him. Their pallid and seemingly betrayed look was for him a slap from which he never fully recovered. But none of that mattered to David Rosen; he was in love. Three months later, he and Dora were husband and wife.

They lived beautiful years, years of carelessness.

And then one day, a new party came to power, and things began to change. Jews were ostracized, beaten, punished, incarcerated. Violence simmered in the city, insidious and treacherous, waiting for its moment. Thousands of Jewish books were burned across the country—including, one fateful night, on the university's central plaza, where David Rosen had met his angel. He had watched in horror from his office window as men and women reveled in the scorching fire, listening to that madman Goebbel's speech. Among his university colleagues—David Rosen was now a professor at the same institution that had educated him—a great many entertained the thought of leaving Germany. He talked about it with his parents. "Leave, but to go where, David? America? To go there, you need a visa, and to get a visa, you need money. Do you have any? We don't; the Nazis took everything from us. Once a week, I have to beg the bank to give me a few *pfennigs*, can you believe it? They drip-feed us the money they stole from us. Do you really think they'll let us leave?"

In 1935, new racial laws were enacted, and David Rosen realized they needed to hurry. So, when his father-in-law, thanks to his connections, said he had found a way to procure visas for his parents, he did everything to convince them. After hours of discussions, they finally agreed. The farewells were long and heart-wrenching, and he never forgot his mother's voice, overflowing her sobs. "Why won't you come with us, David, why?"

But David Rosen could not abandon his angel. Taking advantage of a legal loophole, he continued to teach, while most of his colleagues had been swiftly dismissed from their posts. He spent every weekend with his in-laws—who had welcomed him as a son from the start—spending long evenings discussing politics with Dora's father. This left-wing intellectual, who shuddered at the new regime, had not been able to prevent his son from joining the Hitler Youth, and soon his child would go off to fight this senseless war. To reason with himself, he told himself that it was either that or social downfall, prison, or worse. He also understood the risks of his only daughter being married to a Jew. Troubled waters, a fragile boat indeed, that a false step could crack and overturn at any moment.

From his professor's lectern, now respected by his students, envied by his colleagues—he had published several articles in famous journals—David Rosen saw his country change, fall into madness. Finally, he knew they had to leave, but it was too late: war was declared, the borders were closed. Germany sank into years of misery. Coal and food were sorely lacking. Violence was rampant. Despite his father-in-law's best efforts, he was unable to hold on to his university post any longer, and all of a sudden, he was jobless. Despite all this, David and Dora were together, and they managed to maintain a steady level of joy. During the day, David would roam the city, looking for job opportunities. In the evening, they ate a small dinner, fell asleep together, and woke up in each other's arms the next day; that was already a blessing in itself. But one day—the winter had pressed down harder on the bodies, coal had been impossible to obtain—disease had seized Dora's lungs. At the hospital, the doctor was very clear. Acute, fulminant pneumonia. "We'll try, but I promise nothing." Dora's parents, already weakened by the war, worried for their son fighting somewhere in Europe, were bent double under the weight of the news. They never straightened up again. As for David Rosen, he stayed by Dora's side until the end, never letting go of her hand, never daring to take his eyes off her for even an instant. After several hours, he had to blink, and then it was over.

This is how, on that morning of February 28, 1943, David Rosen found himself, feet planted in the snow of a Berlin cemetery, standing in front of a deep hole. He heard the short, dry words of the preacher, or the priest, he wasn't sure which. He hugged his mother-in-law one last time. His father-in-law passed by him without a glance or a friendly gesture, for secretly he blamed him for not protecting his daughter. Then he remained alone by the coffin, in one of those silences that can last a lifetime.

With only the wind and the cold as companions, he had been standing there for an hour when he heard footsteps; perhaps his father-in-law was coming back to take him in his arms? Deep down, it hardly mattered to him, for he already knew that without Dora, life would be nothing but a burden. So, when the footsteps drew closer and he felt a hand on his shoulder and hard metal pressing against his back, when he heard the voice of a Gestapo agent—distinguishable among all of men's voices by its biting absence of humanity—he was hardly surprised. No, when he heard the words, "You are under arrest, Jew! Your Aryan wife's protection is over! You have tainted the purity of our race long enough!", it was as if those words had been floating in the air for months; finally, someone had dared to utter them. The only thing that surprised him was the woman who, standing before him, radiant with life, was smoking a cigarette.

For even though they had caused him so much misery and sleepless nights, David Rosen had always loved women. So, when he saw the sculptural blonde-haired beauty, the high cheekbones, when his weary gaze lingered on her generous hips and delicate neck, he understood that God—and yet, he was not a religious man—had a sense of humor. It was at that moment that David Rosen felt truly alone. He was back in a world without Dora, where the violence of men and the beauty of women were the two constant pillars of his suffering.

The beautiful stranger observed him with the curious look of a hunter who, after a long chase, finally savors the pleasure of the encircled beast. He locked eyes with her green-flecked blue irises, and a lifetime spent studying souls did nothing to help him decipher exactly what he saw there: instead of murderous madness or feigned pity, he thought he saw deep pain, immense contradiction, a kindness that struggles and loses, that loses and suffers from losing; in a word, he thought he saw hope.

Thus, David Rosen took a step to the side, performed a strange pirouette resembling an exotic dance move, emitted a deep, guttural sound, and with a surprisingly quick movement for a man of his bulk, turned on his heels and began to run.

What followed, only the crows, who watched the scene with indifferent eyes, remember today. There was a scream, then a sharp crack. The compact mass of birds flew up in a rustling of wings, only to settle down a few trees away.

Two hours later, when the snow had covered the woods in a thick white down, the stone placed by David Rosen on his wife's grave stood watch alone over her divine rest.

6

• • •

Monday, March 1, 1943, 3 p.m.

LENA HAD ALWAYS HAD A TASTE FOR CLEANLINESS AND BEAUTY. One day—she might have been eight years old—she had come home from school at midday, walking the four kilometers to change out of a blouse that a bit of ink, escaped from her pen, had had the audacity to stain. Ten years later, when she proudly slipped on her white nurse's uniform for the first time, she inwardly swore to always keep it in pristine condition.

Knee-deep in the mud, Lena had only a distant awareness of those childish concerns. For two days and two nights, she had lived by the rhythm of trucks, crying, violence. She had torn off every usable part of her uniform, making tourniquets and slings, and was reduced, faced with a fresh wound, to asking the youngest prisoners to please provide her with extra pieces of cloth. Outside, at the back of the courtyard, the latrines dug into the ground had quickly overflowed and produced a pestilential, tenacious, omnipresent stench.

Lena worked tirelessly; there was no way for her to sit in a corner and wait for the next morning's relief crew. She would be immediately called out by one of the many guards, she was certain of it. And so, she remained active, indefatigable, focusing on each moment as if it were her last, on each trial as if it were a test of her resilience and compassion. Thus, without even fully realizing it, she fought against despair and the hunger that gnawed at her stomach. Until then, they had only been allowed stingily distributed bits of stale bread and some soup.

So, when a truck appeared in the courtyard and employees of the Jewish hospital got out—she recognized most of them, and couldn't help looking for Sophie—arms loaded with sandwiches and thermoses of coffee, a strange emotion shot through her body, made of warmth and gratitude.

Thanks to her armband, she was served quickly. Clutching her sandwich and cup of coffee to her chest like a treasure, she stepped aside, giving up her place in the queue. While biting into the bread—which unleashed rockets of pleasure in her brain—Lena looked around. The landscape had changed so much since Saturday morning. Everywhere, the space was teeming with exhausted humans. Free spots were now a rare commodity, and a certain order had ingrained itself in the chaos: often, the younger ones would stand up upon the arrival of older prisoners, freeing up a spot on their straw mat. In a corner of the room, stiff, cold bodies were awaiting evacuation.

She took advantage of this moment of calm to put some order in her mind. She had been hearing troubling rumors. Nazis were unleashing their fury in Berlin. Brunner had evidently decided to finish the job, and his minions were now arresting Jews at home, in the dead of the night, or even in broad daylight, setting their dogs loose on anything that resembled a Jew on the run. How long before these madmen turned their evil eye toward the hospital? And then, what would become of Stefan, Arthur, her colleagues? And of herself, if she was ever allowed to go back? The abstract notion of sanctuary was a double-edged sword; how easy it would be for the Nazis to come knocking. After all, what difference was there with the Reich's factories? They too had believed themselves safe.

The soldiers shouted a few orders, and the hospital employees had to turn back. It was time to return to work. Lena resumed checking on prisoners, placing a hand on a shoulder, checking the tightness of a tourniquet. She was crouching by the bedside of an old man when she saw a hand raised. A woman in her thirties, with black, fine hair covering pale, translucent eyes, was lying on her side. Her strength seemed to be failing. A cardboard sign hung around her neck.

"Miss! Please, come here."

Lena finished tending to the old man and moved toward her.

"Hello, madam. Are you in pain? Are you injured? Do you need anything?" The words, aided by fatigue, had become automatic and almost devoid of meaning.

"No . . . fortunately, I wasn't beaten. But I'm worried about my son." She took Lena's hand, and her words were but a whisper. "I know it's too late for me. I know it; don't shake your head. Look at my sign: *Auschwitz*. But for him, there is still time . . ."

"Madam, I don't see how I can help you . . ." Lena wanted to pull her hand away, but the woman's grip was surprisingly strong.

"Shh! Don't say anything. His name is Calvin. He's so kind, he's a little angel . . . understand me, miss. He's only five years old! His father died last year, and I've been trying to raise him on my own. Then, I was told: go work at the factory, you'll be spared! I was going to be able to put food on the table every night, and maybe Cal and I could survive this madness. But, here I am. So, miss, if you can, do something for him. Here, I'll write down his name and address for you."

Before Lena could make a move, say a word to discourage her, the woman had taken out a scrap of paper and the worn-down stub of a pencil. Shielded from the nearest sentinel behind Lena's body, she wrote. "Here," she said. "I beg of you, tell him . . ." Her voice, already thin, broke like fragile crystal. "Tell him that his mother loves him, and that she's proud of him."

For months, without fully realizing it, Lena had been building a veritable wall of ice around her heart. A fortress against which feelings crashed. But Rita's death had breached her defenses, and—was it the idea of a five-year-old stuck in an apartment, was it the cold hand of a mother clinging to her arm—the wall finally broke. And a thousand emotions warmed up, melting the last of her resistance to pour *en masse* into Lena's heart. The immediate consequence of this emotional tsunami was almost inevitable. Lena felt a tingling in her hands, her head, her back. What followed happened very quickly: after casting a circular glance, she reached out for the piece of paper and slid it into the front pocket of her uniform. And the voice that came from her chest, its tone, its thickness, the very words that found a path through her lips, did so from a new place, cleansed, emptied of a burden she herself hadn't suspected the weight of.

"Do not worry, madam. I will take care of it."

Then, it happened without any real logic, with no pre-established plan, but rather simply, as one unrolls a spool of silk. Women slipped her small notes—farewell letters, names, or addresses of children—and Lena, exhilarated, her eyes shining, grabbed the pieces of paper and stuffed them in her pocket.

Thus, when evening came and Lena lay down on her straw mattress, she felt something had changed. In her pocket, it was life that was teeming. And for the first time in months, her gaze softened, her eyebrows lost the tension that created an almost permanent vertical line between her eyes; her mouth relaxed. She quickly fell asleep, a discreet smile drawn at the corner of her lips.

7

• • •

Tuesday, March 2, 1943, 2 a.m.

AT FIRST, ALL SHE HEARD WAS THE RUMBLING OF ENGINES. Muffled, deep, persistent. Feeling like she had barely lain down, Lena opened her eyes; in reality, two hours had passed. Around her, prisoners exchanged powerless looks. An air raid in the middle of the night? Was this to be, at long last, the liberation of Berlin? None of them had been allowed to buy a newspaper in years; their conception of the war's progress was based only on hearsay and fleeting rumors. So, were these the Russians? The Americans? Or had Hitler finally lost his mind and decided to bomb the capital himself?

Like a thunderclap in a stormy sky, the first explosion made the ground tremble. And then, everything happened at once. Like a metronome gone mad, the crisp sound of the anti-aircraft battery set the pace for a deadly symphony of planes, bombs, and the siren's alarm, whose sinister howling drilled into the souls of even the bravest.

Lena, sitting in a corner, took all of this in with a mixture of fear and wonder. Curiously, it seemed to her that Berlin was coming back to life—breathing, exhaling its rage at having been thus violated in its ideological flesh, in its deep vocation as a cultured, refined city. Each explosion made the mud and the straw shiver, as if the city, tired of enduring such violence, wanted to shake it off like a dog shakes water off after a forced bath. Under the tent, after the initial cries of surprise and fear, a tense silence had set in. Everyone understood that escape was not an option. The guards had not left their post, and the air-raid shelters were, of course, off-limits to Jews. So, they waited, shivering from the cold, and listened to the battle. The telltale noise of an exploding shell. The dreaded sound of a plane crashing, sinking into the city. And then, without really admitting it, everyone hoped for a miracle—liberation.

So, when morning came and the proud aviators had turned their wings toward more charitable skies, deep disappointment filled the hearts of the most optimistic prisoners. Others, despite the sign weighing down on their neck, felt a bit lighter, a bit more confident, if not for themselves, at least for the future. Lena got up, unfolded her body, and looked around for her colleagues. This had been their third night in this hell, and they had been promised relief. She was alive; that was enough for her. She had never imagined that a simple air raid would be sufficient to end this war. All she wanted was to leave this place as soon as possible. She had so much to do.

She spotted Ada and the doctor—weary, dirty, exhausted. They looked at each other, unsure of what to say. At that moment, a fresh team of two nurses and a doctor appeared under the tent. Lena recognized one of the girls; they had often worked together. She wanted to talk to her, explain the procedures, the straw, the tourniquets, the signs, but the nervous voice of a soldier brought her back to reality. "Out, night team! You're lucky to have survived! Get out, *schnell*!"

Hence, the two women could only pass each other, and before she could discover this place of apocalypse for herself, the incoming nurse had a look at Lena. She obviously noticed the uniform's decomposed state. She noted the greasy hair sticking to her skull, the shoes encrusted with mud, the hands full of dirt and blood. But it was mostly Lena's gaze that caught her attention: the young ingénue's spark of innocence had all but disappeared, replaced by an expression she could not recognize. It lasted only a moment, and then the new team disappeared into the belly of the beast.

Lena crossed the courtyard where already, despite the night's events, the trucks had resumed their grim comings and goings. In the air, there floated a scent of sulfur and blood. A ray of sunlight broke through the clouds, and under the winter-morning opaline sky, Lena surprised herself by straightening her back, lifting up her chin. Even her shoulders, letting go of their eternal contemplation of the ground, turned toward the skies. Against her heart, she felt the yellow star, all stained with mud. And for the first time since the law forced her to identify herself in this way, she felt pride. It was no longer the Jewish star, but rather the star of a king, King David, whose power had forged his legend.

The small group of caregivers left Rathenhower Strasse behind them and jumped into the first tramway heading back toward the hospital. Neither Ada nor the doctor had spoken much; they probably aspired only to a bit of rest. Lena smiled at them and let her gaze wander over her human brothers and sisters. Never had they seemed so close to her. For their night too had been terrifying. Men, women, children, all eyes were turned toward the city, which through the windows, revealed its newest scars, the deep humiliating cuts of a bombarded land.

Whole buildings lay in ruins, gutted by aerial fire. Craters deformed the sidewalks, revealing the earth's entrails. Fragments of conversations informed her that the planes had been English. English! If England was starting to attack Berlin, then others would follow. She allowed herself, however briefly, the fantasy of imagining her father piloting one of those fierce airplanes. Where was he today? Was he even still in England, or had he managed to distance himself further from this madness? She had no way of knowing. Ada and the doctor discreetly exchanged a satisfied look, but Lena had other priorities than an early triumph.

Spotting a familiar street, she seized the opportunity to slip away. She would have time, later, to find her way back to the hospital; her special armband would protect her for at least a few more hours. Letting the crowd disperse, she found herself almost alone on the sidewalk. A gust made her shiver.

She pulled a piece of paper from her pocket. *Calvin.* Yes, this address was familiar to her. Ignoring both fatigue and the cold, she started walking and soon entered a residential area. For a moment, she worried people would question her—after all, she was still wearing her torn uniform and hadn't bathed in days—but she was quickly reassured. Everywhere she looked, shocked Berliners were too busy discussing the material damage and the dead—apparently, they numbered in the hundreds—to pay any attention to her. She easily found the address, climbed the steps of a small building, and knocked on the front door. Faced with silence, she insisted, even daring to raise her voice.

"Calvin. Calvin! Open up, little one. I'm sure you were told never to open the door to a stranger, but please, you have to believe me; I'm a friend of your Mama's!" After a few minutes, the handle lowered, and the door opened, revealing a little boy. He had eyes that had seen too much for such short years. He wore blue pajama bottoms, a red pullover, and was trying very hard not to suck his thumb.

"Where's my Mama?" he said with a dry voice. Then, Lena had to invent something, stammer useless words, smile, and instinct did the rest. Calvin looked at his feet, turned momentarily toward his home, as if to say goodbye, and held out his hand.

Lena roamed the city for hours, keeping Calvin's hand warmly tucked into hers. Together, they sought out doors. Some remained silent to their calls. Others were already nothing but a pile of wood mixed with scorched stone. Yet others, finally, opened to souls so young that a strange sort of magic was able to take place: the children didn't really understand the gravity of the situation, but they nevertheless offered their absolute trust to this woman, whose eyes revealed everything.

Thus, when the sun reached its zenith, an attentive observer would have noticed, amidst the rubble, the chaos, and the eerie silence that follows a night of war, the frail silhouette of a nurse crossing the city with a sleepy five-year-old dangling around her neck, surrounded by four other children, the oldest of whom was no more than nine years old.

Lena decided they should start to turn back. The military presence in the street was becoming concerning. Their path had led them to the south of the Tiergarten, Berlin's biggest park. Hidden amongst the tall trees, a tower supported the anti-aircraft battery's cannon. All night, it had spat its metallic venom toward the sky. But the English aviators, harnessed in their formidable war machines, had held tight, and it was evident, from where the small group stood, that the garden had also suffered from a deluge of fire.

"My momma told me there's a zoo in this garden, madam," said the oldest of the children. Her name was Anna, and despite hunger, fear, and the shock of suddenly finding herself under the care of a stranger, she was possessed by an irresistible urge to talk.

"Really? Oh, that's fantastic. I've never been to the zoo . . . call me Lena, okay?" she said, smiling.

"Okay, Miss Lena," said Anna. "Then, we'll go together, okay? And I guess you can come, too," she said to the younger ones, who, although disoriented, found it somewhat cavalier to plan a zoo outing without inviting them.

"Yes, that's a great idea! As soon as it's possible, we'll all go to the zoo. Do you have favorite animals?"

"The kangaroo!" said Joseph, who was six years old.

"Very good choice! And you, David?"

"I don't like animals."

It would take some time before they could find joy in life again; she would wait.

Lena was still carrying Calvin, and her back was starting to hurt. "Let's take a short break," she said. "Five minutes, no more."

She wanted to put the child down and stretch, but she realized he had fallen asleep and kept him against her.

"I'm hungry, Miss Lena," said David.

"Me too, I'm hungry, Miss Lena," said Joseph.

"Look at the clouds," said Anna in an attempt at diversion. "Do you know this game? You try and recognize shapes in the clouds. It's loads of fun! Okay, I'll start. There . . . I see . . . a knight riding a unicorn! Do you see it?"

"Meh," said David.

"I see a lion!" said Joseph.

"Where? I can't make it out," said Anna. "And you're not even looking at the sky!"

"Well . . . there!" he said, pointing ahead.

Limping on an injured paw, a golden-mane beast emerged from the edge of the woods. It looked in their direction and, whether it was a sign of despair or an affirmation of its being and rank, it let out a furious roar, a prodigious echo of the time when it reigned over the savannah. It blinked its large, dusty eyelids and decided to turn its powerful body toward the trees, leaving the humans to fend for themselves.

"Wow . . ." said the children in unison.

"Alright, I think it's time to go," said Lena, strangely reassured by the beast's appearance.

They skirted the Tiergarten to the west. Lena knew of a tram stop from where they could reach the hospital. She hadn't really thought about what would happen once they arrived, but for the moment, her main concern was to get off the streets. Fortunately, the tram was about to pull into the station. They were about twenty meters from the stop when the machine's old brakes screeched; Joseph and David covered their ears. A dull noise made Lena realize that the lead wagon had collided with something. She moved closer. A crowd had formed, and lying on the tracks was a woman, wearing a white uniform. Lena stayed still; the young woman was obviously in pain. Her leg appeared to be trapped. Had she slipped? Was she a nurse? Then, what was she doing here, in broad daylight, alone in the center of the city?

Instinct took over.

"We're going to walk around this street, children; come now, I know a much more beautiful way."

The group turned back, looking for a parallel street. Lena tried not to look, but curiosity got the better of her. She turned around and noticed, among the onlookers observing the scene, an extremely well-dressed couple. Far from helping the young woman—who was screaming in pain—they had squatted near her and, aided by men in gray overcoats, were tying her hands behind her back. While the woman brushed a strand of hair from her shoulder, she lifted her eyes and found Lena.

Lena lowered her head, hugged Calvin a little tighter, and walked on without looking back.

8

• • •

Monday, March 8, 1943, 2 p.m.

Among other things, Sophie's new life allowed her some degree of extravagance; despite the late hour, she was still wearing a thick, fluffy bathrobe. Sitting on the edge of the bed, her bare legs dangling, she looked at her feet. It had taken time, but they were finally back to their usual appearance. The weeks spent languishing in that damp cell had terribly withered them; blisters and cracks had formed, and in her rare moments of despair, she had truly believed she would never be able to walk normally again.

But once she had accepted the Gestapo's offer, everything had changed quickly. On that day, she was taken out of her cell, wrapped in a winter coat, and escorted to an official car. "My parents . . . let me see my parents . . ." she had pleaded. But an officer had slammed the car door shut, and the engine had started.

Minutes later, she dozed off in the overheated cabin. When she woke up, they were still driving. Looking out the window, she instantly recognized the neighborhood. At first, she thought it was a joke. After all these hardships, were they simply sending her back, beaten, starved, straight to the hospital? Those weeks of imprisonment would have been nothing more than a farce, the prospect of working for them, a tasteless joke? But the car had passed the main entrance and drove along a parallel street before silently coming to a stop. They got out, and through a back door, they entered a small two-story building located at the back of the park. A guard escorted her to her room.

"Here are your quarters. A meal will be served in thirty minutes on the ground floor."

She had been left alone, unsupervised, for the first time in weeks. Hardly daring to believe it, she'd discovered her new home: a bed, covered with a wool blanket, atop which sat a pillow filled with goose feathers. An oak desk, placed near a window overlooking the hospital park. And a bathroom. Her bathroom. A sink, a toilet, a narrow but clean shower. Fluffy towels spread a scent of lavender throughout the room. As if in a dream, she had undressed and plunged her body under the scalding water jets before collapsing on the bed.

Sophie got up and walked over to the window. Through the misty glass, the park she knew so well stretched out behind newly planted barbed wires; familiar figures walked briskly around the trees. Nurses, doctors . . . yes, she recognized most of them. She hadn't been gone that long. Some of them cast worried glances in her direction. Did they even suspect who was watching them from afar? Did they know of her existence, of her betrayal? Or did they all just accept the fact that she, too, had been claimed by the east? Some part of her hoped they had ceased thinking about her. Oh, she wasn't the only one who had sold her soul. Since her arrival, she'd had time to meet her neighbors: the building was filled with Jews—men and women alike—who now worked for the enemy. She tried her best not to interact with them. She also tried to ignore the fact that in the basement, a few feet under her cozy apartment, dozens of innocents were locked away, awaiting under heavy guard their transport to the dreaded east.

The door opened abruptly. "So, darling, did you miss me?" said Hans in a failed parody of a Hollywood leading man.

"Ah, it's you! You could knock."

"Knock, not knock . . . my dear, none of that between us! We are partners now. Two fingers of the same hand!" He was, as usual, dressed in an elegant black suit. With a smooth gesture, he slid the jacket off his shoulders, revealing, harnessed to his belt, a pistol with a white ivory grip. He approached Sophie and caressed her cheek. She recoiled, barely disguising her disgust.

"Oh, are we playing the coy one today? What's the matter? A moment of emotion, nostalgia for your hospital buddies?"

Sophie adjusted her bathrobe, shrugging.

"Nothing of that sort, Hans. Sentimentality isn't my thing, you know that."

"That's the spirit! It would do you no good to dwell on them. Forget those poor bastards, why don't you! Of all the Jews in Europe, we've got the sweetest deal. Think about it: we're no longer victims. Isn't that what you wanted? No more wearing this shameful star. And we're off the deportation lists. After all, that's the main problem for Jews today, and we're exempt from it? Don't you understand that we're as good as kings!" he said, spreading his arms as if he had just discovered the answer to a millennia-old question. His raptor-like face, always closely shaved, was animated by a malevolent glow.

"No, really, don't waste your time on them anymore. And especially, don't think about Lena. Your dear, sweet Lena, your little educational project! You know, I've got a soft spot for her as well. After all, if it wasn't for her, we wouldn't be here, you and I."

"What about her? What are you babbling about?"

"Oh my, hadn't you figured it out by now? Well, let me explain. After all, you have the right to know."

He sat down and started removing his freshly polished leather shoes.

"Do you remember her night in the Gestapo truck? Yes, it seems like a lifetime ago, I know. Well, I was there with her, as an observer—officially, at least. She must have been traumatized, poor thing. That fat cop was so drunk he shot that girl and her baby before letting loose on Lena with his whip. Well, these things happen. Nothing I could do about it. But before that, I'd had time to work on her. You know my charm has no match, don't you?" He cracked his neck. "Ah, that feels good. So, as I was saying: while we were still alone in the back of the truck, I had time to grill her. I mentioned your name, which immediately loosened her up. Boy, does she have a high opinion of you! Anyway, I quickly steered the conversation toward the subject of your parents."

"My parents? Big deal. She knew nothing about them."

"Be patient! You'll understand . . ." he had a crooked laugh, a sneaky little hiccup. "We talked about our childhood, about those famous Sunday tea parties. By the way, you know that your father's goal with those little get-togethers was to create lasting relationships among the neighborhood Jews. Look at us: I'd say his stratagem worked wonders, wouldn't you? So, I asked her if she knew where your parents were. You know, casually, as if I had just thought of it."

"What of it? I'm sure she didn't tell you anything. Besides, she knew nothing! What did you do to my friend? Did you beat her? You didn't touch her, did you? Tell me you didn't lay a hand on her!"

"Touched her? No, that little virgin's not my type . . . we just had a friendly little chat, that's all." His gaze darkened. "Believe me, I didn't need to insist much for her to start repeating, *Yes, her father loved opera, opera, he loved it, that's all I know!* with her little squeaky voice! Oh, she thought she was doing the right thing, and you could tell it was the first slap she'd taken—she would have done anything to avoid a second one, that's for sure—so she kept repeating that in a loop, and I pretended to calm down, *Okay, little chick, I believe you, don't be afraid!*

"It was hilarious. And clear as day! Of course, the Jews were hiding at the opera. Your father had always fancied himself a great musician. I remember his dreams of grandeur for his pitiful compositions. Intuition did the rest. See, the Gestapo was setting up a new program, and you were an ideal recruit: a beautiful blonde with a vibrant social life, who grew up in Berlin and knows every corner, every alleyway of the city? My word, you were a veritable gold mine for those dear Gestapo clerks! The perfect weapon to unearth those in hiding! All that was needed was a lever to convince you to join us willingly. The higher-ups already knew your parents were hiding. All that was left was to flush them out. So, I thought about questioning Lena, and the rest was child's play: I presented my hypothesis to the management, and they allowed me to keep the opera under close watch. A few days later, bingo. Let me tell you, your father was quite surprised to see what *little Hans* had turned into."

Sophie hadn't taken her eyes off the carpet. Lena. She had been betrayed by Lena . . . what a fool she'd been! She couldn't control herself, could she? Always so weak. Broken by a mere slap? She knew of Hans's strength, his power of intimidation, but still . . . to talk about the opera was to serve her parents up on a silver platter. She thought about them, sitting on the damp floor of their cell, beaten, starved, and her jaw clenched. She had done everything to try to toughen her up. From the start, she had guided Lena through the hospital, holding her hand, explaining how to respond to attacks, to rumors . . . all that, only to be betrayed over a slap! That bitch!

Pain pressed down on her skull. In recent weeks, she had been plagued with terrible migraines. She closed her eyes, trying to reclaim some sense of calm. But it was Arthur's face that appeared beneath her closed eyelids, and another truth exploded in her face. To preserve herself, to live more easily, she had tried to hide it from herself but now, everything was clear. Beneath her prudish exterior, Lena had seduced Arthur. That man, who alone amongst all men, seemed immune to her own charms, she who had only to flutter an eyelash to melt hearts but had never known love. Arthur was different. That man truly moved her. That night, at his bedside, she'd felt herself dangerously close to disappearing into his words. But he had eyes only for that little pest. And now that she had sided with the traitors—there was no doubt in Sophie's mind that the rumors of a spy's nest would swiftly cross the park—she knew he could never love her.

She opened the window; cold air whipped at her face. Lena . . . and to think that after all this, she continued to protect her. After seeing her, alone in Berlin with those five kids, she understood something was afoot. Following her intuition, she began to observe Stefan. It took her no time to notice a new routine. Every day, around eleven o'clock, he would fetch a bottle of milk and disappear from the park for half an hour. After a few days, Sophie quietly crossed to the other side of the barbed wire and followed him, at a safe distance. Dear old Stefan, growing crazier day by day, now interacted more with the cows—inexplicably grazing in a corner of the park—than with humans. He was so out of it that he never noticed her following him down to the basement corridors; yet she was two steps behind when he finally stopped, moved the dusty cart out of the way, and knocked on an old wooden door: three knocks, then two, then one. The door creaked open just enough to confirm what Sophie had already understood. He was bringing milk to those kids. Milk! Had Lena and Stefan both lost their minds? Didn't they understand that none of this made sense? That the Nazis would find out, that all of this was nothing but a temporary respite, that it was only a matter of time before disaster struck?

The storm that had been rumbling in her heart for weeks finally unleashed its organic power, covering her irises in a dark gray deluge. In an instant, Sophie understood she knew hate. Yes, she hated Lena. But that wasn't all of it. She also hated Hans, and the Jews who let themselves be led to the slaughter without a fight, and the Nazis of course—and more than all the others, Hitler. *This man made a Jew out of me!* she repeated to herself endlessly—she who before all this had never seen herself as anything but a Berliner and had been proud of it.

Nausea rose from the bottom of her abdomen like a fierce tsunami, surged toward her lungs, her heart, her throat. She barely had time to leap toward the bathroom and kneel before the white toilet. Her stomach convulsed several times, her breath stopped, tears squeezed through her eyelids. But all that emerged from her lips was a greenish, acidic liquid, like the amniotic fluid of a life ending, of another beginning.

"Come now, don't be a child," said Hans. He had undone his cufflinks, removed his shirt, and was admiring himself in the mirror. "I've put on some muscle, don't you think?" He unbuckled his belt, placed the revolver on the nightstand, removed his trousers and underwear, before lighting a cigarette. He lay his lean, nearly hairless body down on the bed, exhaling smoke at regular intervals.

"You know, if it's any consolation, the Gestapo bigwigs are thrilled with your work. You've become the talk of the streets, a bona fide urban legend! The *angel of death*, the *blonde poison* . . . I must confess, I'm a bit envious of your fame. How many arrests have you made in the last month? Ten? Twelve? And last week, when you thought about arresting old Rosen at the cemetery, that detached look you gave him, as the last clods of dirt were hardly set on his wife's coffin—I must admit that made me extremely horny."

Sophie lowered the toilet lid, flushed, and struggled to stand up. She ran some water in the white sink, splashed her face, and rinsed out her mouth. Then, she looked up. In the mirror, she saw her reflection, but she no longer recognized the woman looking back. And so, without further thought, she undid her bathrobe, unhitched the straps of her pink satin nightgown which silently slid from her shoulders to her ankles, becoming but a small pile of fabric lying on the cold tile. She admired her breasts, which drove men wild. She saw her right shoulder, where Lena had so often placed a friendly hand. Finally, she looked at her hands, once used to soothe bodies and souls, which now served only to point out humans destined to die.

She took a deep breath, emitted a sound halfway between laughter and sobbing, and walked toward the bed.

9

• • •

Tuesday, March 9, 1943, 12:30 p.m.

Walking down the steps of the central staircase, Lena thought that one of the advantages of not having a fixed lunch break routine—Sophie and Lustig's girls nostalgically crossed her mind—was that no one would notice her absence. Reaching the ground floor, she went down another level and entered the basement. She walked by a few colleagues, whom she briefly greeted with a nod, but the corridors were mostly deserted at that hour.

Without Stefan, none of this would have been possible. A week earlier, when she had finally reached the hospital, weary and with five children in tow, she had run into him in the park. "Lena," he had said, "what are you doing with these children? Have you lost your mind? And what happened to your uniform? You look dreadful!" Without him, no, she would never have thought they needed to be hidden. She was about to entrust them to the pediatrics department. "You're not thinking straight, beautiful. They'll be quickly found out, and God knows what the crazies will do to them. Come, come, Uncle Stefan knows the perfect hideout!"

After a few turns, she stopped and positioned her body slightly back, in a niche in the wall. From there, she could observe. One or two doctors walked by without noticing her, their heads buried in their files. She stayed motionless, not daring to move an eyelash, trying to control her breathing. Finally, when she was satisfied with the silence surrounding her, she moved away from the wall and close to an old nurse's cart, which was gathering dust in a corner. She pushed it aside, revealing a wooden door. She knocked three successive times, then two, and finally one last time.

The door cracked open to reveal two large eyes hidden behind brown curls. "Miss Lena! Come in quickly!" said Anna.

Lena closed the door behind her and slid the bolt. She barely had time to turn around before Calvin jumped at her neck. The other children also came forward to kiss her, touch her, simply happy for her presence. And as every time she came down to see them, her heart swung between an intense joy—the warmth of their little hands on her forearms was intoxicating—and the sadness of seeing where these children were spending their days. It was barely more than an abandoned oversized closet, where floor mops, brooms, and old cardboard boxes were piled up. Two worn-out mattresses had been pushed into a corner. They had cleaned them as best they could, but they hadn't been able to get rid of all their four-legged hosts. Already red bumps irritated their young skin.

"Sit down, children." They gathered in a half-circle around her, except for Calvin, who never left her arms. "Here, I've brought you some bread and boiled eggs," she said, handing a bag to Anna, who usually took care of the food distribution. "So, how was your night? Were you not too cold?"

"Oh, no, Miss Lena," said Joseph, with a mischievous smile. "Me and David, we slept under the same blanket, and we weren't cold at all! However," he stuck out his tongue for a moment, "David farted a lot in his sleep!"

"Not true!" said David, blushing. "It was him, Miss Lena, not me! I never fart!"

Anna and Lena stifled a laugh.

"Well . . . anyway, you weren't cold, that's what matters! What about you, Lisa, did you sleep well?"

The little girl, still wearing the pajamas in which Lena had found her, had been the last to join their group. When Lena had knocked on her door, she hadn't eaten for two days. At barely six years old, she had asked no questions, understanding everything with half-words, and simply extended her hand to the young woman, thus offering her eternal trust.

"Yes, Miss Lena, I slept well. And Uncle Stefan brought us fresh milk this morning."

"Ah, Stefan. What an angel!" said Lena.

Encouraged by their initial successes, the Royal Air Force had intensified its raids on the city. It had become common to hear the air-raid siren blare in the middle of the night, followed by the usual ballet of planes, shells, and anti-aircraft fire. While all this was a good omen—finally, someone was fighting for them!—the attacks' immediate result was one of terrible destruction. Every night, buildings, roads, and homes were destroyed; humans perished by the dozens. The hospital, however, woke up intact each morning. It didn't take long for the residents of the surrounding streets to notice this miracle and draw from it truly extraordinary conclusions: the hospital was clearly protected by the God of the Hebrews. Hearing these rumors, Lena thought the Germans were really a strange batch. If the Jews were blessed by the gods, then why did they suffer so much?

Regardless, driven by a survival instinct and this odd belief, a local farmer had decided his cows deserved to graze under divine protection and had transferred his entire herd to the hospital park. The old man, indifferent to the war—caring little who was Jewish or not, and cursing Hitler whenever he was alone with his cows—was surprised, upon moving his herd, to run into Stefan, who was using the milder temperature as an opportunity to try on a new dress.

After the initial shock, the two men struck up a passionate conversation. Stefan had grown up on a farm north of Prague and knew all there was to know about cows. Thus, a friendship formed that only war can foster, and the two men chatted about food, milking, and calving. It all ended in a handshake: Stefan would keep an eye on the herd, and in return, he would be allowed to milk a few animals every morning for his personal consumption. His kind heart did the rest; Lena had not dared to ask him, but whenever he had the chance, he brought a bottle of milk to the children, and in doing so, he had found himself a new family.

"I can't stay, kids, I have to get back to work. I do hope the days aren't too lonely for you down here," Lena said, looking around. The room was bathed in the flickering light of one of the few candles she had managed to provide them with.

"Don't worry, Miss Lena, we're not bored!" said Anna. "Last night, before we went to sleep, I told everyone a Brothers Grimm fairy tale. And this morning, we played hide-and-seek!"

"Yes, look, Miss Lena!" said Calvin. "I found a great hiding place!"

He climbed down from her knees and opened a sort of hatch, hidden in the back wall.

Climbing on an old cardboard box, he squeezed into a space just big enough for him; sitting down, legs crossed, he closed the hatch from the inside. In the dim light, it was indeed an ideal hiding spot.

"But, where's Calvin?" Lena played along. The others burst into laughter.

After thirty seconds, unable to contain himself, Calvin pushed open the door of his hideout. "I'm here!" he said, beaming.

He ran toward Lena and jumped into her arms.

"Come on, kids, I'd love to stay, but I really have to go. I'll see you tomorrow, without fail."

"Goodbye, Miss Lena," they said in unison.

"Goodbye, kids," said Lena. She wanted to say more, but her throat had developed the curious habit of constricting whenever it was time to leave them.

She closed the door behind her, moved the cart back in its place, and returned to her duties just in time for rounds.

"Ah, *schwester* Lena, there you are," said Dr. Elken. "Good, what can you tell me about the patients in beds 1 to 5?"

"Yes, doctor. So, in bed number 1 . . ."

Everyone had noticed a change in Lena: her colleagues, whom she helped more willingly than ever, the head of the department, who in light of her ever-precise answers had made her his go-to nurse, and Arthur. He had thought he would never see her again. To disappear for three days and three nights during wartime was tantamount to certain death. So, when he saw her again, his joy initially prevented him from noticing her profound change. Since then, he had had time to observe her. Yes, she had regained her smile, but it was a more assertive, a more mature kind of smile. Her gait was healthier, almost bouncy. And most importantly, she was talking to him again, looking him in the eye. Sometimes, at the end of the day, she would sit at the edge of his bed, and they would talk. She had told him about her three days in hell, but quickly, like one tells of a bad dream one is trying to forget. Most of all, she talked about her childhood, and also about the future and her dreams. She saw beyond the war, and that in itself was a wonderful gift.

The rounds had come to his bed. Lena was presenting his case to the doctor for the hundredth time. Arthur watched her in silence, admiring the way she elegantly moved between the beds.

"You look well, Arthur!" said Dr. Elken. "But let's keep you here a bit longer, just to make sure you're fully healed . . ."

Arthur knew how lucky he was to still be there. Did he have a secret protector delaying his return to prison? He didn't know, but he was determined to enjoy every moment spent in the company of the one he realized he had fallen in love with.

Lena, for her part, felt a gentle excitement at Arthur's touch, an involuntary smile forming on her lips when she saw him. But her heart lived in the basement. The children were her new family, her responsibility. So, in the evening, when she lay down in bed, Lena no longer heard her roommate's snoring or the rumors—growing louder day by day—of a spy nest set up deep within the hospital walls, operating on behalf of the Gestapo. No, Lena wasn't listening. Thinking about Joseph and David bickering under the blanket, about Anna who told tales and fables from her memory, she smiled. Sometimes, she allowed herself to dream of better days when they could all go to the zoo together, gorging on vanilla ice cream.

She closed her eyes and silently said, barely moving her lips: "Good night, Anna. Good night, Joseph, David, Lisa. Good night, Calvin. Sweet dreams."

Yes, during those few days, Lena was quite happy.

10

• • •

Wednesday, March 10, 1943, 2 p.m.

Lustig's secretary was preparing a cup of tea when they barged into her office. She had grown accustomed to "official" visitors of all shapes and sizes, but something in the demeanor of the three men before her chilled her to the bone. Ignoring her, they walked across the vestibule and nearly tore the director's door off its hinges.

"Lustig! We need to talk," said Captain Bormsen as he entered a dimly lit room, centered by a large oak desk, cluttered with files. A gray light filtered through the window. The man, wearing a dark suit over a perfectly ironed shirt, appeared to be about forty. Each morning, he made it a point to meticulously shave his head—he had read somewhere that it inspired terror in men and desire in certain women—but that day, an area behind his right ear, no larger than a ten-pfennig coin, had escaped his vigilance, giving him the appearance of poorly cleared land. An old scar stretched a vicious smile from his mouth to his left eye. He sat down opposite Lustig and slowly pulled off his black leather gloves.

Feet firmly planted on the floor, the director remained motionless. From his window, he had watched the trucks park in front of the hospital gates. He had then seen representatives of the Gestapo and the Berlin police emerge from an official car and cross the park.

None of this had really surprised him. In recent weeks, the Nazis had deported thousands of Jews taken from the Reich's factories. It was now only a matter of time before the authorities decided to close his hospital, this last Jewish bastion still allowed to survive amidst the chaos that had seized his country. So, the old doctor had tightened the knot on his tie, donned his white coat, and waited for them to come up. He noticed his hands, clenched on the back of his chair, and made an effort to relax.

"Captain, to what do I owe this honor?" he said with a cheerful voice. "It's been a long time since I've seen you. But first, let me offer you all a drink. What would you like: coffee? gin?"

"Keep your coffee, Lustig! We're not here to play games."

"No, of course, captain. I know you, you're a true professional. You have no time to waste. So, tell me, what can I do for you?"

Still cool as a cucumber, that old camel . . . the Gestapo man muttered through his teeth. A few years earlier, still a mere cop in the Berlin police, he had had the unpleasant experience of serving under Lustig's orders. The large man, who had honed his body and his marksmanship all his life, had never been able to stomach how far up the food chain this small, fat man had climbed. After all, he was just a Jew! Disguised as a Catholic, sure, but a Jew nonetheless. All those years, he had always felt as if Lustig looked down on him, but the universe had finally set itself right, and now, as a high-ranking Gestapo officer, the fate of this damned hospital—and, consequently, Lustig's—now lay in his hands. How this Jewish nest had managed to stay open for so long, he couldn't fathom. But the leadership had finally decided to rectify this error, and it was his responsibility to ensure the trucks did not leave the hospital grounds without their loot. As a good soldier, he was determined not to disappoint his masters.

"Enough playing around, Lustig. The order has been given: complete evacuation of the hospital! We need the caregivers, the patients, everyone. Come on! You have one hour. The trucks are waiting."

Lustig felt a tingling sensation tickle the skin behind his ears—an uncontrollable twitch. Deep down, he had expected this answer. All his life, he had mingled with Aryans; he had even married one. He himself had never considered himself anything but a Berliner, and that had always worked in his favor. The first part of his career had been exemplary. His position as a senior officer in the Berlin police had taught him a lot about human nature, while allowing him to rub shoulders with many of the men with whom he had to deal today. And while the circumstances certainly had changed, Lustig always managed to come out on top. He had become a powerful tightrope walker, a grim master of balance; in short, he was not yet ready to admit defeat.

"Captain, I completely understand. You have your orders, and if the hospital must be closed, so be it. However . . ." Lustig walked around his chair and finally sat down. He crossed his legs and smoothed his mustache. "Captain, I was wondering if you could clarify a bureaucratic detail for me—yes, I know, bureaucracy is quite dull, but bear with me for a moment. So, here it is: I wouldn't dare doubt the quality of your orders, but it had always seemed to me that any final decision regarding the fate of the hospital came from the Judenreferat of Obersturmbannführer Eichmann, and not the Gestapo. Is that correct?"

The Gestapo man froze, crushing his pair of gloves in his right hand. The air took on a dense, cutting thickness.

Lustig did his best to appear calm. Yes, he knew these men. He knew their blind obedience to the regime's rules, even as the laws of humanity were but a vague memory to them. He knew the greed, the ego, the hatred that often existed among the leaders of the different departments. And above all, he knew that even though the Gestapo and the RSHA were both under the aegis of SS leader Heinrich Himmler, the real administrative director of the hospital, the true bureaucratic force pulling the strings, was indeed the Jewish Affairs department: the Judenreferat, sub-section B of department IV of the RSHA. And the man who led this sub-section was Adolf Eichmann—Eichmann, that cold and calculating man who spent most of his time behind his desk but was not loathe to visit the hospital himself, shopping for his mortal goods when he was short a few names on his lists. Yet another unremarkable officer he had mingled with during his police career. Ten years earlier, he would never have bet a pfennig on Eichmann, who had since become one of the most powerful men in Germany. So, he often wondered, what interest could such a man have in visiting him several times a month? It couldn't be just to fill his lists; others did that for him. No, there must be another reason, a more personal reason . . . Perhaps Eichmann was hoping, once the place was finally emptied of its Jews—Lustig harbored no illusions on that score—to seize the considerable land for himself, where he could settle more comfortably than in his office on Kurfürstenstrasse? Or maybe he was planning on getting rich as a real estate mogul, building apartments, a luxury hotel? Lustig wasn't sure of anything, but his instincts had rarely betrayed him.

"Indeed, that's correct," said the Gestapo man, his eyes suddenly very dark.

"Good! Then you will surely have no objection, captain, to me calling the Obersturmbannführer himself to confirm your order? Just to adhere strictly to the protocol, you understand. I wouldn't want to be the cause of a squabble between departments."

For a moment, time was suspended, and Lustig thought he's gone too far. After all, what was stopping the colossus from drawing his handgun and smashing his skull with the butt? Or, more simply, lodging a bullet straight into his heart. No one in the room, undoubtedly, would have objected to either option.

But the man did not move. Staring straight ahead, he simply said: "Go ahead, call him. If you really think he's going to answer you."

Lustig let out some of the air trapped in his lungs, tried to silence his heart, which threatened at any moment to burst from his chest. He picked up the phone, dialed a number.

Overwhelmed operators transferred him multiple times. Finally, a neutral but sharp voice answered.

"Hallo."

"Uh, hallo, Obersturmbannführer. This is Dr. Lustig speaking, and I—"

A brief click, followed by dead air. Eichmann had hung up. *Of course*, Lustig thought, his hand clenched on the handset. In the excitement of the moment, he had forgotten that the Nazis had stripped him of his titles. Eichmann would never speak to him if he introduced himself as a doctor.

"That's odd," he said in as calm a voice as possible. "We were disconnected. It happens sometimes. Let me call him back."

"Hurry up, Lustig! We don't have all day!"

"Right away, captain, right away."

Lustig dialed the numbers again, and after two interminable minutes, he heard the supreme leader's voice once more.

"Hallo."

"It's the Jew Lustig, Obersturmbannführer."

"Ach, Lustig. What do you want? You're interrupting me."

"If you'll allow me, Obersturmbannführer, I find myself in a somewhat peculiar situation. I have in my office Captain Bormsen from the Berlin Gestapo. He is presenting me with an order, which I would like, with your permission, to clarify with you."

"Put him on, Lustig! I know that bastard well."

"At once, Obersturmbannführer."

Lustig looked up at the man sitting across from him. He saw fierce hatred mixed with a certain incredulity: how could this little Jew be calling Eichmann on his private line? It was downright remarkable.

"Captain, he wants to speak with you," said Lustig, holding out the handset.

11

• • •

Wednesday, March 10, 1943, 2 p.m.

"I HAVE A BAD FEELING, ARTHUR."

With his free hand, Arthur smoothed his mustache and mustered a brief smile.

"Don't worry, dear Lena. You said it yourself; we live inside a sanctuary. I've been here for months, and it almost seems as if they've forgotten about me. No, really, be at ease."

"I wish I could share your optimism," Lena said softly.

The prison ward's windows offered the nurses a perfect view of the Gestapo trucks, and despite all the work to be done, they found it hard to think of anything else. But after an hour, the trucks drove off, as empty as they had arrived. And when the last of them disappeared around the bend, it was as if the entire hospital let out a long sigh of relief.

"You see, my dear, we have nothing to fear." Despite all the time he'd been there, Arthur was still handcuffed to his bed, and his emaciated wrist bore the scarlet stigmata of the metal cuffs. "Our fearless leader has seen worse, I'm sure. I know what some people think of Lustig—they call him a Nazi puppet, or a coward—but for my part, I have a great deal of respect for him. He will always try and negotiate the best option for the hospital. Believe me, we are in good hands."

"I wish it with all my heart, Arthur," said Lena. "Now, you'll have to excuse me—I have patients to see."

Indeed, she had not left his bedside since the Gestapo's arrival. All that time, the ward's activity had floated in anxious waiting. Was there still meaning in carrying out procedures and cleaning bandages even as the fate of the hospital seemed uncertain? With the trucks' departure, it was as if life, after a brief pause, could resume its course. And yet. Thirty minutes later, a new crowd formed near the window, and Lena understood from the faces of the young women slowly peeling away from the glass that the day's fragile balance had tipped yet again.

"It's him, I'm sure of it! Fritz Wöhrn! I'm not likely to forget him. He had my best friend deported!" said one of the girls.

Wöhrn. Lena had heard enough stories about that cruel man to know his presence boded ill. She risked a glance out the window. Parked in front of the hospital gates were two official cars, waiting in silence. For a few seconds, Lena allowed herself to think of the worst outcomes, then she refocused. Over the past few months, she had learned that trials were faced one at a time, and for now, her patients needed her. So, she got back to work. The hours thus passed more quickly, and soon, the sun set, the temperature dropped a few degrees, and it was time for the shift change. Before leaving the ward, she took a glance out the window. The cars had disappeared.

Lena had set aside a few pieces of brioche, eager to share them with the children; she could already picture them enjoying the treat, and it made her smile. Nevertheless, she decided to take a short walk in the park before going to them. The day had been strenuous, and she was careful never to transfer her budding anxiety to the children. She knew their sensitivity, their keen sense of observation, and wanted to see them with a light heart only.

She entered the garden, which was almost deserted at that time. The moon showed only a shy slice of silver. The sky had cleared of its last clouds. A winter miracle, the first stars pierced the sky's great canvas like thousands of pearls. Lena wandered on the frost-sparkled grass, took a few breaths of air, and it was delicious. The small bead of anxiety swelling behind her sternum felt like it had already been halved. Indeed, she thought, those two visits were not innocuous. Wöhrn had probably come to claim some workers for the Reich factories, or worse. But she was confident. She had the children, her work, and Arthur. Her universe, at last, seemed to take root, to make some sort of sense. She also felt useful enough in the ward to hope to keep her position. She had not forgotten Sophie's words: *Lustig will not hesitate to put on the lists the names of those least indispensable to the hospital's operation.*

Sophie . . . where was she now? Hidden in an apartment with her parents? Or had they managed to get to Switzerland? It would be a miracle, but if anyone could pull it off, it would be Sophie.

The sound of her steps in the snow paced her daydreaming. She couldn't stop thinking about Sophie. A strange anxiety pricked at her chest; it was a tough time to be in hiding in Berlin. In recent weeks, many had been arrested under murky circumstances. There were talks of double agents, traps, false pretenses; it sounded like a cheap spy novel. Lena quickly dismissed these thoughts. No, no. Sophie was way too cautious to be fooled by pseudo-spies. And these were just rumors; who knew what was really going on out there. Sophie was safe, she was sure of it.

Her steps had led her to the large willow tree. Lena placed a hand on the frost-hardened bark, tough as a brown diamond. A gust of wind blurred her vision for a moment, and she thought she recognized, in the knots of the trunk, Calvin's face smiling back at her and sticking out his tongue. She must've been very tired.

"Good evening," said a voice behind her. Still caught up in her reverie, Lena's first thought was that the wind, blowing through the branches, had created that sound. But the voice had the consistency of reality, the thickness of a woman's throat. She turned around, and her world capsized.

"Sophie? It can't be! What are you doing here? Is it really you?"

Two meters away, partly covered in shadows, Sophie stood very still. With both feet firmly on the ground, her body gave an impression of brute force. Lena's first impulse was to rush toward her friend, to throw herself into her arms, to shower her with kisses. But Sophie felt it and took a step back, and Lena stopped her gesture midway.

"Yes, little Lena . . . It's me. Your dear Sophie. You seem surprised." Her voice was surprisingly neutral. Cold, like a white winter sky.

"Surprised? But . . . Sophie, I thought you were with your parents! Hidden deep in the city, or maybe in Switzerland or even in England! What are you doing here? It's incredible! And what's with those clothes?" Lena wanted to laugh. Not just laugh, but also to share that laughter with the world. Sophie had come back! And in a ridiculous outfit that both of them would have joyously mocked just a few months earlier. That purple skirt, such a strange color! And then that green beret, tilted to the side . . . It was downright hilarious! But, despite her joy, Lena felt a cold, viscous liquid cover her stomach, as if there was something deeply, terribly skewed in this apparition.

"You don't understand, do you, little Lena." Sophie pulled out a cigarette case from her inner pocket. Using a beautiful silver lighter, she lit her cigarette, which she brought to her lips with a black-gloved hand. "Let me explain. Remember, when you were calmly thinking about my proposition to join me in hiding? Well. Picture this: while missy was taking her time, thinking about the pros and cons, the Nazis arrested my parents. And then, I don't know if you noticed, but I also disappeared."

"But of course, I noticed! Sophie, it was such a blow for me. I was left all alone, I was . . . actually, I was sure that you had joined your parents."

"Without you? After having offered you to come with me? Is that what you think of me?"

Almost in spite of herself—she had promised herself to be dry and merciless—her self-esteem took a blow. She shook her head. "I should have expected as much. In your mind, you've always had the monopoly on morality. Well, no, I didn't abandon you. On the contrary. I was thrown in jail. I was beaten, interrogated, tortured, but leave without you? No, that, I didn't do." She took a long drag from her cigarette. Her hand shook slightly. "Oh, by the way, before I forget, my parents say hello. You know, my parents, the ones who loved going to the opera."

"The opera? Sorry, Sophie, but now you've lost me" said Lena, already out of her depth. Her own body embarrassed her. Once her initial impulse was blocked in mid-stride, she had tried several poses, letting her hands hang down her body, crossing them in front of her chest, always holding back her desire to get closer to her friend, to hold her in her arms.

"Yes, my parents, who are currently languishing in a Gestapo cell. I wonder how they got there. You wouldn't have an idea, by any chance?"

"But why are you telling me that with an accusatory tone? I don't know anything about it! Besides, you barely told me anything about them!"

"Almost nothing, no, but enough for you to send them to their doom! All while keeping your moral high ground, since it was done inadvertently, wasn't it? No? Nothing? Do you remember your night in the truck? Well, you told Hans just enough to get them arrested. And now, who do you think has to deal with preventing their immediate deportation? One thing is for sure—it's not you. No, you're nice and warm in the hospital, well fed, cooing around your handsome mustachioed man and dropping pieces of brioche to the kids in the basement."

Suddenly, Lena's heart slowed its beat. She took one step forward.

"The children? You know about them?" Her voice was no more than a whisper. "But how? You haven't told anyone, have you, Sophie? You know what would happen if they were found out?"

Sophie also stepped forward, and her face emerged from the shadows. Her hair cut in a bob faintly reflected the moon rays; her lips shone in the crisp evening air. Lena had never seen her like this, and she found her immensely beautiful. But a new light animated her eyes, and Lena, who since their last meeting had lived so much, recognized two new friends, tucked tight in the blue orbs: violence and fear. And, well-hidden at the bottom of her pupil, an immense sadness.

"Ah, finally a topic that spikes your interest. I see that my parents' imprisonment, or what it costs me to keep them alive, doesn't excite your curiosity very much. Well, old girl, you're going to know anyway. But first, tell me: have you ever heard of the *blonde poison*?"

"The blonde poison? Yes, I've heard some rumors about Jewish spies, supposedly working for the Gestapo. I don't really believe them; it all seems utterly delirious. Anyway, I don't see the connection with what we were saying. About the children—tell me, are you sure you haven't told anyone about them?"

"Oh, well this little virgin's starting to get on my nerves!" Her voice had climbed a few octaves and took on the consistency of white-hot iron. "Don't you get it? *I* am the blonde poison. The angel of death! For months, I've had to roam the city looking for hidden Jews. Once I find some, I chat them up, spin them a yarn, and two minutes later, I signal my Gestapo colleagues, who then come to pick them up. That's how my parents are still alive! Are you interested now? Or are you still thinking about those poor kids hidden in their closet? Children, hiding in a hospital! Poor girl, have you lost your mind? Don't you get it? They will never survive the war!"

Her face had turned scarlet. Walking toward Lena, she had shouted the last words, pointing an accusatory finger at the one who had been closer than a sister to her. She realized the volume of her voice, her extended finger vibrating with emotion, and felt a bit ashamed. She folded her finger, and her hand came to rest along her right thigh. Perhaps, at night, lying on her bed, she still wondered how she had become this harsh, violent woman; if somehow, going back was still an option. But it was too late. She had done too much. Only a distant horizon mattered now, which despite her best efforts, she saw only as dark, uncertain, and terribly lonely.

"My God, Sophie, what have you done?" said Lena, whose legs could suddenly no longer support her.

"*What have you done*, she says. But old girl, I did what I had to do." Her voice had returned to an almost undisturbed calmness. "Yes, what I had to do . . . the Gestapo gave me a choice, and I chose. And my parents are still alive. Does that explanation suit you, or are you going to lecture me? I have a new life, now. A new life, which gives me access to information."

She moved closer to Lena, who in the cold air could smell notes of a sweet, fruity perfume. "You've got nothing to add? Good. So, let me explain. For example, I know that this afternoon, the hospital came within a hair's breadth of immediate closure. But that old Lustig performed a sleight of hand he has a knack for, and the officers turned back. A bit later, negotiations resumed, and a compromise was reached: tomorrow morning, at seven o'clock, Lustig must provide the Gestapo with a list of three hundred names; half the hospital. Yes, you heard me right. Don't look so shocked. Doctors, nurses, and patients, too."

The number echoed in Lena's mind. Three hundred. How did one choose three hundred people to deport? It seemed insane.

"Still speechless? Then, I'll continue. I have lots of information. For instance, last night, my commanding officer took me aside and said, 'Sophie, the higher-ups are pleased with your work, but last week, you only caught two Jews in hiding, and this week, only one. So here are the orders: if you don't immediately increase your numbers, your parents will be deported to the east, first thing Thursday morning.'"

"Your parents? In a transport? But Thursday, that's tomorrow! Surely, Sophie, there must be something we can do?"

"Oh, Lena . . ." Sophie crushed her cigarette butt against the gnarled trunk. "Yes, indeed, there is something we can do. And that's exactly what I've done."

Her lips were almost closed tight with anger. She moved closer, close enough to stretch out her arms and hug Lena. Finally, she lifted her chin, and their eyes met. Lena, who had been her best friend. Lena, who so often had cried on her shoulder at night; Lena, with whom she had shared secrets, laughter, and so many trials, too. Her eyes suddenly took on a gray hue. "Yes, Lena, I did what had to be done. They won't be leaving. Not tomorrow, anyway. You will have to . . ." her voice choked up, and at that moment, a new gust—the wind had picked up—blew through the branches, covering her words with a sensitive shadow. "You will have to forgive me."

Then, with surprising speed, Sophie returned to the night. Lena heard steps receding, and a few seconds later—while her eyes scanned the darkness and the air still vibrated with her friend's soul—she saw a few blonde filaments sparkle under an old street lamp at the far end of the garden, dancing in the light.

An acidic taste filled her throat. Forgive her, but for what? Whatever her friend had done, who was she to judge? Wouldn't she herself, given the chance to grant her mother even a few more days, have overthrown regimes and pierced the heavens? So, why had Sophie run away so abruptly? They still had so much to say! They hadn't even talked about the children . . .

Suddenly—and it had nothing to do with the cold—her entire body started to shake. She dropped the bag full of brioche. Then, everything happened quickly. No longer caring about the time or who might see her, she dashed toward the central staircase. She raced down the stairs to the basement and entered a corridor. Within a minute, she had already covered half the distance. A few more turns, and she would see them. Her heart raced in her chest; it had been a long time since she had run. And then, without quite knowing why, she stopped. The air was filled with the scent of tobacco. Spotting a patch of shadow, she slid her body into it and listened, suddenly immobile. The corridor filled with the sound of footsteps. Many footsteps.

Flanked by two armed guards, they walked: Anna, her eldest girl, always proud, chin up. Behind her, the little ones: Joseph and David, holding hands. Joseph stifled a tear by biting his lip. Lisa, in pajamas, lagged a bit. Calvin wasn't there.

Bringing up the rear, a tall man with long bony hands. His hat shaded eyes of a somewhat dirty black, which seemed akin to a still life. Without seeing her, the children walked right past Lena. Hidden in the shadows, she wanted to scream, to protest, to fight, but could only shake with fear. They were almost at the end of the corridor when the man suddenly stiffened.

He seemed to listen, to sniff even. He pivoted and locked gazes with Lena, piercing her heart in the process. He smiled, tipped his hat, and turned around.

Then, they disappeared.

12

• • •

Tuesday, March 10, 1943, 6 p.m.

LOST, THEY WERE LOST. STILL HUDDLED IN A CORNER OF THE basement, Lena tried to control the trembling that had taken hold of her body. She needed to breathe, to regain some semblance of calm. Perhaps there was nothing she could do for the arrested children, but she knew she had to pull herself together because Calvin wasn't with them. She realized the possible reasons for his absence were manyfold, but she decided to cling to one—and only one: he was still out there, and he needed her.

Without thinking further about the possibility of soldiers on patrol—if Hans had wanted to arrest her, he would have done so already—she ventured through the corridors. The sound of her steps on the bare floor was disturbed only by the sound of a clock; somewhere, it was striking six o'clock. Soon, her colleagues would all congregate in the cafeteria, unaware of the drama unfolding beneath their feet.

She quickly reached the children's hiding place. The door had been left open; the deadbolt was shot. She breathed in and entered. Apart from the busted door, the small space was free of any signs of struggle. Instead, it looked as if life had been suspended, snatched in mid-flight: a few books lay open on the floor. Blankets zigzagged across the still-warm mattresses. With trembling legs, she walked around the room, her hand brushing against the walls that still echoed with the children's muffled laughter.

She tried to imagine Calvin hiding in the corridors, naturally making his way to the kitchens, where he would find a stash of cream candies which he would gobble down without a care in the world. "Nonsense!" she said out loud. She understood now that she would not find him. Perhaps he had simply been arrested a few minutes earlier. Yes, she had to go back up. There was nothing more in here for her.

She headed for the exit when the wood creaked behind her. She turned around, listened closely, was about to chalk it up to her imagination when the creaking resumed, followed by a child's voice. "Miss Lena!" With his two feet, Calvin pushed out the door of his favorite hiding spot. His dust-covered face was distorted by a worried smile. "Miss Lena, where are my friends?"

"Calvin!" She ran to the child. "Oh, I'm so glad!" she said as she hugged him.

"I'm happy to see you too, Miss Lena. But where are my friends? Some angry men came in . . . they yelled a lot and took everyone away! We were in the middle of a game of hide-and-seek, so I didn't move, and they didn't even see me. I told you it was a good hiding spot!"

"It's an excellent hiding spot, Calvin. I'm proud of you," said Lena, her whole body shaking uncontrollably.

"So, when are my friends they coming back? We haven't finished our game!"

"Oh, don't worry about the others, Calvin. No, don't worry. I promise I'll take care of them, and I'll do everything I can so you see them again quickly."

She took his face in her hands. "But listen to me: for now, you must absolutely stay in here. Don't open this door for anyone other than me or Uncle Stefan. Do you understand? It's very important."

"Yes, Miss Lena," said Calvin, who didn't understand, and who was starting to get worried by Lena's shaking hands.

"Oh, that's good, that's very good . . . I have to go now. Be a good boy; I promise to come back very fast. Okay? Now, tuck your legs in. Imagine it's a big game of hide-and-seek. It's fun, right? There you go . . ."

"Okay, Miss Lena."

She saw that he was holding back his tears and loved him even more for it.

His little feet crossed under his pants. She kissed him on the forehead and closed the hatch.

•

She returned to the central staircase, trying with each step to bring some kind of order to her thoughts. If what Sophie had said was true, her name might appear on a list the next morning. Then, who would take care of Calvin? Without help, he stood no chance. He would need a new hiding place, food . . . apart from Stefan, no one knew he existed. She finally managed to slow her breathing; her thoughts regained some clarity. Yes, her priority was to see Stefan. With some luck, they wouldn't both be deported, and whoever remained would take care of Calvin.

Running up the stairs, she quickly made it to the psychiatric ward. Under the white light of a rusted ceiling lamp, Laura, one of the oldest nurses and one of her acquaintances, was filling pill dispensers.

"Oh, Laura, I'm so glad to see you."

"Lena! What a surprise. What brings you here? Isn't the prison ward enough for you anymore? Come to check out our collection of loonies?"

Lena tried to laugh, but the sound got stuck in her throat. "No, actually, you know I'm friends with Stefan. I was wondering if I could see him? It's very important."

"That's going to be difficult. You know I don't have the authority to allow visits, even for you. Besides, tonight, Stefan had what the doctor called a major melancholy episode. It happens to him, sometimes. When he came back from his walk in the garden—I don't know what he saw exactly—his face was distraught. He was so pale! He immediately undressed and went to bed. At first, he just lay there, saying nothing. And then he started screaming, repeating the same words, over and over without making sense . . . it sounded like painter, or traitor, or sister, I couldn't tell. The doctor went to check on him and found him still so agitated that he finally loaded him up with tranquilizers. Since then, he's been asleep. Even if I let you see him, I very much doubt you'd manage to wake him."

"Laura, listen: it's absolutely essential that I see him now. Believe me, it's a matter of life and death."

"Life and death? Alright. I'll give you five minutes. But be quick. As you know, if I get caught, I can kiss my job goodbye."

"You're an angel! Five minutes. No more, I swear."

Dimly lit by a nightlight, Stefan lay on his back, absolutely still. Only his lips vibrated in unison, creating a powerful snore with each breath. His eyelids bore the traces of discreet makeup; his arms protruded from the blanket. Lena knelt down and whispered in his ear.

"Stefan, Stefan . . . I need your help. Oh, Stefan, please wake up . . ." But he was somewhere else, floating on a cloud of pharmacology. Frustrated, pressed for time, she shook her friend's shoulder, pinched it, first lightly and then with force.

"Stefan, wake up!" she said, to no avail; his mind was shielded from the world's madness by a nearly impenetrable cottony veil.

Resigned, Lena pulled the blanket up over his bare arms. He looked so vulnerable. Kneeling on the cold floor, she tenderly ran her hand through his graying hair and stayed like that for a while, watching him, really seeing him, as if for the first time.

"Stefan, oh, Stefan," she repeated endlessly, like a simple and beautiful prayer. Then, she got up and returned to the nursing station.

"Thank you, Laura. You were right; he's sleeping like a prince."

"I told you! Come back tomorrow; I'm sure he'll be feeling much better."

"Of course, you're right. Good night and thank you again."

Think, she had to think. If Stefan was out of reach, she needed a backup plan. Whom did she trust . . . the solution presented itself, clear as day. *Of course*, she thought. She climbed the stairs with renewed energy and, upon reaching the fourth floor, greeted the night nurse, who smiled back knowingly; Lena's special relationship with Arthur was no secret, and her tenure in the ward afforded her some degree of privilege.

In the dim light, she approached Arthur's bed. He was reading a book and only saw her at the last moment.

"Arthur?" she whispered.

"Oh, good evening, Lena. I thought I recognized your perfume."

Half-sitting in his bed, his mustache finely trimmed, he watched her.

"You seem worried; do you have any news regarding our rather unusual afternoon?"

"Arthur. I have something to ask of you. But it's a bit dangerous. Will you listen?"

"Dear Lena, listening to you is one of the great pleasures of my life. If I can be of use, then my joy will be complete."

Despite herself, Lena smiled. "Then listen to me, Arthur, for time is of the essence: I've learned—don't ask me how—that tomorrow, half the hospital will be deported. Yes, half. It seems they've decided to finish with us. Nurses, doctors, patients, no one is safe. You must keep this to yourself. But there's more: for the last few weeks, I've been hiding children in the hospital's basements. No! Don't interrupt me. I've been hiding children. Five, to be exact. Oh, they are so kind, so adorable, you have no idea. I took them in after those three terrible days I told you about. And these children have been arrested. All except one."

Arthur said nothing. He just watched the woman he had seen grow up and, in just a few months, transform from a young ingénue into a strong, courageous woman. He had already understood that he loved her; he was now discovering how much.

"Just one? How is that possible?"

"Yes, just one. His name is Calvin; he's five years old." Her voice became a whisper. "He's hidden in a hatch, inside a closet in the basement of building A, and really, Arthur, really, it's no place for a child."

As she spoke, Lena had sat down on the edge of the bed. And in front of this man, from whom she hid so much, her defenses started falling one by one. Was it fatigue? Some kind of mental exhaustion, a backlash from Sophie's betrayal? Her mouth rounded, her eyes dilated, and without being able to control herself, she realized she was speaking much faster than usual.

"Yes, Arthur, he's hidden in a basement hatch, after the third turn from the staircase. Until now, Stefan was the only one who knew. You know him a bit, don't you? He's a charming man, but he's a bit off his rocker at times, like all of us. But you, Arthur, you now have some amount of freedom, don't you? You can walk in the park twice a day, so . . . if tomorrow . . . if tomorrow, he and I are deported, and you stay here, you must promise me"—she leaned in and placed a hand on his chest—"you must promise me, Arthur, that you'll do everything in your power to take care of Calvin."

Their bodies were close now. Arthur brought his hand to Lena's cheek and said, "I promise you, my dear," and never under his fingertips, had he felt life pulsate with such intensity. Slowly, his thumb caressed her smooth, fluid skin. They remained like that for a few seconds, and then Arthur saw a veil form over her misty iris, noticed the quivering mouth that begged him for a child's life, and for a brief moment, there was no hospital, no war, no Calvin, no Nazis—just a man and a woman finally coming together, and Lena slipped into the kiss, the world dissolving around her. It lasted only a few seconds, but for them, eternity mingled with their mouths, their tongues, the crackling of the fire that burned their backs. Finally, their bodies parted, and Lena stood up, slightly embarrassed, her face flushed, and Arthur had never seen her look more beautiful.

"Forgive me, Arthur, I didn't mean to . . ."

Then, she slipped away.

Back in the central staircase, her heart still thrumming with delightful surges, Lena was overtaken by a brief sensation of peace. Calvin might actually be saved! But no sooner had she indulged in her joy than the image of the four children walking like convicts brought her back to reality. Couldn't she have interceded on their behalf, explained to Hans that they were innocent, that arresting children was pointless? No, she told herself, none of that would have helped. For now, all she could do was focus on the next minute, on her next move, and so, her mouth still full with the taste of her first kiss, she headed toward the cafeteria.

There, she found Ingrid, her superior, who was wandering alone in the empty hall.

"Well, *schwester* Lena. You're arriving only now? Where have you been?"

"Oh, good evening, head nurse. Well, you see . . ."

But Ingrid's demeanor that evening was one of resignation; small lines of worry etched the edges of her still-young eyes.

"Don't bother, Lena. Tonight, we're all a bit off-kilter. Surely, you've noticed the Gestapo's two visits this afternoon?"

Lena was taken aback by Ingrid's familiarity; then she noticed the quiver in her chin, and for the first time, she simply saw the head nurse as a woman of her own age. Perhaps they had grown up in the same region, attended the same school; they had never discussed it.

"Yes, head nurse, I noticed. I'm worried too. Do you have any information? Do we know what's been decided?" she asked, suddenly aware of her own duplicity.

"No, nothing has leaked. But, between us, I'd really like to know. Because if it's over for us, there are letters to write, phone calls to make. You know, one has to organize, in this life and the next."

A silence settled between the two women, neither willing to break it.

"Anyway, I don't know why I'm bothering you with this. Maybe you just wanted to grab a bite before heading to bed? If that's the case, I won't hold you up. But just so you know, the dormitory is practically empty. Everyone's gathered around Lustig's office. Seems he and his secretary haven't left it all afternoon. Something's definitely up. I'm heading there myself. Anyway, enjoy your meal."

"Actually, I'm not hungry. Head nurse, may I accompany you?"

"Of course, Lena."

Walking in unison, they emerged into a corridor filled with women and light. Some whispered near the windows, others, exhausted from an overly intense day, sat directly on the floor, backs set against the wall. A palpable anxiety hung in the air, a deep, urgent desire to know.

Toward the far end of the corridor, a few nurses were clustered in front of Lustig's office door. Ears pressed against the solid wood, they waited for a word that, slipping through the carvings, would shed some light on their immediate future.

"Any news?" Lena asked.

"Shh! No, none. All we hear is the sound of a typewriter. And it's been going on for two hours."

"So it's true," said Lena.

"What? What's true?" the mass of white uniforms turned around. "Nothing, I . . . I was just thinking out loud. Don't mind me, girls . . ."

She took a step back. All these women understood, deep in their bones, that if Lustig and his secretary had barricaded themselves in their office at this late hour, it could only mean one thing: the incessant tapping was composing a morbid symphony in which they were the main performers. Lena thought of Sophie's words, and her legs, suddenly, could no longer support her. She let herself slide down the wall until she was sitting on the floor.

She closed her eyes and listened to the hum of voices. Each speculated wildly, from the reorganization of the emergency department to the arrival of new patients in psychiatry. All were deliberately wrong, because it was still possible, because how could they accept that the sound of a typewriter could translate into names on a list, that trucks would be filled with these names amidst screams and violence, and that once again, the next morning, they would have breakfast surrounded by empty chairs? The mind simply isn't built to withstand that. So, they told each other stories, to live just a little longer.

A profound emptiness settled in her chest. But it was too late, or too early—she wasn't sure which—to give in to melancholy. After all, no one really knew what awaited them at the end of those transports. Maybe they would simply reunite with their missing friends in a labor camp? Living conditions there would undoubtedly be harsh, but they would be together, which was what mattered most. She looked around and realized she was surrounded by familiar faces. These women wanted to live above all, and the warmth of the group, united by a common fate, warmed her soul. So, when one of the young women sitting next to her asked, "How are you doing, Lena? You seem a bit pale," she couldn't help but smile and understood she loved them all like sisters. Amidst this war, from which the hospital's inhabitants were miraculously partly shielded, she had built a life. She worked, she ate her fill, and—she thought, blushing—had even discovered the beginnings of love and motherhood. And it was precisely this thought—which had never really left her—that acted as a catalyst.

Before anyone else, she saw Lustig's office door open; she saw his secretary trying, as discreetly as possible, to make her way to the toilets located at the end of the long corridor.

As if in a dream, Lena stood up. She grabbed the secretary's arm, brought her lips to her ear, and the words she spoke, simple and precise, were propelled by an inner strength she herself didn't know she possessed.

"Madame Secretary, I know exactly what role you're playing tonight. I'm aware of the three hundred names."

Over her thick glasses, the old lady shot Lena a look of terror and confusion. How could this young nurse know?

But Lena paid no mind and continued her uninterrupted flow of words. "Yes, I know about the three hundred. And I also know that our director will first rid himself of the people least useful to the hospital. So here's the thing: you must promise me, Madame Secretary, you must promise me, that if you hear Stefan's name, from the psychiatry department, you'll put my name in his place.

No, don't say anything. He's my friend, and besides, I have my reasons. There are still enough nurses for the prison ward, you know it. So, promise me, Madame Secretary, promise me."

Under the authoritative voice of her boss, Madame Kohan had already typed hundreds of names onto lists. Lustig's office door wasn't always thick enough to muffle the voices of the Nazis who came to terrorize her boss; in this woman's heart slept many secrets. Slowly, she turned toward Lena and looked her in the eyes. "Do you even know what you're asking me?"

"I believe I do. Write my name down, I beg of you."

But other arms were already grabbing at the secretary, and questions flew: *What have you been writing for hours? Is the hospital going to close?* and Lena had to let go, uncertain what to make of the look in the old woman's eyes.

She remained there, hands by her side, breathing more freely than she had in days. Around her, the noise level seemed to drop. Her comrades' movements appeared slower, more distant, like the shadow of a memory. Walking very slowly, she left the corridor, heading toward the dormitory.

The air there was deliciously cool. Guided by the habit of hundreds of nights, she walked in the semi-darkness to her cot. Any trace of worry had left her face, replaced by a deep, confident certainty. She removed her cap, her uniform, and placed her worn shoes under the bed.

In a cot near hers, a young nurse, newly arrived—a petite blonde, rumored to have lost her entire family in a bombing—watched her with solitary, worried eyes. Lena easily recognized the expression in her pupils; she had often seen it in the mirror.

So, Lena came closer, stared intently at the young woman with her large dark eyes, placed a hand on her shoulder, and smiled.

"Everything will be alright, little one. Everything will be alright."

Epilogue

• • •

Sunday, July 20, 1975, Lewiston, Maine, USA

A BEAM OF LIGHT PIERCED THROUGH THE BLINDS, SETTLING ON her closed eyelids. Somewhere, a lawnmower engine sputtered, interrupting the silence that cradled the house. Lena had been awake for a few minutes. Lying on her bed, she savored that liminal state between dream and wakefulness. She opened an eye. The clock read 9:30. Since the start of the holiday, she had been waking up later and later; the academic year must have exhausted her more than she realized.

Rudolph had already risen. Even though he had become a true American, proudly flying the star-spangled banner every Fourth of July, her husband had retained a certain taste for order from his German childhood. His neatly folded pajamas hung over the back of a chair. Silently, he had dressed and left the bedroom. *What a thoughtful man I've found*, thought Lena. He knew of her fatigue—at her age, resuming her studies was not without its effects on her body—and did everything to make life easier for his wife.

She pushed back the covers, gathered a little momentum, and swung her feet onto the fluffy carpet. After a quick shower, she slipped into a skirt and a light blouse, buttoning the sleeves just above the wrist. Before heading downstairs, she opened her old jewelry box; her eyes lingered on an old bark pendant, which she had never been able to bring herself to throw away. She ran her fingers over its rough surface and smiled. Then, she decided on a discreet necklace and closed the box.

In the kitchen, her eldest daughter was bustling around the coffee machine. She and her family had been there for only two days, but she had already taken control of the kitchen, which suited Lena perfectly.

"Ah, Mom, you're up! Well-rested?" said Pauline. "You're just in time; I've made some coffee, nice and strong, just the way you like it."

"Thank you, darling. Yes, I feel invigorated and ready for the day! This last semester tired me out, but the English literature courses were absolutely fascinating." She kissed her daughter on the cheek. "What about you, did you sleep well? And my grandsons? Are those little monsters already up?"

"Oh, yes! They've been playing in the garden for hours . . . they found the ball you gave them last year, and they won't let go of it!"

Lena adjusted her glasses and leaned toward the window. The two boys were bouncing their little legs on the freshly mown lawn. The elder had placed his T-shirt on the grass, marking, along with the trunk of a sun-stunned birch, the imaginary boundaries of a soccer goal.

"Little angels. What about your father? Has he left for his tennis game yet?"

"Yes, you know him. He would never miss a doubles match with Dr. Fishman. Plus, it gives them a chance to compare their most interesting cases of the week, in addition to keeping them fit!"

Lena sat at a wooden table in a corner of the kitchen—she reserved the dining room table for Shabbat meals, when her whole tribe gathered in a joyous mix—and accepted the university-emblazoned mug her daughter handed her.

"Hmm . . . this coffee smells wonderful. Thank you, my dear."

Pauline kissed her mother on the forehead and went out to join her children as they attempted to catch a squirrel.

Lena brought the mug to her chest, feeling its warmth seep through her body. What joy to have her daughter with her. When Pauline had told her she was moving to Europe with her husband, Lena had initially recoiled, before catching herself. After all, France wasn't Germany, and the war had been over for a long time. But she still missed her daughter terribly. Fortunately, every summer, she and her family traveled to New England. It would have been hard not to see her grandchildren grow up. Aged two and four, they adored their grandma and never missed an opportunity to leap into her arms. Yes, she was lucky indeed.

She poured herself a small bowl of Froot Loops—they might be children's cereal, but they were darn good!—and added milk, some dry cookies, and a drop of maple syrup. While putting away the milk, she noticed the kosher "K" symbol, discreetly printed on the label, and thought America truly was a wonderful place, where one could buy kosher milk in the local supermarket's refrigerated section, surrounded by neighbors and friends.

A thud signaled the arrival of the mail. Old Earl had taken a well-deserved vacation, and his substitute, the neighbor's son, didn't stop as he did to chat about neighborhood news. No doubt in a hurry to catch up to his friends on the baseball field, he simply slid the mail through the slot designed for this purpose in the front door before moving on to the next house.

She walked to the living room, gathered a pile of letters, and her *Herald Tribune*. Subscribing to a newspaper had been one of her first acts as a citizen. From the start, she had wanted to blend into her new country and never missed a day of "the news," always reading the daily from front to back. Plus, she did enjoy the *funnies*, which her grandsons always went straight to. An additional package caught her attention. A large brown envelope, bound with string. Her name was written in beautiful black ink calligraphy. Examining the stamps, the forceful postmarks, she finally understood what was bothering her: *Deutsche Bundepost*, it read. A package from Germany? Her heart skipped a beat. She dropped the rest of the mail and tore open the brown paper. Inside, she found a small envelope and a stack of sheets, bound by a black spiral.

With slightly trembling hands, Lena opened the envelope and extracted three neat pieces of paper. They were covered in fine, precise, almost nervous handwriting. Through the blinds, a golden light filtered. The lawnmower had stopped. But Lena, her eyes fixed on the letter, heard neither the sound of birds nor the children's shouts. All that echoed in her heart was the sound of the first words she read, over and over again, not quite daring to believe them.

> *"Hello, Lena, I'm not sure if you remember me. My name is Calvin, and if what I've discovered is correct, you saved my life."*

Suddenly, her legs wouldn't support her. She dropped the letter, sought support, and finally, sat down heavily on the couch. *Calvin.* She never thought she'd hear that name again. Not after all those years in the camp, not after watching all the others leave, one by one . . . Slowly, she collected herself and looked around. Over the upright piano, which she had taught herself to play—simple tunes from her childhood, mostly—stood the portrait of her husband as a soldier in the US Army, eyes full of confidence in his new country. Family photos and official diplomas decorated the beautiful living room wallpaper; after raising her children, she had decided to resume her studies and now pursued a leading academic career. Yes, she had rebuilt herself. But she had thought of him so often.

The children were still playing outside; her husband wouldn't be back for another hour. Lena picked up the letter, sat up straight on the couch, adjusted her glasses, and took a deep breath.

I grew up on a farm north of Berlin. I was seven years old when, at last, the cannons fell silent, and the time came for rebuilding. For the longest time, I had no memories prior to that date—my child's brain having presumably deemed it wise to seal away the war file in a tightly locked chest. The relative void didn't bother me; I was fortunate to have two loving parents, and despite the privations and material difficulties, I can boast of having had a happy childhood.

Apart from some recurring nightmares (trapped in a dark room, I heard children's voices calling my name) and a few unique quirks—I could never stomach a jam sandwich, for some reason—I was, by all accounts, a rather easy child to live with. Inherently sociable, I quickly became the neighborhood darling. My schooling proceeded without incident, and even in an astonishingly brilliant manner. It seemed mathematics and science came naturally to me, as did a musical talent that my parents, who could hardly tell the difference between the sound of a tuba and the mooing of one of their beloved cows, watched bloom with fascination.

Anyway, I won't recount all my youthful memories; let's move on. Having finished high school with grades that opened the university doors to me, I decided, almost on a whim, to enroll in medical school. No deep passion drove me there, but by some kind of primal instinct, I felt this was a field where I could be useful. That very evening, I announced the news to my parents, and even today, when I close my eyes, I can see their look, that curious mix of approval, surprise, and understanding.

I threw myself into my studies with the abandon of youth, passionately indulging in everything; the lectures, the evenings spent debating with my classmates around ever-full steins, the first steps inside the hospital, wrapped in a white coat that I donned for the first time with a feeling of pride.

For me, this was also the time of the discovery of women. I was fortunate to see them approach me with good intentions, probably finding something to hold onto in my large dark eyes and rebellious curls. I thus floated from conquest to conquest, finding all of it quite natural and wildly enjoyable. But abundance is often the sister of indigestion, and almost without realizing it, I fell in love with a first-year student who relegated all others to ancient memories. I discovered happiness in its purest form, and six months later, we were engaged.

If you'll allow me, dear Lena, we'll speed up a bit here; I'll gloss over the study years, my wedding, and our settling into a loft apartment in the center of Berlin. There were six months left before graduation; Alice and I were eagerly awaiting our transition into professional life. She had chosen pediatrics, while I was drawn to internal medicine. One evening, after leaving the ward, I felt the urge to visit my parents. I started out toward the farm. The half-hour walk, my mind still buzzing from my day's work, whetted my appetite, and I was already daydreaming of the cookies my mother always kept in a terracotta jar in the center of the kitchen. As I approached, our neighbor Frederick called out to me. "Doc Calvin!" he said. "There's been a tragedy. Your father stumbled while milking the cows and hit his head. He had to be rushed to the hospital." I noted the address and hurried there. The Jewish hospital was only a few kilometers from the farm. I passed it every day on my way to medical school, but curiously, I had never gone in. I walked through the main gate and into a leafy park. A nurse happened by, and I asked for directions. "The emergency department?'" she said. "I was just heading there myself. Follow me. It's quite the maze here."

We took a broad central staircase and descended a floor. "We'll go through the basements; it's a shortcut," she told me. Our footsteps echoed in the dry, cold air. For some reason, those corridors made me uneasy. Suddenly, I had to stop, kneeling down. Dizziness overcame me; children's laughter, akin to the one from my nightmares, echoed in my head. But this time, they seemed more real, more present, as if those children were actually hiding behind one of these doors, ready to burst out at any moment. "Calvin, will you play with us? Come on, we'll count to ten and then come find you! Calviiiin!" Their laughter pierced my skull, Lena. "Sir, are you alright? You're very pale!'" the young nurse said to me. As my mother had taught me during my childhood, I focused on my breathing until I regained control of myself. "It's nothing," I said, standing up. "Just a brief spell of lightheadedness, that's all." The young woman helped me to my feet, and we were on our way.

A few minutes later, we emerged from the basements. The young woman wished me good luck and left me in the care of the emergency department's doctor. I introduced myself and, still shaky on my legs, was led to my father's bedside. He looked pitiful: this robust man, who had spent his life among animals, seemed tiny in his hospital bed. A white bandage, tinged with pink, was wrapped broadly around his head. "Ah, my son . . . you're here," he said. "Come, come, sit down." My mother was seated on the bed. She had nestled her tiny hand in my father's large paw and smiled weakly. Both of them looked at me as if, in a curious role reversal, I had become the patient whom worried parents were visiting.

And that, Lena, is how I came to learn the truth. My father, perhaps thinking his final moments had come—I can reassure you on that count, a week later, he was frolicking again, armed with a good story to tell his buddies—had found the perfect opportunity to reveal everything. I don't hold it against him, of course; he had kept all this in his heart for such a long time.

So, I had been adopted. He told me about Stefan and Arthur, who came to see him one day as he was herding his cows in the park—yes, the very park visible from the hospital window. It was one of those terrible days when dozens of Jews were leaving the hospital under Nazi guard. That sight had always made him sick: with rage, and powerlessness, too. Stefan and Arthur looked dreadful. Stefan, usually so jovial and ready with a joke, simply said: "Lena's children have all been arrested. All but one . . . tell me, old man, do you want to save a life?" My father, not a man of many words—the story he told me that day was, to my memory, one of his longest speeches—simply nodded, without asking questions. Stefan then disappeared, leaving my father alone with Arthur. That man, he told me, looked profoundly sad. "Lena was deported this morning," he had said, "she made me swear to save this child. It's all I have left of her . . ." My father was bewildered. He knew neither Arthur, whom he was meeting for the first time, nor this Lena everyone talked about. But the war repulsed him; plus, he told me with a mysterious air, he had his reasons. So, when a few minutes later, Stefan reappeared with a five-year-old boy clinging to his shirt, face smeared with charcoal, my father had smiled. "Calvin," Stefan said, "This gentleman has promised us he will take good care of you!" Unperturbed, the boy agreed, took my father's hand, and they both quietly left the hospital, never looking back.

Understandably, Lena, my first reaction was a mix of anger and denial. I had no memory of that scene. So, after kissing my parents goodbye, I excused myself. I needed to walk. My legs carried me across the city. I passed buildings rumored to have been Nazi torture centers. I walked by the old headquarters of the Kommandantur and saw it as if for the first time. The war, in this city that was barely beginning to recover, was something most of my peers avoided discussing. No one wanted to stir up the still-raw wound of defeat and humiliation. The youth wanted to live, to feel, without thinking about the stories lurking around every corner; here, a child was shot, there, a pregnant woman was tortured . . . No, no, we preferred to avoid these images and drink life to the lees. Moreover, we knew very few Jews.

A Jew . . . Was I Jewish? I thought back to all those post-match showers in my soccer team's locker room. Still a teenager, I had observed, embarrassed, my teammates' genitals, so different from mine. My father had explained my circumcision, citing multiple childhood infections. I had never questioned this explanation; I had even gotten into a locker room fight when another kid had called me a Jew. Now, questions swirled in my mind, each generating ten more: if my father was telling the truth, then who were my real parents? Had some of my family survived the war? And who was this Lena, who, apparently, had saved my life?

With my heart still racing, silently cursing my parents, the war, and the madness of men, I wandered the city for a few more hours. Eventually, I returned home. I climbed the stairs to our apartment, then, without a word to my wife, still fully clothed, I lay down on the bed and fell asleep immediately.

The next day, I woke up a different man. A blazing sun shone on the city. After speaking to my wife, I headed to the hospital. First, I visited my father (avoiding the basements this time) and asked him to tell me more. But the good man had already told me everything. He had only frequented the hospital park during those few months of 1943, when the director, a certain Dr. Lustig, had allowed him to bring his cows there. He was already feeling much better and almost seemed to regret his monologue from the day before. I reassured him; I was glad he had told me everything, and as for him, he would always be my father. Leaving him, I took the opportunity to explore the place. I walked the large park, admiring the old trees, searching for memories, perhaps inventing some . . . had I sat on this bench with Lena or Stefan? Where exactly was the spot where I had changed hands? A giant chessboard unfolded before me, and I immediately knew that I had to solve it.

The last months of my internship left little time to satisfy my newfound curiosity. However, I never stopped thinking about the mystery revealed by my father. Once graduated, one of my professors arranged an interview for me with one of the heads of the Jewish hospital. I must have seemed trustworthy enough, as two weeks later, I started my job as chief resident in the internal medicine clinic. What years those were!

A fascinating and challenging job, always rewarded by the satisfaction of having helped my patients, of learning a bit more about medicine and human nature . . . but I never lost sight of my goal: whenever my schedule allowed, I sought answers. There wasn't a kitchen clerk or a nursing aide who hadn't endured my grilling. Finally, after a few months, I found the person I was looking for. Ingrid had been the head nurse during Dr. Lustig's time. After the war, she couldn't bear to leave her haven.

She now held an administrative position, and it was during a visit to her office to sign off on my vacation days that I asked her the question. "Yes, yes," she said, "I was here during the war. Lena? Of course, I remember her . . ."

At first, she was reluctant to dive back into those memories and only gave me information in dribs and drabs. But I wasn't discouraged and visited her whenever I could, each time bringing a different offering: a very sweet black coffee, her favorite pastry bought at the corner shop . . . my efforts eventually softened her, and she started to open up. Our meetings gradually became part of our respective routines, and one evening, as I entered her office a little later than usual—carrying a beautiful butterkuchen under my arm—she greeted me with a knowing smile. "Dr. Calvin, I was beginning to think you'd forgotten me. So, where were we?"

Sometimes, we roamed the city in search of clues. Here, a factory had been emptied during the Fabrik Aktion. There stood the old stables where Jews had been gathered before their transfer to the east. Before my fascinated eyes, Ingrid spoke, and Berlin took on a new texture.

It was also Ingrid who guided me into the world of Judaism, and while I did not become a religious man, I am now aware of my origins. She was there with me, the day I stepped into a synagogue for the first time, awkwardly placing a kippah on my head. But when the rabbi began reading the Torah, his clear and melodious voice—which seemed to harbor the suffering of thousands of deaths—touched me deeply. It was as if, through prayer, I heard the voices of my vanished parents. "We're here, Calvin, and we're proud of you. Everything's alright, Calvin. Everything's alright."

Years passed. Ingrid had become part of the family, and every Saturday, she visited us. In the meantime, I had experienced the joys of fatherhood, and my son always jumped for joy upon seeing her enter the living room. We had lunch before getting to work. Gradually, we reconstructed the fates of our main characters. Stefan, deported to Terezin in 1944 (did you see him there?), was later transferred to Auschwitz, from which he did not return. Arthur remained at the hospital until the end of the war. Afterward, he apparently emigrated to a small village in Switzerland, where he lived a quiet life. Then one day, Ingrid spoke in a mysterious tone. She had information about Dr. Lustig: on the day Berlin was liberated, witnesses had seen him being pushed into an official car by Red Army soldiers. His trail ended there.

Information about Sophie was harder to come by. At the end of the war, she had simply vanished. I had almost lost hope of learning more when, a few months ago, I stumbled upon an article about a certain Sophie Gollschmidt, who had spied for the Gestapo . . . yes, Lena, our Sophie, I am sure of it. Convicted of treason by a post-war Russian court, she had served ten years of forced labor in Siberia. Returning to Berlin, she likely longed for nothing more than a few years of rest, but a new trial had started, this time ordered by the German justice. The article showed a photo of her—a still-young woman, but with eyes devoid of soul. I was very tempted to contact her, but I could never bring myself to do it. She lived a few months, waiting for the hearing. Perhaps there were men, laughter, a few rare moments of fleeting happiness. But probably not enough; one evening, she decided it wasn't worth it anymore. She climbed over the railing of her fifth-floor balcony and jumped.

As for you, Lena, I naturally sought to learn your story. Sure, we had found your name on Lustig's list heading to Terezin in March 1943, but after that, documents were scarce. As for the children, "Lena's children," as Stefan had called them, optimism was hard to come by. So, after many false hopes, I had almost resigned myself to your disappearance. Precious few had made it back . . .

My meetings with Ingrid grew less frequent; she was getting older, and we had already discovered so much. Over the years, I filled dozens of notebooks with notes. Then one evening, I sat down in front of my typewriter. What if I imagined Lena's arrival at the hospital? And Stefan? I'm sure he was funny; why not imagine their exchanges, their sufferings and their laughter . . . At first, it was just for me. But I got carried away, and everything followed. Everything I had discovered—the incongruous details, the historical landmarks, the anecdotes told by Ingrid—all crystallized in my heart, in my hands, and through my fingers on the typewriter, onto sheets of paper.

One day, I looked up, and before my eyes, was our story. Only the ending was missing. What had become of you after saving me? I dared not invent a fate for you, as you had given me mine.

And then one evening, Ingrid called me, her voice filled with palpable excitement. This admirable woman hadn't given up on you! Without telling me about it, she had traced your path. Toward the end of the war, murky negotiations had taken place, and amid the convoys heading to Auschwitz, she had noted an anomaly: in February of 1945, a train full of prisoners had left Theresienstadt for Switzerland. Intrigued, she had dug deeper. The trail led to an article published in the New York Times *on April 7, 1945, titled "1,200 Jews from Theresienstadt Sent to Switzerland by Nazis." Among the amazing facts explaining this miracle convoy—seeing the end of the war approach, Himmler had negotiated the release of Jewish prisoners with a Swiss politician called Jean-Marie Musy, hoping to be judged less harshly by posterity!—she found the real hidden gem: a list of names, one that was not tinged with the scent of death but with the sweet tang of life and hope. The passenger list. When she told me you had been on that train, I couldn't stop smiling for at least two hours. So, you had survived! I imagined you stepping onto that train, finally leaving that wretched place, ripping off your Jewish star, and, after a few days of traveling, setting your eyes on the magnificent colors of winter in Switzerland. How happy you must have been! The trail then led to the United States. New York! I dared not believe in such good luck. You were alive, you were alive! "Yes, yes," Ingrid said. "And I have an address."*

So here it is, Lena. Overjoyed, trembling with excitement, I finished this book. This book is our story, my gift; my words, my affection, my all. I have very few memories of my mother, but I know this: she chose you to save me, and that's what you did. And one day, after much deliberation, as one would hesitate to revisit a youthful love, I decided to write to you.

There, Lena. It's time to end this letter.

Just know that every day, I try to honor your example. If, after a night shift, dreaming only of getting home, I find a worried woman whose father has been placed under my care waiting outside my office, I think of you. If, in the midst of hell, you found the strength to save me, then I can well fight off sleep a little longer, lay a reassuring hand on her shoulder, and smile. And every morning, as I lean over the crib of our second child, I think of you, of the gift you gave me, and of all those who weren't as fortunate as me.

One last thing, before I leave you. Our second child is a girl. We named her Lena.

Lena placed the letter on her lap. Her hands were shaking slightly.

Jonathan, her youngest grandson, likely tired from chasing squirrels, burst into the living room. His cheeks were rosy from the heat, and his large eyes sparkled under his brown locks.

He climbed onto the couch and looked at his grandmother. "Grandma, why are you crying? Did you get bad news?"

"Oh no, my boy. Quite the opposite." She turned to him and stroked his face. "This is good news. Very good news. I'll tell you all about it when you grow up."

She smiled, winked, and said, "you know, we have a little time before lunch. How about a game of hide-and-seek with your old grandma?"

"Yeah!!!"

So, they played.

A Note from the Author

• • •

THIS BOOK WAS A LABOR OF LOVE, MORE THAN TEN YEARS IN THE making. If you are holding it now, I want to thank you—sincerely—for spending time with these characters and carrying their story with you.

If this story moved you, there is one simple way you can help it live on: share it. Leave a few words about it, recommend it to someone you care about, pass it forward.

Stories like these only endure when they are carried from one reader to another.

Thank you for being part of that chain.

This novel is inspired by the true history of Berlin's Jewish hospital, one of the last Jewish institutions permitted to operate under the Nazi regime. Throughout the war, the hospital became both a place of care and a fragile refuge, a paradoxical island of survival within a city increasingly organized around persecution and deportation.

My grandmother, Gerda Haas, worked there as a young nurse during the war. Her memories—shared with me over many years—formed the emotional foundation of this book. Some of the events she witnessed—the moral dilemmas she described, and the atmosphere of fear, solidarity, and quiet resistance that surrounded daily life at the hospital—have been woven into this narrative.

While certain historical figures, institutions, and documented events appear in these pages, this novel blends historical reality with fiction. Some characters and storylines are drawn from real individuals and testimonies, while others have been created or adapted to serve the narrative and to reflect broader human truths of the time: the impossible choices people were forced to make, the fragile bonds that formed under pressure, and the small acts of courage that often went unnoticed.

I have tried to remain faithful to the spirit of this place and period, while allowing the freedom of fiction to explore what official records cannot always capture: the inner lives of those who lived through it.

Any remaining inaccuracies are mine alone.

Acknowledgments

• • •

TO MY GRANDMOTHERS, GERDA AND EVA: WATCHING YOU LIVE, love, and rebuild after the cruelest of times taught me more about courage than any history book ever could. This novel is for you—and for those who did not make it home.

Amanda Sthers, you were among the very first to believe this story could become what it is today. Your generosity, your openness in sharing the craft of storytelling, and your early encouragement came at a moment when they mattered most. I will never forget that gift.

To my agents, Jonathan Bronitsky and Sarit Catz: thank you for trusting this story and for your strategic vision, guidance, and unwavering professionalism. Jonathan, you have been everything an author could hope for in an agent—steadfast, thoughtful, and tireless in your advocacy. Sarit, your early involvement, insight, and belief in this project's broader potential helped shape its trajectory in meaningful ways.

I am deeply grateful to my editor, Kathryn Riggs, whose intelligence, rigor, and sensitivity guided this manuscript with exceptional care. Thank you for believing in this story and for helping shape it into the book it was meant to become. My thanks as well to the entire team at Skyhorse Publishing for their trust, professionalism, and support.

To Ashley Rindsberg: thank you for the innumerable conversations about this book, for your sharp mind, your enthusiasm, and for being a true believer from the very beginning. Your intellectual generosity and constant engagement helped sharpen this story more than you know.

Carly Schabowski, you came onboard at an early stage and never looked back. Your trust in this project, your generosity, and your steady encouragement carried me through many moments of doubt. And if Stefan lives and shines in these pages, it is partly thanks to you.

I owe special thanks to Daniel Silver, whose patience, generosity, and historical insight were invaluable during the early stages of this novel's development. His knowledge of the Jewish hospital of Berlin helped anchor this story in truth. I am also profoundly grateful to Serge Klarsfeld for taking the time to read this work and for his words of encouragement, which carried immense meaning.

My sincere thanks as well to Heather Morris, Georgia Hunter, and Graeme Simsion for reading early versions of the manuscript and for their thoughtful support. Their generosity toward this project will always stay with me.

To my family: Ania, whose patience knows no limits—thank you for the endless late-night conversations about "our characters," for your honesty, emotional intelligence, and constant presence. I truly could not have written this book without you.

To my daughter, M—I love you.

To my parents, and especially to my mother, thank you for the meticulous proofreading, the encouragement, and the quiet faith that carried me through moments of doubt.

Finally, I thank the nurses, doctors, and forgotten voices whose courage inspired this novel. May their humanity continue to echo beyond the silence history tried to impose.